LET NOT THE DEEP
AND OTHER STORIES

Let Not The Deep

and other stories

by

BILL HAWKINS

SERENDIPITY

First published in 2002
by Serendipity
Suite 530
37 Store Street
Bloomsbury
London

British Library Cataloguing-in-Publication data
A catalogue record for this book is available from the British Library

ISBN 1 84394 025 6

Printed and bound in the UK by
Bookcraft Ltd, Bath

CONTENTS.

To my late wife Valerie
and lifeboat men everywhere

LET NOT THE DEEP

Chapter One

'Now that's a trim little craft, m'dear,' observed the elderly gentleman to his lady companion as they stopped, briefly interrupting their morning walk along the town quay, to admire the appearance of the trawler that lay alongside the ancient stone quay that for centuries had been battered and scarred by early sail trading schooners and present day small coasting steamers, 'for a fishing boat, that is,' he added knowledgeably, his eyes proclaimed expert by the nautical badge on the pocket of an immaculate navy blue blazer and the miniature flag motif on a neatly knotted tie as he surveyed every inch, from stem to stern. 'Yes, very trim indeed.'

Behind them, carrying a bulging cardboard carton inexpertly stuffed full of provisions for the forthcoming voyage, stood Joe Tomlin, the stockily-built, middle-aged skipper and part owner of the vessel under scrutiny, waiting patiently for them to allow him to get aboard.

Puffed with pride at hearing the compliment, he softly nudged the nautical gentleman with his carton, muttering in a grossly exaggerated West Country accent, 'Beggin' 'e pardun, zur, can oy git boy?'

The naval type, slightly startled, moved to one side, embarrassed that his comment had been overheard, then made off along the quay, his lady clutching timidly at his blazer sleeve as his hands felt for each other behind his back. He had seen Nelson walk like this, on the telly.

Joe threw his leg over the wooden gunwale of his boat, balancing the cardboard box precariously as he twisted his body inboard and awkwardly organising his other sea-booted foot to follow. He was still giggling – a little childishly – at his charade with the 'Admiral', and glowing with the compliment.

Skilfully negotiating the obstacle course that is the deck of any fishing boat he made his way around the after end of the superstructure and, opening a heavy wooden door, stepped over the knee-high coaming into the small but fastidiously clean compartment that was the home he shared with his two shipmates. It was little more than a steel box.

A table, flanked by two locker-seats covered with flattened cushions, took up half the available space while the remainder was sparsely

furnished with two sagging armchairs, screwed into the iron deck, and
a few luxuries such as a radio and a bookshelf stuffed with a first-aid
box, boxes of odds and ends, a packet of tea-biscuits, a crib-board and
playing cards, and a few tatty, dog-eared paper-back books.

Apart from his own personal cabin, a six by six feet space with a bunk,
minute table and chair that barely left standing room – this was his home.

He loved it.

Carefully he lowered the provisions on the table just to one side of
the papers that were carefully being studied by the balding, slightly
overweight figure of his engineer and co-owner. The cardboard carton
all but collapsed as he took his supporting arms away,

'What's this then, Ted,' he said by way of a greeting, 'A-levels?'

He was ignored except for an obscene finger-gesture so, lifting the lid
of the locker seat opposite, began stowing the tinned groceries from the
carton into the space beneath.

Ted, a craggy-faced Geordie whose weather-worn features belied the
fact he was still in his mid-thirties, also lived on board, having no home
or family ashore, and enjoyed a private cabin equally as small as Joe's.
They were good mates, having met many years ago when in the Navy
serving on the same ships and sharing many adventures, some of which
were frequent topics of conversation between them, others best forgotten,
but it was only in the last two years that they had joined together in
buying *Bonnie Lass* with their meagre savings.

'I reckon to get under way just before noon,' Joe continued without
looking up from his unpacking. 'That's if Ben gets aboard in time, and
your box of tricks start-up,' he added, referring to the diesel engine –
Ted's pride and joy – waiting patiently to perform down below in its
dark oil-laden compartment.

Ben was their paid-hand. A young fresh-faced twenty-year-old with
passions for the sea, the *Bonnie Lass* and girls – not always in that order.
He had joined them shortly after they bought *Bonnie Lass* and was a
good reliable hand who knew his fishing having crewed on his father's
boat since leaving school. Ben lived ashore with his parents when in
their home port and slept in his beloved hammock slung over the mess
table when at sea. It was a good arrangement.

Ted, the engineer, had acquired a rather paternal attitude towards him
and secretly looked on him as the son he had always wanted, not that
that stopped them from having the occasional wild spree ashore together
when away from home.

Still there was no response from the huddled figure.

'That'll be on the top of the tide,' said Joe, apparently to himself, 'so
we'll have the ebb to push us down-channel.' He looked at the top of is
partner's head seeking a response from the immaculate parting.

'Why don't you belt up,' retorted Ted at last. 'I'm trying to sort out these bloody accounts and can do without your rabbiting.' He paused and slammed down his pen in false anger. 'Ah! What the hell, I'm fed-up with them anyhow,' and shuffled the papers neatly together. Glad of the excuse.

'I was just saying,' continued the skipper – putting the last tin away and closing the locker lid – 'we can get a good run down-channel before the weather breaks. The forecast's pretty lousy but if we get down as far as Leemouth, or even Nesterdon before it gets too bad, we can get a good sheltered anchorage until it blows over. Then we'll only be a few hours from the grounds,' he said, referring to the fishing grounds they were currently working.

Ted looked at his fingers, blotchy-stained from the leaking ball-point pen.

'Yeah, we might just as well do that as sit here scratching our arse,' he muttered. 'Let's hope we get a good catch this trip,' he added as an afterthought.

The boat gave a slight lurch. 'That'll be young Ben,' said the engineer intuitively, and a few seconds later the young man opened the door to prove him right.

'Mornin', you two,' he greeted. 'We goin' fishin' or staying in 'ere all day?' He smiled to dispel the disrespect in his words.

'Captain to you, son,' directed the skipper in mock severity.

'Balls,' came the laughing reply.

The two elder men stood up slowly and Ted shook his head in a semblance of despair, then grinned. 'Let's get the show on the road then.'

In the wheelhouse, a slight trembling felt through the soles of his shoes told the skipper that Ted's beloved engine had once again started its faultless performance. Looking aft through the rear window, he saw Ted's blue-overalled figure emerge from the engine-room hatch and give him the thumbs-up signal before going to tend the stern mooring ropes. A quick look forward and he saw young Ben had singled-up to a slip rope and was waiting his command.

A swan thrust its way past, wings half raised in annoyance, its beak turning from side to side like a searching periscope as it skilfully avoided the flotilla of empty plastic containers and lumps of wood beginning to float seaward on the early ebb.

'Let go for'rd,' he called, then turned to look aft. 'Hang on to the spring, Ted.'

He eased the engine throttle back and the slowly turning propeller pulled *Bonnie Lass* astern against the tension of the back-spring, forcing her bow away from the quay.

A scruffy, tousle-haired lad sat disconsolately on a near-by vacant bollard, his eyes following the fishing line draped over his forefinger and disappearing down into the murky water alongside the quay, yearning to catch just one decent size fish to take home to Mum instead of the endless crabs that lay smashed around his feet.

Pushing the throttle into neutral, then slowly forward, Joe again called aft, 'Let go, Ted.' A splash of rope in the water and they were away, rapidly widening the gap between them and the quayside.

Happily, Joe steered *Bonnie Lass* seaward, along the length of Town Quay with its usual sprinkling of spectators. A late holiday-maker gave a cheery wave while the locals looked on with a mixture of interest and disinterest, some critical, some wistful. Past the local lifeboat snugly and conveniently moored to a buoy opposite the Royal Victoria pub, her dark-blue topside contrasting dramatically with the orange superstructure placed top-heavily in appearance on her fast cruiser-like hull, making her look more like a millionaire's gin-palace than the efficient sea-boat that her record had proved her to be. A lanky figure, with overalls down around his waist tied by the sleeves, leaned over the lifeboat's taffrail, staring unseeingly at the dark-blue dinghy trailing astern on its jerking painter, a fag dangling precariously from the corner of his mouth. He raised his head as the trawler slid gracefully by and lifted a tired hand in salute. 'Awright Joe?' came his call across the few feet of separating water. Joe glanced over at the full-time mechanic of the lifeboat. 'Fine, Smelly,' he answered, sticking his head out of the wheelhouse side window, smiling to himself at the perfect nickname for someone whose surname was Feates.

On past the weed and slime covered slipway that led up to the old granite lifeboat station that used to house the rowing lifeboat way back in the early part of the 1900s but which now stored the rusting and rotting accoutrements of the town's fishermen and where industrious gulls strutted disdainfully in their perpetual foraging.

Then gliding quietly by the wooden bench full of retired folk sleepily nodding-off in the weak midday September sun, their enigmatic smiles confessing to dreams of past love affairs or conquests as they sheltered from the cool southerly breeze in the lee of the Harbour Master's hut on the stone mole from where a cap-less uniformed official raised a languid arm to acknowledge the passing of *Bonnie Lass*.

At the very end of the granite-stoned breakwater, under a miniature red-and-white striped lighthouse with its grey-white cap of seabird droppings, two anglers stood alongside their unmoving rods, leaning on their elbows against the flaking red-rust railings in companionable silence. Shoulders drooping in unrewarded anticipation, they stared unblinkingly at their floats bobbing on the water, willing them to be sucked under by an inquisitive fish as a third man hopefully cast his weighted hook far out across *Bonnie Lass*'s bubbling wake with an over-arm sweep of his rod that would have done justice to a tennis player serving an ace ...

On through the two ranks of wooden poles that marked the entrance channel and provided perches for the great black-backed gulls arrogantly reviewing their passing, as they hopefully inspected every scrap of flotsam on the water for its edible quality, kwaw-kwawing to each other like a group of army pensioners reliving past battles.

As they came abreast of the most southerly channel marker, a concrete pile crowned with a resting cormorant – black wings spread wide as though airing its armpits – sitting on the flashing light that could still be clearly seen even in broad daylight, Joe turned the wheel spoke by spoke, swinging the trawler's bow to the westward.

Chapter Two

'Shipshape and Bristol fashion', that's how the skipper liked everything to be, thought Ben as he replaced the cover of the small hatch in the foredeck through which he had just stowed the mooring ropes of *Bonnie Lass*. 'A place for everything and everything in its place,' he muttered silently to himself while twisting the butterfly screws that tightened the iron clamping bar across the hatch to make it watertight.

He sensed the skipper's eyes checking his every movement from the wheelhouse window but felt no resentment, just the skipper being a good seaman and leaving nothing to chance. A leaking hatch in the foredeck would be disastrous in heavy weather, but this was not the problem that worried the young fisherman.

Fishing had been his life since he had left the tired, dilapidated town school with its cream and brown painted walls and geriatric teachers, at the worldly age of fourteen. Starting as a 'deckie' on his Dad's boat he had learned the trade in misery with his father treating him more as a skivvy than a son. It wasn't a case of cheap labour, more a Victorian parent's idea of a strict upbringing that considered love to be soft and unproductive when it came to character building.

Most people remarked how wonderful it was for father and son to work together. It made him puke. What the hell did they know about it? They should have been in his shoes, or those of his poor Mother who had to contend with the worry of two of them away together. If she lost one she would probably have lost both.

Ben senior, a rough, tough, hard-fisted fisherman of the old school, had been pretty upset when his son left him to join *Bonnie Lass* and to this day had still not completely forgiven him, not that this worried Ben too much, they had never been really close. Ted and Joe now, were different, great guys, even though Ted was a bit of an old woman at times and tended to treat him like a little kid. Still, better that way than like his Dad, and they were good to him in many other ways. The money was good as well. One good trip was worth more to him, in wages and bonus, than most of the local lads earned in a month.

He straightened up and, catching the skipper's eye, gave him a thumbs-up signal, getting a nod and a wink in return.

He walked aft along the narrow planked deck – lovingly scrubbed white in harbour but soon to be stained by the refuse and detritus trawled from the sea-bed with the fish, then dumped on the deck or overboard for the inspection of scavenging gulls that appeared from nowhere as soon as the first net was hauled aboard, hovering like clouds of exhaust fumes over the trawler's wake. He was completely indifferent to the passing scenery as they motored out of the harbour, his mind occupied with the problem of what he was going to do with his life as he stepped into the small compact galley and flashed-up the twin-burner oil stove. Mentally, he was pulled in three different directions and the trouble was, he wanted all three!

Scooping a couple of handfuls of potatoes from the sack under the worktop he dropped them into a plastic bucket and added a few pints of precious fresh water. With the bucket between his knees he sat uncomfortably on the edge of the door coaming and began to peel them thinly with the enthusiasm of a blind man watching television. No slap-dash chunks or the skipper would have his guts for garters. 'Best part of the spud wasted,' Joe would cry if he saw thick peelings in the bucket.

His eyes were oblivious as they swept the gaunt horizon but his brain was as active as a humming-top as he returned his attention to the lumpy 'King Edward' he was scalping.

It would be awful to leave the boat, he thought. Like betraying his two shipmates who had given him so much. But there seemed no alternative if he chose either of his other two options. He had told no one, not even Joe or Ted, but he desperately wanted to go deep-sea proper, not fishing. He wanted to join the Merchant Navy and see something of the world. Every day he would watch the huge tankers and cargo ships going to and fro, up and down the Channel, and he longed to be on board each one of them, sailing to far away ports with wonderful names like Singapore, New York, Calcutta, Hong Kong, Melbourne. Each conjured up exotic sights and smells he had dreamed of and read about.

With a worried frown creasing his forehead he transferred the bald spuds into a pot and placed it on the stove.

Everyone thought he was happy and contented with his job aboard *Bonnie Lass* and in many ways he was, but he wasn't doing anything with his life. He wasn't going anywhere! Hell, he hadn't been further than Penzance, and then only to shelter from a storm. His experience of 'abroad' was limited to an occasional call into Falmouth or somewhere. Not exactly 'foreign' by any stretch of the imagination.

Yes, all the other lads in the town envied him like mad and would swap their mundane lives for his any day but the novelty of what they saw as an exciting, adventurous and well-paid job was wearing thin. He wanted to spread his wings and see the world.

The potatoes were bubbling merrily on the stove and getting furry around the edges as he turned down the flame under the pot and watched absentmindedly as the water changed from the frothy turmoil of a witches' cauldron to a clear gentle simmer.

Taking a heavy iron frying pan from its hook on the stove's side frame, he positioned it over the second burner then, slicing a liberal chunk from a block of lard, slid it into the already warming pan, watching it spread like oil pollution on the surface of the sea. When it was hot enough to spit back at him, he stabbed each one of the row of sausages lined up on the worktop and launched them, one at a time like torpedoes, into the pan with a sweeping movement of his arm in fair imitation of the Jap dive bombers attacking American ships in the war films he had seen.

As he stood watching the sausages sizzle and swell, his thoughts pondered the third of the options that were tormenting him. His romance with Lisa. It had become serious and very important to him. He had known her for years, just another girl at school and around town at first, one of many and nothing really special. Then he had met her at a 'do' in the Co-op Hall a few months ago. It was the first time he had really looked at her. With her long blonde hair and summer dress she was a gorgeous picture and they had danced together most of the evening. She felt good in his arms and her scented body excited him in a way no other girl had done before. Everyone else ceased to exist. He couldn't keep his eyes off her and when she agreed to go out with him again he had been over the moon. He felt so good and contented with her and felt sure she felt the same way about him.

She was one of the few local girls without a reputation for being 'easy'. A few of his mates had had dates with her but no one – not even the boastful ones – ever got further than a cool kiss. It was as if they were meant for each other.

Yesterday, he had asked her to become engaged to him. At first she just looked at him and he was sure she was going to turn him down. Then he saw the tears in her eyes as she threw her arms around his neck and whispered, 'Yes, oh yes!' He thought his heart was going to burst – he felt so happy. Proudly she had told him that she was still a virgin. She wanted to stay that way until her wedding night, and he believed her. He told her, honestly, that he was too; not that he would have admitted it to anyone but her.

That had been the beginning of a terrific evening, at least right up to the very last moment when they were saying 'Goodnight' in the alleyway near her home with some really heavy petting. He was very embarrassed with a rock-hard erection and he curved his thighs away from her hoping she wouldn't feel it but she hugged him close to her, crushing it against her stomach and giggling, 'Oh! ... what's that, then?'

Things were beginning to get out of hand and he was losing control of himself when Lisa whispered breathlessly in his ear, 'I want to be all yours, Ben. I want to give myself to you, but if you want us to be married you will have to leave the sea.' Her words hit him like a bucket of cold water and his shocked reaction startled her.

'I'm sorry, love,' she continued, 'but I wouldn't want a life like your Mum has had. Nothing but worry all the time you're away. Worrying when there's bad weather. Worrying all the time if you are all right, worrying that you won't come back. Worry, worry, worry. That's no life to lead.'

He remembered mumbling something about thinking it over and having to go because he was sailing early in the morning. She had just stood there with tears in her eyes. They both knew that the magic of the moment had been lost, and there was little of the earlier passion in their goodnight kiss. He loved her dearly and wanted her like mad but how could he think of leaving the sea, especially now when he wanted to go into the Merchant Navy. What could he do ashore? ... Work in an shop? ... Sit in an office? ... Carry bricks on a building site? ... Queue up at the dole? No way. What a dilemma!

He drained off the spuds and mashed them angrily into a pulp, adding a big dollop of butter before spooning three equal portions onto pre-warmed china plates – no cheap tin plates on Joe's boat. Then he pushed a couple of bloated sausages into the mash, like brown zeppelins entering a white-wool cloud, and sprayed each with a generous splurge of tomato sauce.

Ted had re-started his struggle with paperwork, the table littered with books and scraps of paper, as Ben entered the tiny mess-room juggling two plates.

'Grub up,' he announced.

The engineer looked up and a grin of hungry appreciation lit his face as his arms swept a clear area on the table in front of him.

'Snorkers, good-oh!' he cried, and they both laughed having seen the film *The Cruel Sea* and recalled the famous catchphrase of HMS *Compass Rose*'s First Lieutenant.

'Sling your plate in the galley when you've finished,' ordered Ben over his shoulder as he made his exit to deliver the skipper's meal, but Ted's mouth was already full, chomping away at a sausage.

In the wheelhouse, Joe stood alone, hunchbacked over the varnished steering wheel, dreamily watching the trawler's bow nodding up and down through the ragged skyline that was becoming increasingly irregular with the rising sea. His thoughts had drifted far away as he fantasised about being the owner-skipper of a deep-sea Arctic trawler, earning thousands of pounds each trip. Having a huge palatial home in the country, with a posh car and gorgeous wife to enjoy between voyages. Some hopes he had – he didn't even have a girlfriend.

He loved the peaceful solitude. No one else to worry about. No one to entertain. Just him and *Bonnie Lass* – together. He broke wind and felt better for it, wrinkling his nose. He couldn't smell himself but nevertheless, he opened the side window an inch or two – just in case.

His head turned with a start as the door clicked open and young Ben entered carrying the meal that immediately started his taste buds going.

'Ah! good on you, lad,' he said, 'I could just go that lot.'

Ben hated being called 'lad' and his annoyance obviously showed causing the skipper to quickly add, 'This looks lovely, mate,' as he took the plate and placed it carefully on a folded piece of paper to protect the highly polished console beside the gleaming binnacle.

'Want a spell?' Ben asked unenthusiastically, puckering his nose like a sniffer dog detecting an alien scent. Usually he loved to steer the boat and took every opportunity offered but today he wanted to be on his own to think. His lack of sincerity was not lost on the older man.

'No thanks, mate, I'm okay,' he replied. 'I'm sure you've got other things to do.'

'Right,' agreed Ben, having identified the smell and deliberately hooking open the wheelhouse door to show his awareness as he left, leaving the skipper a little concerned and wondering what had got into him.

'Perhaps he's in love,' he grinned to himself as he forked half a sausage into his mouth and returned to his make-believe world.

Back in the galley, Ben again sat on the door coaming, this time balancing his dinner plate on his lap, but he had no appetite. His mind was in a whirl. If he stayed with *Bonnie Lass* he would surely lose Lisa and the chance to travel abroad, so that was a non-starter. That left two choices: either join the 'Merch' to see the world and take a chance on Lisa not meaning what she had said, or pack it all in and marry her. What would he do then, become a postman or something? If she loves me she takes me for what I am, he thought with a belligerence he didn't feel.

He finished his meal without tasting it, throwing a piece of uneaten sausage over the side to be fought over by squadrons of swooping gulls, as he desperately sought an answer to his problem. How could he stay at sea and still have Lisa?

His thinking was interrupted by the engineer returning his empty plate.

'That was great, kiddo. Just what the doctor ordered,' said Ted gratefully, then, noting the coolness of his reception, stepped back out of the galley onto the outer deck.

'I'll be down in the engine-room if I'm wanted.'

Ben quickly washed up the two plates and replaced them in their rack, wishing he could talk to someone about his problem. He knew his two shipmates would be sympathetic listeners and undoubtedly give him good advice and guidance, even though they would naturally be upset that he was considering leaving *Bonnie Lass* and them, but he shied away from making an approach. Somehow it didn't seem to be the manly thing to do. He would have stand on his own two feet and make up his own mind before the end of this trip. He just wished they would hurry up and get to the grounds and start fishing to take his mind off it all. He wouldn't have the time, or energy, to think then.

Chapter Three

Down below, the gloom of the cramped compartment was lit by a single electric light bulb caged at the end of a wandering lead, swinging from a hook in the cluttered deck-head above the rumbling engine, creating ever moving light and shadow with the movement of the boat.

Mention the word 'engine-room' to the average land-lubber and he would conjure up a picture of a vast, thundering, cathedral-like steel space, with a massive shuddering piece of machinery as its centre-piece, surrounded by a framework of open-grated metal walkways at varying levels joined together by shining steel vertical ladders with hand-rails burnished bright from the abrasion of generations of greasy-handed watch-keepers as they climbed into every nook and cranny in their ceaseless inspection of their domain.

One such ladder would rise through the oily heat haze up to the multi-framed skylight from which rays of sunlight probed downwards, sweeping across the tangled web of pipes and machinery in concert with the rolling gait of the ship, occasionally spotlighting a white-overalled technician, wearing ear defenders for protection against the thunderous roar of thousands of horse-power, standing before a control panel of flashing indicators, tell-tale gauges, valves and levers.

Bonnie Lass was not like that. Her engine-room was exactly as described – room for an engine – just. Barely eighteen inches separated the sides of her diesel from the surrounding bulkheads and into this gap a body had to squeeze and squirm like a contortionist whenever there was a need to inspect, lubricate or repair.

With only five feet of headroom, the engineer must stand with a permanent stoop and move very carefully to save his scarred skull from further conflict with spiteful fittings. Her control panel consisted of a couple of gauges, and a battered blue-painted tin box full of well-worn tools, standing on the oil soaked teak decking beside a grease-blackened softwood stool which doubled as a work-bench and currently bore the weight of her puzzled attendant.

Ted's brow wrinkled in an ageing frown, squinting his eyes and twisting his head to put his best ear forward like a housewife listening in on her neighbours over the garden wall. The engine was chonking away nice and sweetly. Everything seemed fine as his experienced fingers touched, felt and probed the warm oily machinery like a doctor examining his patient. The steady heartbeat of the pistons, the chattering of the tappets, the whining hum of the spinning shaft were like a faultless orchestration to his sensitive ears, yet instinctively he knew something wasn't right.

For the umpteenth time his fingers rapped gauges but the flickering needles trembled only in tune with the vibrating engine, recording correct pressures and temperatures.

He bitterly regretted letting the skipper talk him into allowing the marine fitters from Bellwood's Yard fit the new camshaft during the last two days in port.

'You won't have time to do it yourself,' had been Joe's argument, and of course he was right, but if he had stuck to his guns and insisted that he do it himself they would have lost a day or two's fishing but saved the cost of using Bellwoods. Moneywise it was as broad as it was long. Besides – and this was the real reason – he didn't like others messing around with his engine. He had always been the same, even with cars. He had had several in his time, for short periods in between service postings, and had always serviced them himself. Apart from saving money he felt safe knowing a job had been well done. He hated being technically reliant on others. In fact, it had been a long, long time since he trusted anyone – except for Joe and Ben, of course – and even they didn't know everything about him. He hadn't told them.

Mentally, he opened the cupboard door and looked at the skeleton inside. He had started a four-year apprenticeship as a boiler maker at a Tyneside shipyard when he was sixteen and by the time he was nineteen he was married to his childhood sweetheart. A girl who was everything a man could wish for. A beautiful, warm, loving wife, a wonderful friend, and a wild, passionate whore in bed. Life with her had been idyllic even though they had very little money, but then he went and spoilt it all in a few stupid moments that he could not even blame on drink.

He met this girl who flattered his ego. On the very first night he had walked her home and they found a dark spot at the rear of a pavilion in a school's playing field. With a lot of encouragement from her he had her skirt up around her waist, then moved his hands to her breasts only to find her brassière full of crumpled tissue-paper. She was flat-chested. His first thoughts were, 'Christ, it's a boy,' until he realised that a few moments previous, with her knickers at half-mast, he had found she certainly wasn't. His second thought was, 'She's only a kid.' In a panic, he asked how old she was. 'Sixteen,' she answered. He backed off like a scalded cat, much to her anger and annoyance.

Subsequently, she reported him for molesting her but fortunately the Magistrates, having heard his story and learning of her bad reputation, found him 'Not guilty'. Unfortunately, his wife didn't agree with the verdict. She packed her bags and left. That's when he joined the Navy and met Joe.

Once again his eyes, ears and hands went over the throbbing engine painstakingly, half hoping to find fault in Bellwood's work that he could then rectify and ease the niggling worry he felt. All of his years dealing with machinery, up to his elbows in grease and oil, had trained him to listen and diagnose technical faults before they became serious enough to cause damage or stoppage. Now he was listening damned hard, and looking, and feeling. Why did he have this awful feeling that something was wrong? Perhaps he was hoping, too hard, to fault Bellwood's, and his failure to do so was hurting his ego.

In vain his eyes swept over the small compartment then, in utter frustration, he gave the engine-casing a quick wipe-over with his ever-ready oily rag before climbing the three-rung iron ladder out of the engine-room, promising himself a few hours kip before their arrival at the grounds where a decent night's sleep was about as likely as a cold pint of draught beer in the Sahara.

Emerging from the hatch he felt the cool breeze on his cheek. Like most men of his calling he was at home in the oily, warm fug of an engine-room and didn't find the damp, salty air at all refreshing. For the life of him he couldn't understand what there was to like about always being cold, wet and windswept. 'Deckies' are a weird breed, he decided.

Making his way along the narrow side deck towards his cabin he looked out across the sea which was, to him, as exciting as a blank television screen. They were in a world of their own with not a ship in sight, nor sign of land in view. Nothing but the ubiquitous seagulls wheeling and screaming across the cloud-streaked sky. The sea was getting up a bit with wave tops being torn off by the wind. If it got any worse, he thought, they'd be in for a dirty night. Still, that was Joe's worry and they had been through bad weather before, plenty of it, and the bright spot was that it usually brought a good haul of fish.

Perhaps the fish were reincarnated 'deckies', he laughed as he grasped the handle of his cabin door just as a circling gull, obviously seeking revenge for the non-appearance of an expected meal, narrowly missed him with a dive-bombing effort that splattered against the bulkhead, inches from his head.

He looked up trying to identify the culprit but they all looked the same so, gripping the handles of his imaginary twin-barrelled machine-gun, he sprayed the sky with lethal streams of lead.

'Rat-a-tat-a-tat,' he spluttered, then guiltily swivelled his head, embarrassed in case his shipmates had witnessed the childlike act. The empty deck was a great relief.

'I'm going stark raving bonkers,' he said aloud to the empty sea, and was answered by another gull dropping its message on the gunwale in front of him.

'Blasted kite-hawks,' he cursed, entering his cabin.

Chapter Four

The view forward through the wheelhouse window, dappled with sea-spray, was exhilarating. The short, white-capped waves rushed to meet the thrusting bow of *Bonnie Lass* as she bobbed towards the setting sun that was slowly disappearing behind dark boulders of cloud collecting threateningly ahead. Under her bluff counter the pounding propeller churned a fringe of white foam pointing back in the direction of her home port whose sheltering harbour she had left just a few hours ago.

Her skipper leaned contentedly against the small steering wheel; the warm fug of the small wheelhouse made him pleasantly drowsy as he proudly surveyed his command. Yes, she was a trim little craft, he thought, recalling the words of the naval type that morning, and he loved every inch of her fifty-foot, work-worn hull.

She was a stout craft built on the lines of the war-time MFVs and he was confident she was equal to anything the elements could throw at her. Slowly he turned his head, eyes panning across the wheelhouse woodwork, all expertly grained and polished, making a perfect backcloth to the gleaming brass-work of the compass binnacle. A rare sight to be seen on a hard working fishing vessel. This was his home as well as his place of work and every minute of his waking day – when not actually fishing – was spent lavishing his care on her appearance.

Continuing his turn, he gazed out of the rear window over the rounded stern and along the white ribbon of the boat's wake that was bordered by an agitated spray on the weather-side and a calm oily edge to leeward, until it mingled several dozen feet astern with the rest of the wind-whipped surface of the sea then disappeared, erasing forever all traces of their passage.

A solitary seagull, its unblinking eyes scanning the sea-surface like radar, skimmed gracefully over the wave tops, swooping from one quarter to the other, its wings rarely moving in an effortless glide. Did this beautiful scavenger of the sea recognise *Bonnie Lass* as a fishing boat, he wondered? Did it follow knowing the sea around the boat would eventually be strewn with a rich feast of fish guts? Or was it merely following for the morsels of waste and galley scraps that all ships threw overboard?

Slowly his gaze returned to the compass card in an instinctive check on his course.

The wind was blowing up a bit, he noticed, with spray beginning to break over the port bow, but that was only to be expected. The marine forecast hadn't been at all good but what the hell, he wasn't out here for a pleasure cruise. Nevertheless, he estimated with a frown, the wind had increased by a good ten knots in the last hour or two and was now a strong breeze. His eyes swivelled to the clock on the bulkhead over the small chart-table. Six o'clock. He consoled himself with the thought that it was nearly time for tea and he licked his parched lips. Nothing like a good cup of hot char.

He hadn't seen either of the other two all afternoon but he knew that they would be either resting or fully occupied at something or other. The frown eased his forehead and dreamily his mind raced down memory lane, through his years in the Navy where he had first met Ted. Theirs had been an unusual alliance with Ted being a stoker and he a seaman. Chalk and cheese. They saw little of each other on board ship but nearly always managed to wangle shore-leave together and the good times far outweighed the bad. Like the time in Singapore when they had picked up two gorgeous girls only to find out, luckily before they had spent all their money on them, that they were boys ... Hah!

Five years ago they had even been de-mobbed together, well, almost together, within a few days. Ted got a job in their home town, in a garage, and he had realised a lifelong ambition to own his own fishing boat. His first, *Cockle*, had only been small; barely twenty feet long with a wheelhouse just big enough to hold him alone. She had never given him a minute's worry or anxiety. Life with her had been good and rewarding and in only two years of hard graft he had put enough money in the bank to enable him to accept an invitation from Ted to jointly buy a larger craft.

Selling *Cockle* hadn't been pleasant. Like parting with a faithful dog. He had taken great care to ensure she went to a good owner, even refusing one offer from a chap who wanted her 'for pottering around at weekends'. No way would he have seen her rot on a beach somewhere, or end up a rotting skeleton in some muddy back-water for the rest of her days. Eventually, a local chap bought her and the last he heard was that she was fishing out of Plymouth.

When he first saw *Bonnie Lass*, lying unkempt and scruffy alongside a rickety old wooden jetty at Littlehaven, Joe fell in love. She was a beauty but, as he stepped onto her cluttered and unscrubbed deck, he felt an uneasy feeling of unfaithfulness come over him. Poor old *Cockle*, would she ever forgive him for deserting her?

He had looked around *Bonnie Lass* with a critical and professional eye then, in true sailor tradition, soon forgot his last love.

The next two years had been idyllic. Ted was a good friend who worshipped his engine. The pokey, cramped engine-room was kept relatively spick and span and the engine itself, when not thumping away merrily, always had some part or other being stripped down for cleaning and maintenance. He was also a good fisherman and did more than his fair share on deck. They worked hard, long hours for the first two years, spending as much time at sea, fishing, as possible. Putting money into the bank. Enough, eventually, to afford to take on a paid-hand to ease their heavy workload.

The opening of the wheelhouse door brought him back to reality and a strong draught of refreshing salt-laden air hit him as young Ben entered carrying a tin tray on which he balanced two steaming mugs of strong tea and a plate piled high with thick sandwiches, obviously made from the sausages left over from dinner. Joe saw the liberally applied tomato sauce oozing out from between the slices of bread and licked his lips in anticipation as he moved to allow the lad to place the tray on top of the locker beside the steering wheel.

'Tea up,' cried Ben, late and unnecessarily, sniffing the air experimentally as the two men exchanged smiles of welcome.

Gratefully Joe lifted his mug and eyed the circling bubbles on its deep-brown surface before sipping cautiously at the scalding hot liquid, like a bilge-pump sucking air.

'Bloody hell,' he exclaimed, 'I needed that.' He replaced the mug and grabbed a sandwich. 'Where's Ted?'

'Got his head down for a bit,' came the irreverent reply, 'must be getting old.'

Joe sank his teeth deliciously into the sandwich and a blob of sauce edged out under pressure and fell to the deck, narrowly missing the locker top.

'Leave it for the sweeper,' moaned Ben resignedly, knowing that the cleanliness of the wheelhouse was one of his many chores as he pulled a handkerchief from his trouser pocket and collected the splattered ketchup, like a dog-owner with a poop-scoop.

For the next couple of hours the two men discussed every subject known to man, thoroughly enjoying each other's company and putting the world to rights. Outside it began to get dark. Inevitably their conversation turned to the topics of seamen the world over, the weather and women. The latter was of more interest to the youngster but Joe was paying more heed to the weather. As skipper, he took his responsibilities seriously and was becoming slightly concerned at the rapid increase in wind strength, and the height of the seas. He wasn't in the least bit worried about *Bonnie Lass*'s seaworthiness but if matters became much worse he would have to run for shelter until it improved. The boat was plunging heavily now, disdainfully cleaving her way through quite big seas. Decision time was fast approaching and he began to consider his options, turning a deaf ear to the lad who was still recounting details of an earlier amorous adventure.

Ben dearly wanted to raise the subject of Lisa and his future. He needed Joe's advice and guidance, but with the weather deteriorating rapidly he questioned if now was the right time. He looked out of the window as the last strands of daylight faded away on the far side of the leaden, overcast sky.

Then the engine stopped.

For some long seconds the two men looked at each other unbelievingly, before understanding hit them.

'Get Ted,' ordered Joe sharply, knowing full well the engineer would be out of his bunk and halfway to the engine-room by now.

Ben crashed out of the wheelhouse leaving its door swinging until the wind slammed it shut. He almost collided with Ted who was frantically pulling open the sliding hatch to the engine-room, muttering something that sounded suspiciously like 'Fuckin' Bellwood's.'

Bonnie Lass quickly lost steerage way and her bow was paying off to starboard away from the wind. Joe cursed as he foresaw the motion and danger when she became broadside-on to the sea. He pushed open the door of the wheelhouse and hurried forward along the deck to where the sea-anchor was stowed near the stem-head, becoming soaked with sea-spray in the process. Undoing the locker he looked at the contrivance of tarred canvas and metal spreaders he himself had made two years ago. This was the first time it had been used in anger. He couldn't even remember if he had tried it out; he must have done. Well, he thought, it will certainly be tried out now!

Mentally crossing his fingers he lifted its unwieldy weight clumsily on to the gunwale. As he did so *Bonnie Lass* dropped her bow sharply and lurched to starboard. A solid sea came over the side and hit him in the chest, making him gasp, almost tearing the sea-anchor from his hands. The water felt icy cold even though it was still only September.

'I should have put my oilskins on,' he said loudly to himself, puffing salt water from his mouth. 'Too bloody late now.'

He dropped the canvas shape into the sea and paid out the rope, trying to recall if it was better on a short line or a long one. He knew an ordinary anchor worked best on a long length of cable so he paid out all the line available, securing the last few feet to the bow bollard. Now, he thought whimsically, we will see if God looks after heathens as well!

At that moment a solid, breaking sea thudded against the bow and he was thrown across the winch. He felt no pain, no nothing, except a rising flood of fear that seemed to inflate his chest. He was choking, and panic was overpowering him. He wanted to run – but where to? Staggering back to the lee of the wheelhouse he deliberately took several deep breaths, packing his lungs to capacity each time before letting the air blast out between his teeth. It hurt his chest but made him feel much better, and calmer, as he slowly collected his thoughts.

He was well aware that Ted and Ben would be doing their best down below, wedged firmly between the engine-bearers against the irregular gyrations of the heaving hull, and he took comfort from the knowledge that, if anyone could get the engine going again, it would be Ted.

'Please God he does,' he prayed silently, deciding not to ask about progress so soon. Down in the bowels of *Bonnie Lass* those two poor sods had more than enough on their plate without his badgering, though he dearly wanted their company and some crumb of hope to hang on to.

Suddenly he felt very alone as a cold shiver surged through his body. In his mind's eye he saw his own lifeless body floating face down in a grey sea and for some inexplicable reason wished he had married.

It was no good, he couldn't stay where he was on his own, so making his way a few feet further aft he reached for the engine-room hatch and slid it partially open.

Bracing himself in the opening he peered down into the darkness where two shadowy shapes were huddled over the silent engine. The warm smell of oil and diesel rose to meet him and his stomach, though hardened by a lifetime at sea, heaved. Even in this weather, he told himself, I'd rather be up here than down in that hell-hole.

'If you two buggers don't hurry up and get your fingers out we're going to end up on the beach before long,' he shouted down with a cheery nonchalance he didn't feel.

A white, sweat-stained, oil-streaked face turned upwards, smeared with blood. Even in the howling din of the gale the voice that reached him sounded as though it came from the depths of a tomb.

'What do you think we are, bloody magicians?'

Joe forced himself to lower his head further into the engine-room, reaching for one of the ladder rungs until he was almost upside down.

'Well, I don't want to worry you but I reckon we're only about a mile or so from a lee shore and the sea-anchor ain't that bleeding good,' he said, more as an incentive than a warning.

He waited for the expected response but none was forthcoming so he pushed against the iron rungs and reversed back out onto the deck, closing the hatch behind him. A worried frown creased his forehead as he made his way back to the wheelhouse, staggering in concert with the violent motion of the boat, trying to remain upright on the wildly gyrating deck. It must be blowing a Force seven or eight now, he guessed. What a time to have their first and only engine failure!

Twinges of fear gripped his stomach as he turned his back to the wind, eyes trying to pierce the spray-laden darkness. Somewhere to the north of them, too close for comfort, lay an uninviting coastline towards which they were being helplessly and relentlessly blown, like a scrap of paper in a storm-drain.

From the corner of his eye he saw a brief flash. Was that a light?

He stared until his eyes ached, knowing that their position should be somewhere not too far from Gostone lighthouse, but he saw nothing except the white wave-tops rushing past in the otherwise solid darkness.

Thank goodness the sea-anchor seemed to be working okay, holding them bow to wind and hopefully reducing their rate of drift, he thought, climbing up into the wheelhouse, painfully aware that his arm and chest were hurting.

The bow of *Bonnie Lass* climbed rapidly up the slope of a menacing wall of grey water and broke submissively through the wind-torn crest. Then she dropped sickeningly down the other side, burying her stem deeply into the base of the next advancing sea charging towards them like an unstoppable horde of Kamikaze warriors. Joe bent his knees as the deck rose beneath his feet then straightened them for the stomach-churning drop down before relaxing them again to buffer the sudden deceleration as the hull sank gunwale-deep into a trough.

Normally, he would have revelled in this sort of weather. He was one of that rare breed of men who honestly enjoyed a rough sea. But this was different. *Bonnie Lass* no longer thrust her stem into the sea. There was no spindrift or solid water driving over her bow. What there was came slopping onto her deck. She was dead, wallowing and pitching at the mercy of Mother Nature's whim, her bow held to wind by a flimsy device of man.

He jumped, startled, as the cuddy door opened and the howling wind came in.

'It's no good, Skip, she won't start.' Ben's strained voice came to him like a comforting arm, and his panic drained away. 'Ted reckons we should send out a distress call.'

Even this disastrous news came like a reprieve. At last he could get on and do something instead of just waiting helplessly. He reacted gratefully.

'Right, let's see how the other half lives,' he answered, reaching for the radio telephone on the bulkhead beside the clock, trying hard to remember the right procedure for calling out the rescue services. He didn't even question the possibility of a lifeboat coming out to them. He knew they would.

He felt calmer now that he had something to do and was slightly ashamed of his earlier weakness. Thank God there were no witnesses. 'I wonder if the Captain of the *Titanic* felt like I did?' he mused.

The radio handset felt strange in his grasp as he looked at it, mustering his thoughts. He had only ever used it for routine messages. It was then he saw his hand covered in blood, and again a weird thought crossed his mind ... 'Good job I'm not wearing a white shirt.'

He pulled the handset to his mouth, straightening the curling spring-like cable. He took a deep, painful breath and, pressing the transmit button, spoke into it.

Chapter Five

'*Sacré* – rotten – *bleu*,' lamented Ray Pearman, cursing his luck as he combed his fingers through his thinning hair, still trying to regain his breath. Why did it always happen to him? Twenty minutes ago he had been at home, fast asleep, tucked up in his warm bed, wrapped around his Missus, and would still be there now if he hadn't been Duty-dog when this gale blew up. He'd only been asleep for a few minutes when his Regional Control Centre rang to tell him he was required to stand a rough-weather watch owing to the strong winds that were expected to reach Force 9 or 10 in the next few hours. He had already done a full day's work patrolling the coastline, so it was with bad grace that he reluctantly climbed out of bed trying not to disturb his sleeping wife who grunted, belched and turned over as he stumbled around the bedroom in the dark looking for his socks, wondering how it was that one of them always wandered off, playing bleeding hide and seek.

Downstairs, still wearing his pyjamas under his uniform, he dashed the few yards separating his front door from the Land Rover standing forlornly in the driveway. Then drove off through the windswept, sleeping village, the noise of his engine being drowned by the howling wind. Turning right at The Jolly Taxpayer he left the tarmac road and climbed the rough, pebbled track to the top of Leemouth Head. The strong, blustery wind hit his vehicle, rocking it alarmingly. 'Sod this for a game of soldiers,' he grunted sourly as he parked in the lee of the tower and fought his way up the wooden steps. So, now, here he was stuck up in a stilted wooden tower on top of Leemouth Head.

'Rough weather watch indeed!' he snorted derisively. All he could 'watch' were the surrounding wooden walls of the tower and the spray-splashed windows streaked by the wind, reflecting his sleep-deprived face like a mirror. 'Look-out Tower,' he sniffed in disgust, more like a 'Look-in'. It was as exciting as an empty boxing-ring.

Eight years in the Coastguard Service and he still wasn't used to such a variable routine, controlled as it was by the vagaries of wind and weather.

It was a great job in the nice weather, driving around the countryside in his Land Rover or patrolling the local beaches full of bikini-clad, sun-bathing beauties, but when it was like this it was crap. Unless of course you were one of the medal-seeking, gung-ho types who longed for bad weather to throw themselves down vertical cliffs to rescue silly buggers, or to organise beach-rescue teams for stranded ships. He had done his Rambo bit in the Royal Navy. All he wanted now was a quiet life.

'I'm going to jack this lot in,' he promised himself for the hundredth time, knowing, but not admitting, that he really got a kick out of the job. It gave him all he wanted. Security, being near the sea and ships, a feeling of unspoken pride in doing something worthwhile, and being a respected member of the community.

'Sod it,' he swore, as he sat down and tucked his feet up under the stool, slowly rocking his buttocks to ease the numbness. He knew that comfortable seats were sleep-inducing during a long watch, especially when there was nothing to see outside, but did the issue ones have to be so bloody hard? 'If the bosses, or the bloody civil servants, had to sit here they would have plush seats,' he said to himself, quietly truculent. Even the illicit cushion brought from home was wafer thin and he recalled with a smile the annoyance of the District Inspector when he found the plush cushion taped to this very same stool during his last visit, and the childish memo received as a result. The thought amused him. What else could be expected from an ex-Naval pig? He'd had his fill of them during his time in the Andrew; all education but no common sense, or as the lower-deck would say ... 'All gold-braid and bullshit'. He laughed as he recalled the description of a Naval Officer given him by an old three-badge AB who said, 'The reason they're officers is because the ain't got the brains to be a sailor.' He shifted his weight and stretched one leg to the floor. What a life! Roll on my twelve.

He stared absentmindedly at his blurred image in the window. Faintly he saw a dim glow of diffused red light smear across the glass but his brain hardly recorded it. His perch in the tower came within the red sector of Gostone Point lighthouse that, under normal conditions, would sweep the interior of the tower every eight seconds. Tonight however was different. It was particularly nasty outside with very restricted visibility and he was aware that, with the lighthouse nearly three miles away, he would rarely see its sweeping beam.

He leaned forward, placing his elbows on the chart-covered table in front of him, and raised his binoculars to eye level. It was a futile move, made out of boredom. He could see nothing through the salt-caked windows that formed three sides of the tower, but what the hell, it was something to do. He tried thumbing the milled adjusting wheel to bring the tear-drops of water on the window into focus, altering from one extreme to the other, without success. The marvels of prismatic engineering! With them he could see every detail of a ship ten miles away but at a range of a few inches they were bloody useless.

The whole structure of the tower shook before another violent blast of wind, yet without apparent concern, he lowered the binoculars to the table and glanced down at his Log, idly running his eyes over the entry recorded a few moments ago.

23.50 hrs. Wind S by W. 35 knots gusting 40. Viz ¼ mile reducing. NTR.

'Nothing to report.' Thank goodness there wasn't. He wondered at the possible fate of anyone at sea in this weather, gaining little comfort from the knowledge that, if anything did happen, there was little he personally could do about it. He could call Doctor Stewart, the Leemouth Lifeboat Secretary, but he probably wouldn't agree to launching the Atlantic 21 class lifeboat. It was only supposed to be used up to a Force Six – or so the Regulations said – and it was well past that now. More like eight.

He could call out Langley Coastguard Cliff Rescue Team with their Breeches Buoy apparatus if he had a casualty close to shore, but they had nearly ten miles to come and by the sound of the seas thundering upon the rocks below him at the foot of the Head he doubted if they, or anyone else, could be of much help.

A feeling of inadequacy came over him. He couldn't just sit here while someone drowned. He'd have to do something, but what? Even the offshore lifeboat at Melhampton could hardly be expected to render assistance with thirty-odd miles of heavy seas intervening. 'I'm as useless as a fart in a colander,' he said to himself gloomily. 'I might just as well wrap up and go home.'

Such thoughts depressed him so he rose from the stool and taking his oilskins from their hook, put them on. If I can't do anything else, at least I can wipe some of the salt off the windows, he decided. It will wake me up too. Turning the doorknob, he pushed gradually and carefully, inching the door open. Then the wind took charge and despite all his effort literally tore the door from his grasp, crashing it back against the tower's wooden side. He winced as he heard the splintering of wood.

Stepping through the opening onto the terrace-like platform around the tower, the wind hit him like a bomb blast. The buckled door had bent the catch on the side wall that held it open and he had to fumble for a few minutes before managing to get it secure. His eyes closed to slits as he turned to face the wind and leaned forward almost horizontally. It dragged at his oilskins, flapping the loose material wildly, threatening to rip the buttons off as he tried to keep the two sides together with one hand while hanging on to the rail with the other. His hair flattened on his scalp as he edged his way forward and around to the front. He laughed, humourlessly, at the stupidity of what he was doing and pulled the chamois leather from his pocket but, as he raised his hand to the window, the leather was whipped from his fingers. He gave up and turned away from the wind, using both hands to hang on grimly to the rail as the gale shoved him in the back like a shunting train. His oilskins ballooned like a sailing ship in a typhoon and his feet were almost blown from under him as he was pushed back to the door. How he closed it behind him, he didn't know. He remembered waiting several times for what seemed like ages for the wind to ease off sufficiently to let him do so. It had taken all his strength and left him breathless and exhausted. He was more than grateful to get back inside out of the mind-numbing wind. The door handle was broken and one of the panels split. He wedged it closed then sat back on the unyielding stool to contemplate the wording of his damage report. He'd have to think of something plausible. They would certify him if they found out he had been trying to clean the bloody windows in a howling gale. He must have been crazy.

His eyes searched around looking for inspiration, then locked on to the wall-clock with its second hand jerkily making its circuit around the white face. Lighting an illegal cigarette he inhaled the calming smoke deep into his lungs then exhaled luxuriously, blowing smoke like one of St George's dragons, watching it being caught in numerous draughts of air swirling around the tower.

He jumped as the VHF radio on the wall came to life and an urgent voice filled the tower.

'MAYDAY, MAYDAY, MAYDAY. This is the fishing vessel *Bonnie Lass*, *Bonnie Lass*, *Bonnie Lass*. Does anyone read me? – Over.'

Chapter Six

A distant jangling filled the room, drawing nearer and nearer with the speed of an express train approaching from out of a tunnel, until it burst through the thick fog of his sleep-sodden mind. He woke with a start.

Instinctively he stretched an arm from out of the warm snugness of his bed and felt for the telephone that was dancing sadistically on the bedside table. Slowly, and with a great deal of effort, he lifted the leaden weight of the receiver across to his ear, grateful that the cacophony of bells had stopped.

What on earth made him choose a profession where people could get him out of bed at all hours? Especially tonight when he had only arrived home a few hours ago from a rather bacchanalian dinner at the Lodge.

What was it this time, he wondered. Someone with a toothache or perhaps Liz Kendall's baby? ... Whatever it was he wished it could have waited until the morning. He was desperately tired.

His eyes remained steadfastly closed but his mouth opened a fraction and a furry hoarse voice emitted from his gravelled throat – 'Doctor Stewart.'

'Leemouth Coastguard here, Doctor,' said the metallic telephone.

He jerked into full consciousness and the fog cleared from his mind. Nature had bestowed her gift of mental clarity upon him whenever situations of stress or urgency arose, and even though it was an immense asset to him in his chosen career, it was especially so in his role as Secretary and Launching Authority of the local lifeboat: an office of which he was inordinately proud to have held since coming south from his native Scotland some fifteen years ago.

He recognised the voice, and queried, 'Yes, Ray, what can I do for you?' pleased to hear the calmness of his own voice.

'I've just received a Mayday from a fishing boat called *Bonnie Lass*, Doctor,' reported the Coastguard. 'Her engine is kaput and she's riding to a sea-anchor. Her skipper says she's in a pretty bad way, only about a mile offshore and roughly sou'west of my Look-out. I reckon with this wind and tide she'll be up on the rocks within the hour, then there will be no hope of saving her.'

'How bad is the weather Ray?' It seemed a totally unnecessary question because, even in the relative shelter of the village, his own house was being shaken by very strong gusts of wind, and long strands of thorny bramble roses, climbing the outer walls, were aggressively rattling against the windowpane of his bedroom as if demanding sanctuary from the storm.

'To be perfectly honest, Doctor, it's bloody awful,' Ray replied with excessive loudness, as though trying to outdo the weather. 'It's blowing about Force Eight from the sou'west and there's a hell of a sea running.' There was a brief pause and the doctor could hear the drone of the storm outside of the Coastguard's tower, over the phone.

'I was in two minds whether to call you or not,' he continued, 'but there's not much else I can do, though I shall call out Langley CRS in a minute, just in case. Not that they can do much either.'

'Any idea how many people on board, Ray?'

'Yes. Her skipper said three all told.'

'Well,' said the doctor, pondering his dilemma, 'it sounds as though it is too bad for me to authorise a launching, Ray, but you know what Geoff's like. Leave it with me for a minute. I'll give him a ring and come back to you.' Then as an afterthought he asked, 'Have you contacted Melhampton offshore lifeboat?' knowing full well that Ray didn't need anyone to tell him his job. 'It would be as well to put them on stand-by at least, don't you think?'

Replacing the receiver he hesitated for a fraction of a second, wondering how he could ask the crew to launch on a night like this. Geoff, the coxswain, would be furious if the launch was refused without even consulting him – not that he had to, but he admired the man and had the greatest respect for his nautical professionalism. He was a damn fine seaman even if inclined a bit towards recklessness, which wasn't a bad thing as far as sea-rescue was concerned. Over-caution could, and did, mean people being left to drown, and had no place in the RNLI.

Geoff is always boasting about how good the boat is and swearing he would take her to sea in any weather, but then, it's all right for him to talk. It's still my responsibility!

With typical Scottish frankness he rebuked himself for such an unfair thought. After all, it was Geoff who would be taking the boat to sea, not him!

Nevertheless, as Station Hon. Sec., *he* was responsible, and he couldn't delegate such a burden.

Momentarily he made up his mind not to give his authority and reached for the phone to inform Ray. Then he remembered the three men on the fishing boat. Could he deliberately let them go to their deaths without at least giving Geoff the opportunity to consider attempting a rescue?

Picking up the receiver again he dialled the coxswain's number, feeling decidedly guilty at his lack of courage. He should have said a categorical 'NO' to Ray. What was he about to start? Geoff and the crew would go without a second thought, given the chance. Was it fair to place the onus on them? Torn with indecision he stared unhappily into the blankness of the dark bedroom, groping carefully like a blind man in strange surroundings for the main light switch somewhere on the wall above his head.

The telephone clicked and a voice barked, 'Ross!'

Chapter Seven

It had been a long, frustrating and demoralising day. Everything had gone wrong for Geoff Ross, or so it seemed. Why was it, he asked himself, that when he had one problem everything else seemed to go sour? He supposed a head-shrink would label it with some highfalutin name and say it was his own fault, and he would probably be right, he admitted begrudgingly, but that didn't make him feel any better.

It had all started at the breakfast table that morning. What had begun as an everyday discussion with his eighteen-year-old son David, had developed into a heated argument ending with both sides sulking angrily. David had risen angrily from the table calling back over his shoulder, 'Trouble with you, Dad, is that you still think I'm a kid,' as he threw on an anorak jacket and stormed out of the house slamming the front door behind him.

It had left him depressed. There was something drastically wrong with their relationship. They just could not communicate. Other fathers appeared to get on well with their sons, why couldn't he? Was it his fault? he asked himself. He so wanted to be good friends with his only child and made every effort to understand the workings of a modern teenager's mind, but the more he tried the worse things became. He would give anything to be like 'Gravy' Browning, the builder, and his son. They went everywhere, and did everything, together.

Then his wife got shirty. With two grown men in the house sulking and quarrelling like children he couldn't really blame her, but she did seem to take Dave's side most of the time. It was either maternal protective instinct or his own twisted imagination. Whatever it was, it only made him feel worse, and he had left for work, earlier than usual, feeling very irritable. On top of everything, today was the day his Area Manager was due to call on his regular fortnightly visit. He could well do without that horrible little man's sarcastic nit-picking ways. He knew the man detested him and would jump at any opportunity to get rid of him. Just because his brother was MD of the firm he thought he could treat people like dirt and get away with it. Unfortunately he could. Geoff needed his job. There was no other work anywhere in the area.

The short walk through the lovely seaside village did little to improve his petulant mood, but at least the crisp fresh air swept away the beginnings of a headache that tightened around his forehead, as he

strode purposefully along the uneven paving stones, kicking venge-
fully at the occasional weed that had the temerity to show between the
cracks.

John Thomas, the unfortunately named postman, called 'Good morning Geoff' from across the street, hefting his mail-bag into a more
comfortable position, burping loudly from the acidy burn in his chest as
he regretted the bacon-and-egg breakfast that aggravated his hiatus
hernia. Geoff nodded a silent acknowledgement, then said 'Good morning' to the bent back of old Mrs Dains, on her knees scrubbing the
front-door step of her tidy little terraced house on the corner of Cross
Street.

He reached the pub at the corner, walking abstractly beneath its dilapidated sign that hung, rusted and fatigued by years of almost continuous
wind-driven swinging; some village people used it as a weather-gauge
saying they could tell the wind-force by the sound of its screeching and
grinding. They could well be right. It made a horrible noise. How nearby
residents could stand it was beyond belief. All it needed was a bit of
oil ... and a chipping hammer.

He turned left along the cobbled waterfront street, past the red-brick
Lifeboat Station on the opposite side. Reaching his office, he pushed open
the heavy weather-worn front door and went along the short, dimly-lit
entrance hall and entered the dingy main outer office where his terse
greeting brought raised eyebrows and an exchange of knowing glances
from the two girl-clerks who had hurriedly put away the magazine they
had been sharing when they heard his approaching footsteps.

Walking straight past them with a grunted greeting, he entered his
own small office, and dropped heavily into the battered-leather swivel-
chair with a sigh, feeling very sorry for himself.

Swinging the chair around with a twist of his hips, he sat looking out
of the window with unseeing eyes, lost in a mist of confused thoughts.
The small harbour lay before him with its two aged, granite-stone
breakwaters curving out from the shoreline, forming a harbour that
embraced a handful of small dinghies and scarred fishing craft lying
quietly at their moorings, ignoring the solitary white sailing-cruiser
whose owner contemptuously shunned the plush marina at nearby
Langley, preferring the delights of this pleasantly attractive west-country
village.

Ten years ago this same harbour had been a hive of activity, its busy
fleet of fishing boats so numerous that pleasure craft were virtually
excluded by reason of space. Moorings were at a premium. During the
summer season yachts would tie up three abreast alongside the embrac-
ing breakwaters. Latecomers who had not booked a berth would be

reluctantly turned away and directed to Langley Harbour by the Harbour Master, loath to forego any addition to his bulging bag of Harbour dues.

The Jolly Taxpayer, Leemouth's one and only pub, would be packed solid with the transient 'Yachties,' from opening time to the moment the harassed, but contented, publican called 'Time gentlemen, please.'

Local villagers, having been admitted by the back door a few minutes early by a landlord who was only too aware that he must keep their goodwill to carry him through the winter, would spread themselves out in the 'snug' and greet the visitors with withering glares should they attempt to enter their 'reserved' territory. The generous 'Yachties' however, in general, took no offence. To them the residents' behaviour was part and parcel of the local 'charm and character', and many a pint of foaming brew found its way onto the 'snug' table – courtesy of the gentleman at the bar wearing yellow 'wellies'.

Now, most of the yacht owners and fishermen had succumbed to the new and better facilities at Langley, where the new marina had attracted a host of small shops, restaurants, chandlers and other conveniences that Leemouth lacked.

These days, the busiest user of Leemouth's little harbour was its lifeboat housed on top of the slipway across the narrow street from Geoff's office. She was his pride and joy.

He had joined the crew more than a decade ago when the lifeboat had been a wooden-hulled eight-knotter which, despite its slowness, had been a fine sea-boat, with an impressive record. Four years ago, it had been replaced by the RNLI with a revolutionary new fast boat, much to the anger and displeasure of the crew who were mostly fishermen and thought the 'new boat' was nothing more than a toy.

This new craft had a rigid glass-fibre hull with inflatable rubber sponson tubes fixed along either side, from stem to stern, acting as gunwales. Her twin 40 hp outboard engines gave her an astounding speed of thirty knots and made her a very lively boat.

The whole crew, except for Geoff, resigned. Most did so without option to comply with the RNLI Regulation that no one over the age of forty-five should serve on this ATLANTIC 21 class of boat, owing to the possibility of kidney damage resulting from the pounding the crew were subjected to in heavy seas. The remainder left in disgust that they be expected to go to sea in what they considered to be an overgrown 'rubber-duck', fit only for pleasure boating.

Within a very short time, this boat, and her new crew of young men, with Geoff as the coxswain, proved herself time and time again. The whole village was proud of her achievements. Everyone, that is, except the few former crewmen who still retained their bitterness. They would sit at the extremity of the breakwater watching the lifeboat set out on exercise, calling derisive comments such as 'Mind you don't run over a pin!' Seldom were these same men around when she sailed 'on service' in bad weather, and even less frequently did they voice their opinions in the bar of The Jolly Taxpayer, where the walls were covered with photographs and newspaper cuttings of the lifeboat's activities, and the only 'charity-box' on the bar-top was an RNLI one that launched a little plastic lifeboat down a slipway each time a coin was dropped in the slot.

How long Geoff sat there trance-like, he didn't know, but he was rudely brought back into the land of the living by the sudden appearance, in the office doorway, of a none-too-pleased Area Manager whose sarcastic 'Did I wake you up Mr Ross?' did little for Geoff's mood. He almost told him to go back out and knock before entering but thought better of it. That would be playing into the creep's hands. He was an arrogant little man who took advantage of his seniority and derived great pleasure from the embarrassment he was able to cause this so-called 'hero' of the local community. 'Ross might be top-notch in a boat,' he thought maliciously, 'but he was mediocre as a manager.' And he had told his brother this, on more than one occasion.

With sadistic pleasure he began delving deep into the office books, raising petty queries that he knew to be exasperating, and it was way past normal lunchtime before he eventually departed, much to everyone's relief, leaving the girls to sort out and re-file the documents that had been so thoroughly scrutinised, and Geoff to irritably face his own full-day's work load.

It was gone seven in the evening before he was able to lock up the office, and thankfully get out into the fresh air. Mentally and physically exhausted, he uncharacteristically failed to notice the deterioration in the weather as he made his way home, his mind occupied with the hope that both his wife and son had mellowed during the day and that there would be no more awkward silences. He was so fed up with being miserable.

He knew the answer as soon as he opened the front door. The unspoken accusations. He was late. He could have phoned. His dinner was ruined.

David had already gone out for the evening and Geoff's wife sat in the living-room watching telly, engrossed in 'Coronation Street'. 'Why did women get so involved with other people's lives,' he wondered, as he sat alone at the table contemplating his meal that, even though he was two hours late, was hardly dried up, and had obviously been lovingly tended.

Was it all his fault? he asked himself for the umpteenth time. Was he becoming a crotchety old bastard who couldn't be spoken to?

He looked at himself in the kitchen wall-mirror as he washed and rinsed his plate. 'Christ,' he blasphemed. 'I'm only forty, yet I look ninety.'

The evening passed quietly, wife and husband each absorbed in their own unhappiness. At one time his wife had placed her hand on his and he had responded just enough to signal his acceptance of the silent gesture. He wanted to take her in his arms and love her but his obstinacy held him back and she released herself with an excuse to go into the kitchen to make a pot of tea.

By ten o'clock, he could hardly keep his eyes open and his suggestion of an early night was readily agreed to. Wearily they got in bed but whereas he fell asleep almost immediately his wife lay listening to the wind that, by now, was roaring about the house and rattling the bedroom door and windows until, almost like a lullaby, it brought sleep.

It took several seconds for the distant tinkling to reach deep into Geoff's exhausted mind and register as the ringing of his telephone, probably because he was completely submerged under the blankets. Automatically his arm emerged into the coldness, reaching for the phone, knowing that – at this time of the night – it had to be a lifeboat 'shout'. Raising himself up on one elbow he leaned over the edge of the bed and brought the receiver to his ear. He could hear the howling wind outside and thought, 'Who the hell is at sea on a night like this?' In that split second he became fully awake and heard the urgency in the husky voice coming from the phone. 'Hello Geoff ... Doc Stewart here. We've got a call for the lifeboat.'

Geoff's feet were already swinging out of the bed as his free hand groped in the dark for the light switch. His wife, fully awake by now, lay fearfully looking at the dim shape of his bare back. She put out her hand to touch him but he was engrossed in his conversation, while struggling – one handed – to get into his clothes.

'Of course we'll go, Doc ... yes, no doubts.' He stopped, staggering to pull on a sock.

'I *know* it's your responsibility ... Yes, the boat will be fine,' he answered the string of concerned questions. Then irritably, 'Well somebody's got to go for them!' A final pause. 'Okay, I'm on my way if you will fire off the maroons. See you at the boathouse.'

With that, he dropped the phone back on its cradle, quickly finished dressing, then leaned back across the bed to kiss his wife tenderly.

'Don't worry, love, it's not as bad as it sounds.' He backed off the bed then, opening the door, called back over his shoulder, 'See you in a mo.'

Chapter Eight

Twenty-one year old Bob Denning, the youngest member of the lifeboat crew, lay snuggled up in bed staring into the black void above him, listening to the storm beyond the insulating walls and hearing, in the lulls between gusts, the strident grinding of the inn-sign outside The Jolly Taxpayer, around the corner. It must be blowing a full gale out there now, he judged. That means there's no chance of a Service launch tonight. Too rough for the '21'.

Even if the Q.E.2 did a *Titanic* under Leemouth Head the Hon. Sec wouldn't let us go, he thought. They would get the 'big boat' at Melhampton to launch. Yet, from the warm security of his bed he half hoped that at any moment he would hear the two maroons explode, calling out the crew.

Deep, way back in his subconscious mind, he was honest enough to admit to his own lack of experience and realised that his bravado was probably due to there being no likelihood of the coxswain choosing him as a crewman in this sort of weather, even if they did launch. His 'lot' was rescuing wind-surfers and dinghies on nice summer days although, he recollected proudly, he had gone out on a night-search once in pretty naughty weather, and Geoff had praised him afterwards.

He knew the time would come, one day, when he would be an automatic choice on bad jobs, but for now at least, a 'turn-out' tonight would be something to tell his envious mates about, at work tomorrow, even if he only helped with the launching.

He had gone to bed early. Telly was the usual load of rubbish and he was flat broke in any case. Mum was depressed and pretty rotten company, but this had been her way of life ever since Dad died two, no three, years ago. The heart had gone out of her and all his efforts to cheer her up failed. Now, when he stayed in, he just sat quietly with her, respecting her silence and getting miserable himself. He wished, with all his heart, that she would find herself another man. She was still a youngish woman, and attractive. He didn't fancy the idea of his Dad being replaced so soon but he also didn't like to see her so unhappy and miserable. She still had a life to live and, after all, he wasn't going to be around forever. He wanted to do things and go places but, at the moment, the lifeboat was his life, just as it was the hub of the village life now that the fishing had died off.

He considered himself lucky to get a place in the crew by being in the right place at the right time. He had been one of the enthusiastic 'helpers' at the lifeboat station at the time the 'Atlantic 21' replaced the old boat. Geoff Ross got the job as Boss-man and he'd been looking for new blood for his crew. Bob was there, right at his elbow and had been one of the first to be given the coveted job, much to the envy of his mates and the admiration of Jenny, his girlfriend.

He would never have stood such a chance in the days of the old boat, with its ancient crew. You had to be over thirty in those days to even be their tea-boy. Talk about dead men's shoes!

He liked and respected Geoff, as did almost everybody in the village. He envied him his reputation and the medal earned for an extremely daring rescue several years ago that he modestly never mentioned, even though there were several framed newspaper reports of it hanging up on the pub wall.

Bob imagined himself lined up with the rest of the crew along the quayside on some flag bedecked occasion with a shiny new award for bravery of his own pinned to the right breast of his RNLI jersey, being jealously watched by the local lads; and was that 'blonde bird' over there looking at him in awe and admiration?

Fantasy followed fantasy, but sleep evaded him. Some chance of fame he had with a mere ten rescue services to his credit, and even they had only been 'bread and butter' jobs.

Geoff and the other crewmen were good blokes though, and he was learning fast. They kept telling him he was still young and had a lifetime ahead but his impatience demanded everything now! He saw himself as coxswain of the lifeboat, spray smashing into his face as they sailed through the harbour entrance where TV cameras and floodlights recorded the start of yet another epic rescue.

An extra strong gust of wind rattled his bedroom window bringing him wide awake. Blimey! he thought, I'm getting a right Walter Mitty.

From the corner of his eye he saw a blurred smudge of light. Turning his head he recognised the luminous dial of his wristwatch. He lifted his head from the pillow and focused his eyes onto the faint glow. Surprisingly it was only a little after midnight. He expected it to be three or four o'clock at least. Would his over-imaginative mind never let him sleep?

His head dropped back on to the cushioning pillow and he screwed a fistful of duvet tightly up under his chin, willing himself to go to sleep.

BANG – a short sharp explosion like a pistol shot, heard loudly above the howling wind, reverberated around the room.

He froze … 'Jesus,' he said, irreverently shocked wide awake. 'That was a maroon.'

Hardly daring to breathe, his heart pounding, he listened expectantly and fearfully. Would there be a second one to summon the lifeboat crew?

Chapter Nine

'Arr, Jim boy,' exclaimed old 'Tommo' Grayling in his best imitation of Long John Silver, as he poked his head into the 'snug' of The Jolly Taxpayer. 'Oy thart oyd find thee in yer.'

He hobbled in, his two good legs unconvincingly playing the part of one good one and a peg-leg.

'The windy's a blowin' up, and thar's a couple of boats in the 'arbour that 'e moyght loyke to 'ave a look at afore they sinks.'

Jim Tucker put his pint back on the table and turned his head just in time to see Tommo's grizzly back, shaking with amusement, disappear from the doorway to escape the expected reply.

'Just my bloody luck,' he cursed, as his fist closed again around his glass. 'Trust Tommo to know I'd volunteered to stand in for the Harbour Master while he was away at his daughter's wedding.' He lifted himself a few inches off the cushioned seat to peer sideways out of the salt-stained window. He could see the deterioration in the weather by the little white-capped waves already showing among the bobbing boats, and the scraps of village debris being blown along the street like tumbling racing-cars.

Swallowing the remainder of his drink he gazed into his empty glass, like a fortune-teller deciphering tea-leaves, then got up and nodded towards the landlord as he returned his glass to the bar and went out, noting that the clock on the wall behind him showed the time as ten past eight which meant it was just eight o'clock.

It was a long, exhausting, three hours later before he was back in his small bedroom staring at his thirty-two year-old reflection in the cracked wall mirror. 'Bloody hell!' he thought, 'I look like an old man.'

The last few hours had been a hard battle, going from boat to boat, replacing and reinforcing mooring ropes, rigging new fenders, bailing out flooded dinghies and the hundred and one other jobs needing attention in the small, gale-lashed harbour. His hard callused hands were sore and he knew that tomorrow, when he returned to his own job, he would have a few colourful bruises to show for his stint as Acting Unpaid Harbour Master. He felt shattered.

Crossing the landing he went into the bathroom and turned the tap of the water-boiler, on the wall above the enamelled iron bath, on full; adding a liberal measure of Radox Salts to ease his tired body. Wearily his aching fingers fumbled with stubborn shirt-buttons and trouser belt-buckle as he dropped his wet clothes in a heap on the floor. Then, with a pleasurable sigh, he gratefully lowered himself into the deep hot bath wishing that, at times like this, he had someone to rub his back and cook a good hot meal.

With these thoughts drifting through his mind he dozed, and slipped lower into the hot luxurious suds. The whistling of the wind, screaming through the cracks of the ill-fitting window frame, was nothing more than a lullaby to his eardrums that had taken such a pounding during the last hours, and he slid uncaringly into an aquatic drowse, dreaming of his Army days and the good times spent in Hong Kong. Those were the days. Booze, babes and more booze, with an occasional military parade thrown in to break the monotony. Like a fool, he had left the Army at the insistence of a woman who had then spent all his money before leaving him for another bloke who, to rub salt into the wound, was still in the bloody Army!

Sadly, he returned his thoughts to the present, and his lonely, mucky, part-time job on the farm just outside the village. He hated it. He must change his life, even if it meant moving away. If that happened, he would miss his involvement with the lifeboat. That was fun, and rewarding. He even enjoyed turning out on cold, wet and windy nights in the middle of winter. He must be a masochist, but the social life and comradeship among the crew was well worth the occasional discomfort. But, he had to be realistic. The farm job didn't pay very well and he earned very little extra from his couple of days a week fishing from his boat. He caught plenty, but had no buyers except for the pub and one or two regulars in the village. It was barely enough to live on, let alone lead a normal single man's life. He couldn't afford a girlfriend and had to limit his drinking. If only he could find a steady job, earn a decent wage, and be happy.

A sharp, whip-crack explosion of a maroon, seemingly within inches of his bathroom window, brought him abruptly and shockingly awake. He shot out of the bath like a Polaris missile, knowing instinctively that another maroon would surely follow.

Fumbling with buttons, he threw on his damp clothes without drying himself. His brain, jolted into life, raced ahead of his reluctant body and by the time the second detonation reached him he was stumbling half dressed down the stairs.

Even after his earlier experience in the harbour he was still unprepared for the violence of the wind that hit him like a blast from a cannon as he stepped out of his house opposite the pub and fought his way onto the deserted cobbled street. For the first time ever, in his life as an active fisherman and lifeboat-man, he felt the ruffling waves of concern deep inside. He staggered, wind-blown, the few yards to the lifeboat station, passing the row of unlit cottages that sheltered their elderly occupants. Past the trees with boughs streaming unwaveringly downwind and constantly quivering, unable to spring back against the pressure of the unrelenting gale. Rounding the corner where the sign outside The Jolly

Taxpayer swung violently from its bracket, screeching raucously, like a tinny church-bell tolling a mournful warning, and onto the quayside awash with the spray and spume from the brutalised harbour seas.

At the door of the boathouse he collided with the coxswain who was fumbling with a key in the lock, his face streaming sea-water and a piece of seaweed decorously plastered across his shoulder.

They exchanged joyless grins and hurriedly entered the comparative peace of the dank darkness. Geoff switched on the light, swiftly running his eyes over the grey and orange hull nestling comfortably on its launching trolley, yet giving the impression of being poised, ready to spring into life and charge off into action, as he crossed to the telephone hung over the desk, to get an up-date from the Coastguard on the casualties situation, while Jim went about his appointed tasks with an outward show of calmness he didn't feel.

Almost immediately, young Bob Denning burst dramatically in the door, closely followed by an exhausted Doctor Stewart and 'Doggy' Barker who, at the ripe old age of forty-eight, was the Head Launcher. Within seconds they too were joined by Pip Langman and Dave Fulton, two of the remaining members of the crew.

'Stodger won't be coming,' one of them called breathlessly across to no one in particular. 'He's laid-up wiv a broken toe.'

Geoff replaced the receiver and turned to find the Honorary Secretary behind him.

'Well, Doc,' he reported, 'it looks like this fishing boat has had it, unless we do something bloody quick. The Coastguard reckons it'll be on the rocks in no time flat. He can't see anything, but the people on the boat reported that they caught a glimpse of the lighthouse loom earlier on, and thought they saw broken water to leeward.'

A worried frown flitted across the doctor's forehead. 'I can't let you go out in this, Geoff,' he pleaded, as he watched the coxswain climb into his two-piece weatherproof suit. 'It would be sheer bloody murder.'

'Aye,' came the grunted reply, 'and we'll be the ones doing the murdering if you don't okay the launching.'

'But it's my responsibility, man,' said the Scot defensively. 'I'm the one that's got to answer if anything happens to you.'

'Well, one thing's certain, Doc. We can't waste time arguing about it so I'll make it easy for you,' replied the coxswain impatiently. 'We've got to go, with or without your authority. We are the only hope they've got, and that's what the job is all about.'

The obvious sincerity in the words removed all the sting from this rebellious response and the doctor's answer was equally decisive.

'If you've got the guts to go, lad, then I must find the courage to support you. I'll approve the launch.' As he spoke these words he felt the weight of responsibility heavy on his soul, knowing full well he was wrong. But, he consoled himself, they would have gone in any case and taken the consequences of an action he was too cowardly to approve. 'I'd never be able to face them, or any villager, again ... ever,' he said to himself, as he offered a silent prayer.

Decisions made, Geoff became a man of action. Turning to the expectant faces of his crew, who had been busily readying the boat and themselves for sea, he gave his orders.

'Right, lads.' He spoke just loud enough to be heard above the buffeting the boathouse was taking. 'This is going to be a naughty one so, irrespective of seniority and experience, I'm only taking the two single men on this trip, and I don't want any argument, so let's get on with it.'

Each man returned to his allotted task and the doctor, being a keen observer of human nature, saw the bitter disappointment on the faces of the men ordered to stay behind. How they contrasted with the eagerness of Jim and Bob, both flushed with adrenaline as they hurriedly nodded their heads into life-jackets and tightened the waist strap before crouching down with knees apart to pass the crotch-strap between their legs.

Were these brave men, or just perverse? Was it courage that drove them, or stubborn refusal to be beaten by Mother Nature? Were they filled with humanitarian desire to save their fellow man or just determined to deprive the cruel sea of another victim? As men, they were no different from others. They came in all shapes and sizes. Good and bad, drunk and sober, religious and otherwise, but as lifeboat-men they became a breed apart. Dedicated and professional, but certainly not fearless, as he could see by the tightness of their lips and taut features. Yes, they are certainly human all right, he thought, as he watched them prepare themselves for the onslaught to come.

He picked up the telephone and dialled.

'Leemouth Coastguard,' came the abrupt, metallic voice from its bleak perch up on the headland.

'Hello Ray, Doctor Stewart here. We will be launching in a minute or two. What's the situation now please?'

'Launching?' came the astonished reply. 'It's blowing a fortnight out there!' ... a slight pause then, 'Well, I still can't see a thing but they must be on the rocks below me by now.'

The doctor could sense the utter frustration in Ray's voice as he continued. 'They were calling me a few minutes ago but then their transmission stopped after the first few words so either their radio is US, or they've had it. I've been calling them continuously since then, but there's no answer. Melhampton boat is launching but it will be hours before they get anywhere near here, in this weather. Langley CRS are on their way but they will take at least an hour, providing the roads aren't blocked. Don't think much of your lads' chances either, Doc,' he added.

'Thank you, Ray,' replied the Hon. Sec., as casually as he could manage, as he replaced the receiver. At that moment, he was blasted by what felt like a violent explosion that had him staggering deafly for several seconds before his reeling senses recovered enough for him to realise that the big doors comprising the entire seaward end of the building had been slid open, exposing the boathouse interior to the blasting wind and stinging sea-spray.

Geoff was yelling his instructions out of pure necessity to be heard above the howling wind, as the six men pushed the boat on its trolley, out of the boathouse onto the brink of the slipway where, held by the restraining hawser, it paused trembling, as if with excitement at the challenge it was facing, its bow pointing down the slope towards the turbulent water that rushed, wind-driven, halfway up the incline before admitting defeat by gravity and retiring to regroup for another assault.

Geoff, Jim and young Bob clambered aboard, already life-jacketed, to take their seats and ram their sea-booted feet into the safety stirrups on the decking.

Dougie, the Head Launcher, grasped the recovery hawser firmly with both hands as he waited anxiously for the signal to slip. Above the noise of the storm he heard the first engine burst into life followed by the second. He tensed expectantly, then seeing Geoff drop his raised arm, loosened his grip on the rope allowing it to run freely through his hands and around the staghorn bollard at his feet. The trolley, free of its restraining leash, ran smoothly down the slipway, meeting a climbing wave as it reached its zenith and being swept down with it into the harbour.

Jim and Bob slipped the trolley securing straps and the lifeboat, released from its carriage, nosed almost eagerly into the wind-streaked sea, nasty enough even though still within the harbour, as Geoff thrust the engine throttles forward.

Back at the boathouse, standing exposed in the open doorway, the four men peered into the darkness, hands over their eyes in futile protection from the driving spindrift. They could see little except the brilliant white stern-light of the lifeboat as it drove across the small harbour towards the blurred whiteness that they knew, to their horror, was the storm-lashed cauldron of sea at the gap between the two break-waters marking the harbour entrance.

They watched in fearful awe. The light bobbed away, getting fainter and fainter. Then suddenly, as it merged into the white hell, it vanished.

Chapter Ten

Bonnie Lass was not enjoying the last minutes of her life. All hope of re-starting the engine had gone. She was just a lifeless hulk drifting downwind towards a sudden and violent death.

Ted climbed out of the tiny engine-room to report to his skipper in the wheelhouse that there was a total fuel blockage somewhere that would require a major strip-down to locate.

After the heat and stuffiness of the confined engine-space he was soon numbed by the ferocity of the wind and noise that struck him as he emerged from the hatch, angrily cursing the incompetent idiots at Bellwood's who, he was certain, were the culprits – and blaming himself for not checking more thoroughly. The motion, as he stood on the deck recovering his breath and stretching his legs for the first time in ages, seemed ten times worse than it felt down below. Huge seas, their white crests torn off and blown high over the trawler's wheelhouse, rushed past on either side as the boat rode sluggishly over each one, as though too tired to resist any more. Solid seas broke over her low-lying foredeck as she lurched from side to side until jerkily checked with a jolt by the restraining sea-anchor, and brought back head to wind.

Normally the angry cresting seas would not have worried him to any great extent but in the boat's present disabled condition he was more than a little concerned. Placing his back briefly to the wind he looked astern but all he could see was a few yards of wind-strewn sea disappearing into the solid darkness. He turned and forced his way forward, leaning into the wind and being soaked by flying spray.

Dragging open the wheelhouse door with great difficulty against the pressure of the wind, he squeezed himself into the small square space alongside Joe who stood gripping the useless wheel and staring out of the window.

'No good mate,' he reported, looking at Joe's strained face. 'Not a hope in hell.'

Joe turned, and Ted chilled to see the glazed look in his skipper's eyes. A moment passed, then Joe replied quietly, 'Neither have we, chum.'

The two lifelong friends looked each other straight in the eye and Joe took a deep breath. 'We've got a duff radio and a lee shore within spitting distance.' He paused again, then squaring his shoulders, made his decision.

'Get Ben up here and batten down everything. I want both of you in here, in life-jackets. Make it as quick as you can,' he added ominously, 'because as sure as hell we're going to hit the beach soon so put on as much protective clothing as you can. We're going over the side and take our chances as soon as we get near the shore. At least the sea-anchor's holding, that's something.'

Ted, suddenly fearful for young Ben, shouldered his way out of the wheelhouse to carry out the instructions. He met the lad at the engine-room hatch and together they secured the hatch cover. Then, going into the crew quarters, they dragged on extra jerseys and donned life-jackets.

'Got to take me photos,' Ben said calmly, as he pulled them from the bulkhead by the bookcase where they had been pinned, and placed them carefully in his pocket. The older man looked at him with a mixture of love and admiration. The lad was certainly a cool one. He wanted to say so many things, of comfort and assurance, of how he felt towards him, and how he would protect him, but all he answered was, 'They'll get bloody wet.'

Together they went back out on deck to return to the wheelhouse, carrying a life-jacket and a couple of jerseys for Joe. As Ted made his way hand over hand along the rail of the superstructure, bracing himself against the plunging and rolling of the stricken vessel, he heard Ben's fearful scream. He turned in panic expecting to see the lad being washed away over the side, but he was still there, facing aft away from Ted, and pointing.

In horror, Ted's eyes followed the outstretched arm, and his blood froze.

Less than fifty yards astern, the seas were pounding onto jagged, evil-looking rocks, throwing spray high into the air where it appeared to hover briefly, as though admiring the view, before collapsing back with a tremendous roar. The darkness was lit by the incandescence of the boiling sea and behind the rocks a denser, higher shadow showed the blurred shape of a cliff face.

Grabbing Ben's arm, Ted hauled him forward and hammered on the wheelhouse door, skinning his knuckles in a frenzy to get the skipper's attention. The door was pushed open from the inside and Joe started to help them into the sheltered cuddy but stopped when Ted screamed, 'Look!' The skipper's mouth fell open and his heart stopped, as he took in the frightening scene astern. A wave of nausea and panic swept through him, then just as quickly subsided, leaving a feeling of strange calmness.

'Inside, you two,' he snapped.

They huddled together, each searching the other two faces for comfort, or sign of fright. Inwardly their souls were in torment, daggers of fear twisting their guts as blood seemed to freeze in their veins. Outwardly they showed calmness for the sake of their shipmates, but they were scared. Bloody scared.

'We will stay in here until she hits,' instructed Joe with as much confidence as he could muster. 'Cover your faces from the breaking glass and when I say GO … we go. And heaven help us. Don't try to swim. Let the sea take you and conserve your energy until you hit the shore. Then you will need all the strength you have. And get those bloody sea-boots off.'

They held on to each other closely, each taking strength from the other, waiting, helplessly, for the inevitable.

They were impotent, petrified spectators as *Bonnie Lass* drew ever closer to the black, foam-covered rocks, until with a splintering crash, they struck. The deck reared like a wild horse, throwing the three men brutally against each other and smashing the steering wheel. Shards of glass and loose items filled the air and a scream of agony, or fear, from one of them rose above the indescribable noise of the sea's assault on the unyielding rocks.

Again and again the vessel lifted dizzily, tossed sideways like a small toy onto the barbed granite teeth until she was swept right over them, ending on her beam-ends. Hungry seas poured into the gaping holes in her hull as momentarily she lay still and waterlogged, in a relatively sheltered area between the rocks and the looming dirty-white cliff.

'Let's go!' screamed Joe, and the three drenched, battered fishermen extricated themselves from the debris of what remained of the once immaculate wheelhouse.

Grasping Ben's life-jacket strapping, Ted clambered over the broken gunwale and together they fell into the foaming turbulence. Joe saw them go and painfully made to follow them. His arm and back hurt like hell and he knew for certain that he had a nasty injury somewhere. Exactly where he wasn't sure. He seemed hurt all over, and vaguely remembered being thrown against something bloody hard. He felt faint, nauseous and very weak.

He felt the boat lifting again as he started to climb over the shattered siderail. At that instant, a huge breaking sea smashed over the rocks, pouring down onto the doomed vessel's hull like a waterfall, and struck him hammer-like in the back, washing him head-over-heels into the scuppers, towards the stern. Seawater gushed into his open mouth, silencing his terrified scream. The last thing recorded in his mind's eye was a faint flashing blue light amidst the fog-like spray.

Chapter Eleven

'Give the Coastguard a shout and let them know we're on our way!' yelled Geoff over his shoulder as he balanced the two engine-throttles alongside his right knee. 'Ask if they've got a fix on the casualty yet.'

He felt, rather than saw, the nod of acknowledgement from Jim sat behind him at the VHF radio, then heard his muffled call.

'Leemouth Coastguard – Leemouth Coastguard – Leemouth Coastguard. This is Leemouth Lifeboat – Leemouth Lifeboat. Do you read? Over.'

'Lifeboat, this is Leemouth Coastguard. Read you strength four. Casualty believed to be on the rocks beneath my Look-out. Over.'

'Roger, Coastguard. Proceeding. Out.'

'Did you get that, Geoff?' shouted Jim, inches from the coxswain's ear.

Geoff nodded, leaning forward and flicking the console switch to activate the blue-flashing 'police' light at the stern in the hope that it would be seen by the fishing boat's crew and give them hope.

His main concern at that moment, however, was in conning the lifeboat across the darkness of the harbour, avoiding the moored craft and floating lines on the vacant buoys. He would look pretty silly to pick up one of those around his props before even getting out to sea.

He was already half blinded by the needles of spray driven into his face but, even so, he could still make out the solid mass of white foam at the harbour entrance ahead of him. The sight was horrifying. He felt fear constrict his throat and his chest seemed to solidify as he instinctively eased back the throttles. A hand touched his shoulder and although he couldn't hear what was said it had a calming effect, and he forced himself to relax.

His jaw ached where his teeth had been clamped tightly together and his thighs hurt through gripping the console seat between his knees. Thankfully, the tension eased off and he concentrated on his formidable task.

He kept as close to the southern breakwater as he dared in the knowledge that, when he cleared the seaward end, he would be pushed well downwind before being able to get the boat's head to starboard and pointing into those vicious waves. He shivered involuntarily. The frightening gap looked terrifying. He desperately wanted to check with his two crewmen sat behind him, and to feel the comfort of their presence, but he couldn't take his eyes from the menacing entrance, that looked more tempestuous as they came closer.

Then they were there.

A huge crested wave hit the end of the southern breakwater. One half

of it, balked by the unyielding sea wall, threw solid sea and spray high
into the air as the remainder swirled angrily around the curved knuckle
of stone worn smooth by an age of ceaseless conflict with the elements.

With helm hard over to starboard Geoff tried to meet it bow-on but
it caught the lifeboat on its beam and contemptuously flung it across the
entrance, narrowly missing the northern mole.

Before he could react, another heavy, curling breaker hit them, pouring
over the side sponson and filling the boat, but thankfully the two engines
purred away contentedly and he offered a silent tribute to their manu-
facturer. Breathlessly, he shook the water from his face and fought to
regain control of his semi-submerged command as the sea-water drained
away over the stern, between the engines. Manipulating helm and engine
speed he brought the boat's bow up into the wind and seas. Using all
his experience he clawed slowly to windward, avoiding the worst of the
breaking combers and cascading crests as they appeared from out of the
spray-laden darkness. It was like weaving through moving valleys
bordered by towering mountains, trying to dodge the most dangerous
ones and hanging on for dear life when he didn't.

He had no thought for steering a compass course. The only direction
he could go was directly into the eye of the storm; any other would have
been suicide, and as that was the way he wanted to go in any case, he
had no worries. Or did he?

The sea was filled with a wild hate that threatened to smash the lifeboat
over on her beam ends if he let the bow pay-off the wind too much, and
he had no doubt that his two crewmen were as scared and battered as
he was, more so probably. At least he had a job to occupy his thoughts;
they had nothing to do except hang on and hope.

Surprisingly he didn't feel quite so frightened in among the seething
white water. It was scarier when viewed from the outside. It was an
almost arrogant feeling of satisfaction to challenge and survive each of
the murderous white-crested watery mountains. He made a mental note
to ask the others if their thoughts had been the same.

An enormous white-topped wave, larger than most, appeared out of
the gloom, racing towards his starboard bow, and he turned the boat to
meet it head-on. Up and up went the bow, climbing the face of the wave
almost vertically as he cut back on the throttles. He wanted to 'flop' over
and through the crest with just enough speed to maintain control. Too
much would drive the bow over and expose too much hull for the wind
to catch, and possibly blow the boat back, bow over stern.

Wave after tremendous wave bore down on them like ranks of charging,
suicidal troops, each one a challenge to be met, but never to be beaten. As
his confidence grew so his strength began to slowly drain. He began to
feel weary fighting this endless battle, so he was more than grateful to feel

a hand grip his shoulder followed by an outstretched arm and finger pointing to starboard of his heading. He peered into the spray-filled murk but could see nothing except yet another steep-sided sea roaring down on his Cockleshell of a boat. The wind tore great lumps off it and he sensed the whole boat submerge until they were a fair imitation of a WWII human torpedo, with only their heads above water.

Surfacing, he wiped a hand over his streaming face to clear his salt-filled eyes. Again he peered ahead, squinting, scanning his limited horizon. Still nothing. Then he saw her.

'God Almighty,' he spluttered, more as a prayer than an oath. There she was, smashed to hell, barely afloat and hardly recognisable as a fishing boat.

Beyond her, to seaward, the terrific surf pounded on Leemouth rocks with appalling savagery, yet she herself was being pitched and tossed about like a sodden cigarette end in the comparative calm swell between the rocks and the cliff. Carefully he edged the lifeboat to starboard to gain shelter for himself in the lee of the rocks. Surely the stricken craft hadn't been washed *over* them, he questioned, incredulously.

Yet again, a hand fell on his shoulder and, although he couldn't understand a word of Bob's excited shout, he followed the finger pointing to the right of the wreck. At first, all he could see was a mass of confused water covered in flying spume then, momentarily, he saw a round black object which immediately disappeared. He stared at the spot, still watching the sea ahead out of the corner of his eye. There it was again! It was a man's head – no two!

Cautiously he inched the lifeboat over to starboard and nearer, gradually feeling the shelter of the rocks, hearing as though from a distance Jim's voice shouting into the hand-mike of the radio, reporting to the Coastguard.

Despite the violent motion of the lifeboat, he could still feel movement behind him as his two crew went through the much exercised routine of preparing to receive survivors.

They were getting close to the two bobbing heads so he began to ease back on the engine throttles, releasing them for a second to raise his right hand shoulder high and outstretched to indicate to his crew his intention of a 'starboard-side to' approach to the men in the water.

Concentrating on positioning the boat while keeping her as head-to-wind as possible, he played no part in getting the two fishermen aboard. This took a lot longer than normal and he knew it had been far from easy.

He waited patiently for the next move in the carefully rehearsed drill of sea-rescue but it was ages before a hand cupped over his ear and he heard Jim's awaited report.

'There's another one somewhere, Geoff,' he yelled. 'These two aren't too bad. They got off before the other bloke. They haven't seen him since so he could still be on board ... can't raise the Coastguard either.'

In reply, Geoff pointed to the wallowing wreck, now rolling dramatically with her deck awash. So low in the water was she that she disappeared from view in the troughs of even the smallest of seas still smashing their way to destruction on Leemouth beach and breakwater.

Slowly, the lifeboat edged forward as the crewmen wrapped the two survivors in heat-retaining foil blankets and secured them to the sponsons to prevent them from being washed overboard.

Geoff had no option but to approach the waterlogged fishing vessel from its lee side despite the tangle of cordage and netting streaming downwind threatening to enmesh the lifeboat's propellers.

As soon as safety permitted, he idled the starboard engine to reduce the danger of fouling and made his final approach on port screw only. He screamed into the wind as he spotted the seemingly lifeless life-jacketed body of the third fisherman being swirled back and forth on the wreck's flooded deck, but his warning was snatched away by the wind.

His first attempt to get alongside was foiled by an immense sea that came from nowhere and only his quick flick of the throttles, and a lot of luck, saved them from being caught under the casualty's deck-house and the damage that would have done to their rubber sponsons. The derisive fishermen back in Leemouth might call the 'Atlantic 21' a floating fender but puncturing a sponson on a night like this was the last thing he wanted.

Warily he eyed the swirling maelstrom around him, trying to judge when and how to make a second attempt.

Perversely, the floundering hulk was turning slowly into the wind and Geoff quickly realised that very soon he would have no lee at all from her. It was now or never. Thrusting both throttles forward, he again yelled to his crew to hang on but whether or not he was heard he never knew.

The distance between the two craft shortened alarmingly. Then, to his horror, he saw the wreck lift violently and tilt towards him as if on a giant hand. He snatched at the throttle levers as he felt his own bow dipping down and down, the stern coming up and over, pitch poling, and he was hurtling, head first, onto the splintered wheelhouse of the wreck as the two craft came together.

Chapter Twelve

Lt. Commander John Godfrey RNR, Divisional Inspector of Lifeboats, sat his heavy frame back into the worn upholstered armchair and looked at the group of men assembled around the table in the small room above The Jolly Taxpayer pub, each uncomfortably perched on one of a variety of stools and stacking chairs. A roaring fire spluttered cheerfully in the hearth but there was no cheer on the solemn faces before him.

He shuffled his papers awkwardly on the lid of the briefcase across his lap as he sought to find the right beginning.

'Gentlemen.' He cleared his throat, wondering it there were any right words to use on such an occasion.

'Thank you for coming at this very distressing time ...,' he paused, 'but, as you know, I am required by the Institution to make a preliminary investigation into the tragic accident that occurred two nights ago. I realise this isn't easy for any of you but I'm sure you will appreciate the necessity for such an early inquiry.'

He hesitated, unsure how to continue. 'I must emphasise to you that my examination of the facts relating to this Service call will be informal insofar as I shall only be making notes to record your verbal accounts.'

He looked around at each of the men and was a little unnerved to see that all but one of them were sitting with head and eyes lowered in a posture of grief. The exception was the stern, craggy face of Doctor Stewart who was unflinchingly staring straight at him.

He felt a strange affinity with this likeable character and knew that, given similar circumstances, he would probably have followed the same course of action as the wretched doctor had taken. Unfortunately, however, he thought to himself, I'm not an individual. I am an Inspector of Lifeboats with rules and regulations to uphold, and he dreaded the unavoidable conclusions that were inevitably to be in his report to Head Office regarding the Lifeboat Secretary's involvement.

'I'd like to do this in two separate parts,' he continued. 'Firstly, gentlemen, I will ask each of you to describe, in your own words, the happenings on the night of the tragedy as you saw it, up to and including the actual launching.' He paused then, lowering his voice, continued, 'Then we will go on to the subsequent occurrence.' Again he cleared his throat and looking towards the Coastguard Officer said, 'Mr Pearman, may we start with you please?'

One by one the group told their story, unfolding to the Inspector a vivid picture of the wild night and the agonising problems and decisions borne by these exceptional people.

Each narrative complemented the other in all but minor detail until a clear and concise sequence of events was established. He was especially moved by the Honorary Secretary's report in which he openly and honestly accepted full responsibility for authorising the launching, without mentioning the coxswain's bellicose attitude or seeking to lessen his own accountability.

The Commander had been making copious notes and his wrist ached from the unaccustomed chore. He placed his pen along the centre-fold of the pad and looked up.

'Thank you, gentlemen, I think now is a good time for a little refreshment before we continue,' and he pressed the bell-push on the wall, licking his dry lips in anticipation.

Quickly a lad appeared from the bar below in answer to this summons and took orders from each of the eight men in a feat of memory that attracted the admiration of them all.

'He ought to be on "Mastermind",' observed Pip Langham, as he excused himself to go to the toilet.

Within minutes they had settled down again and already pint glasses were half empty. Pipe and cigarette smoke filled the small room with a not unpleasant fog and the general air of tension seemed less evident, even though no one present was looking forward to the next session.

'Right, gentlemen,' began the Inspector, bringing the group back to informal order. 'We are now at the stage where the lifeboat was launched. Will you take up the story now, please, Mr Taylor?'

Jim didn't look up straight away. This was the part he had been dreading: to have to re-live that dreadful night and recall each appalling incident that he had been trying to put at the back of his mind for the last forty-eight hours. He knew he could never forget. It would be with him forever, terrorising and re-living the fear and panic of those hellish moments.

'Mr Taylor?' the Inspector repeated kindly, looking at Jim with raised eyebrows.

'We were all right until we left the lee of the breakwater,' said Jim quietly, his throat thick with emotion, 'then all hell broke loose.' He looked down at the white knuckles of his hands, clasped tightly in his lap.

'Sea and spray was everywhere and we were thrown around like a cork. To be honest, I kept my eyes closed most of the time 'cause it really was terrifying. I just held on like grim death. We were practically underwater most of the time and how the hell Geoff ever managed I'll never know, he was fantastic. Anyhow,' he closed his eyes briefly and took a deep breath, 'to cut a long story short, we eventually found the casualty and got two men out of the water. They were both completely knackered and we wrapped them up in the foil sheets. The younger one said there was a third man in the water somewhere and pleaded with us to look for him, so I told Geoff.' Again he stopped as though mustering his confused memories. His eyes misted over as he visualised the happenings of the next minutes and for several moments no one spoke until the Inspector said softly, 'And then, Mr Taylor?'

Jim bit his lower lip. He was close to tears. Twisting in his chair he pulled out a handkerchief and blew his nose, hard and unnecessarily, but it did the trick and his emotions ebbed sufficiently to allow his voice to work.

'Geoff took us alongside the wreck and we could see this chap floating about on the deck that was well awash. Then a bloody great wave, bigger than the others, rushed down on us and Geoff put us astern out of its way. I was pretty busy securing our two survivors with Bob when I felt us go ahead again and I looked aft. There was this mountain of a sea coming at us from ASTERN!' he said incredulously. 'I can only think now that it was a freak rebound off the breakwater. I turned forward to warn Geoff and saw another sea, even bigger, coming at us over the rocks. I was petrified. It lifted the fishing boat and just threw it at us just as our arse-end lifted and we surfed on the front of this stern sea.' His voice broke, choked with grief, and he cleared his throat noisily as he made a visible effort to pull himself together. The others could see his eyes full of tears and looked away embarrassed, remaining quiet and waiting.

'We smashed straight into that bloody wreck,' he continued, a few moments later, so softly that he was hardly heard. 'I saw Geoff slam into the top of her wheelhouse and could almost hear his head cave in.' He shuddered, remembering the nausea and horror. 'I guess that's when I was hit 'cause the next thing I knew I was coming to on the beach.'

He hung his head silently and after a few minutes the Inspector said sympathetically, 'Thank you, Jim.'

They all sat silently, deep in their own thoughts and misery. Then the Inspector spoke again.

'Mr Denning, may we have your version please?' He shook his writing wrist violently to ease the cramp that was setting in.

Bob nodded. A pint and a double rum had rid him of his initial awe of the Staff Officer. He didn't much like having an audience like this though. The Doc was all right and had been very kind to him, but the others were always taking the mickey out of him, up to the accident anyhow, and now they would be putting the blame for all this lot on him, he supposed, feeling sorry for himself.

'It's just like Jim said,' he started, then stopped, tongue-tied.

'Yes, I accept that, but what happened when the two craft collided?' prompted the Inspector, a little testily in a tone, immediately regretted, that was not lost on the young man.

'Well, I can't remember it very clearly, Sir,' he continued, sitting up in his chair respectfully. 'I was working aft with Jim making the two survivors comfy. It was all so bloody hectic and we were being chucked about all over the shop.' He paused in vivid recollection, seeing the huge lumps of sea towering above him. 'I was frightened, know what I mean?' he queried, looking straight at the Inspector.

The Staff Officer nodded, the picture clear in his mind. He knew all right but he kept silent, not wanting to break the lad's train of thought.

'I was crouched down I think 'cause I remember looking up and seeing Jim standing there like a statue. It seemed like the trawler was right over on top of us and dropping like a ton of bricks. Something big, it could have been a mast or a derrick, swung across and clobbered Jim and he went down like a sack of spuds.' He could see it all so clearly. 'I thought at first he was going over the side so I grabbed him and held on. I don't know if I was trying to save him or me, honest.'

He raised his eyes and tried to smile, but the smile turned into a grimace.

'All of a sudden everything seemed to quieten down and I saw we were lying in a patch of fairly calm water. It was all white, like a bowl of suds, and when I looked up the fishing boat was on our other side.' His eyes opened wide, showing his amazement. 'We must have been washed right over her!' He looked around the room expecting to see disbelief, but all he saw was an intense interest etched on each face.

'I don't know how long it was,' he said, 'but suddenly I realised that apart from Jim being out for the count, Geoff seemed to be as well, 'cause he just sat there slumped over the wheel. His head was a mass of blood and the collar of his lifejacket was almost torn off his shoulders. I didn't know he was dead!' He choked and felt bile rise in his throat. Leaning across to the table, he picked up his glass and took a large mouthful of beer, swallowing some then washing the remainder around his mouth before letting it trickle down his throat rinsing away the vile taste.

'I pulled him off the seat and laid him on the deck with Jim,' he went on, almost dreamlike. 'The steering wheel was broken but I moved it and it seemed to work okay. Then I tried the throttles. Port side was dead as a dodo. Starboard one seemed all right though and I felt the engine chunt into gear. I remember looking around wondering what the hell to do next. I knew the harbour was downwind and I should go that way but the big seas really scared the shit out of me.' He looked up at the Inspector in apology but the Officer was head down scribbling his notes.

'I remembered our training with Geoff when we exercised using the sea-anchor as a drogue in a following sea, so I got the thing out of its bag and threw it over the port side to keep it clear of the good engine. I remembered,' he said almost to himself, 'that we used to rig it through the quarter cleat but this time I couldn't and it seemed to work okay. I got into Geoff's seat and gently opened up the starboard throttle, steering straight downwind. When we got back into rough seas again we were thrown about something rotten and I'm certain it was only 'cause of the drogue that we weren't pitch-poled end over end. Next thing I knew was seeing seas coming back at us and I reckoned these were rebounds from the breakwater which must be almost dead ahead. I didn't want to smash into that so I brought her bows around to starboard a bit, very carefully. Mind you, Sir,' he emphasised, 'we were being hit from all angles and the bows were pointing everywhere at once. I tried to keep her roughly with the following sea just slightly on our starboard quarter and I got to admit it was all by guess and by God. I didn't really know what I was doing or how I was going to do it,' he admitted. 'I looked over me shoulder to see how the other blokes were but I never did see them 'cause I just caught a glimpse of the old lighthouse on the end of south breakwater in the dark murk just abaft me port beam. I'd gone right past it, thank God, and I remembered thinking that I was dead lucky. A few more yards further away and I wouldn't have seen it at all. Any nearer and I'd have been swimming. Anyhow, no way was I going to try to get into the harbour. I remembered what it had been like in the entrance when we came out!, so I looked on me port bow to see if I could spot the north mole, but I couldn't, so I judged when I was well past it and then came round to port to try and get in the lee of it. It worked,' he cried triumphantly, 'and I was soon getting into calmer water. I still kept her coming round to port, then I saw the dark shape of the mole on me bow so turned a bit to starboard hopefully heading in for the beach. It was quite calm by then and I could see flashing lights ahead which looked like torches so I just kept going towards them. Then I hit the rocks, Sir, and you know the rest.' He stopped. No one spoke. As though by mutual agreement they waited, no one wanting to be first to break the silence. Several moments passed before Bob lifted his head and everyone could see the anxiety that pinched his pale face. 'I'm sorry, Sir,' he addressed himself to the Inspector. 'It's my fault the boat's wrecked! I forgot about the rocks on the beach.' As though that was the worst happening of the night.

It was Doctor Stewart who finally broke the heavy silence in the room. His soft voice full of compassion. 'That's the last thing anyone is worried about, Bob.'

'I agree with the doctor,' concurred the Inspector, looking kindly at the young lad. 'Please don't concern yourself about the boat. No one is blaming you. In fact, you did a damn fine job out there.' He stopped abruptly, not wanting to make known his personal thoughts on what he considered to be a very heroic effort by the young lifeboat-man. His gaze shifted across the room to where the dour Scot sat, eyes downcast, staring unseeing at the drink held in his large yet sensitive hands, and a feeling of pity swept over him knowing the anguish that was tormenting the poor man.

'Can we come back to you now, Doctor?' he asked almost apologetically. 'Take it from where you saw the lifeboat passing the harbour entrance on her way back.'

The doctor's bowed head nodded jerkily, then gradually the bushy eyebrows lifted and his unhappy eyes looked directly at the Inspector. He cleared his throat noisily, attracting everyone's attention, not that it was needed as everyone was already poised to hear how their Hon. Sec, would phrase his difficult version.

'We had been on tenterhooks for what seemed like ages as we stood on top of the slipway,' he began, measuring and weighing each word for the effect it would have on his position as Station Secretary. 'I cannot describe how bad it was. I don't have the words,' his voice quavered. 'It was blowing storm force but I don't think any of us had a mind for anything except those poor lads out there. We could hear the pounding of the seas outside the breakwater, even above the screaming wind. I was convinced we had seen the last of them. God it was awful!' He drew his lips into a firm line, reliving the horror.

'I called the Coastguard but their news was that they had lost contact with both the lifeboat and the casualty, and that made me feel even worse, if that were possible.'

He pinched his nose with his thumb and forefinger. 'We tried hard to pierce the dark fog of flying spray as each assured the other that Geoff would bring it off.

'It was then that I heard young Dave's voice cry out and I turned to see him pointing towards the harbour entrance. I stepped closer to him and he shouted that he had seen the blue-flashing "police" light of the lifeboat. Disbelieving, yet prayerfully hopeful, the rest of us strained our eyes in the direction of the boiling dark-whiteness at the end of the breakwater. I lifted my binoculars, knowing they were useless in these conditions, then dropped them back onto my chest. "There!" screamed everybody, as we all saw it together. It was the lifeboat.'

His voice reflected the joy of the moment. 'We saw at least three blue flashes as it crossed between the two breakwaters and then disappeared behind the northern one. We knew then that Geoff was wisely and deliberately avoiding coming into the harbour because of the dangerous seas piling up in the entrance. He would be aiming to come ashore in the lee of the northern mole. Our hearts lifted as we threw ourselves at the large boathouse doors and fought them closed. With the wind shut out, the silence was deafening and at first we continued shouting at each other. A lot of this was excitement I suppose.'

He stopped and sipped at his small glass of undiluted whisky, taking the opportunity to rub his handkerchief back and forth across his mouth and nose. 'Then we had a quick council of war,' he went on, 'and unanimously decided we should go to the beach and guide them ashore. I made a quick telephone call to the Coastguard to tell him the news and our plan of action, and requested he arrange for the ambulance, already on its way, to meet us by Geoff's office. As we reached the beach we could clearly see the boat's "police" light flashing close under the lee of the breakwater, but as there were no visible side-lights, we couldn't make out the course he was steering. It quickly became obvious they were closing on the beach so Dougie waved his torch furiously, pointing it to sea then waving it to his left trying to signal the boat away from the rocks near the breakwater. We shouted as loud as we could, realising Geoff had forgotten their existence in his preoccupation with getting ashore. The dark shadow of the boat became visible beneath the winking blue light and our torches lit the orange hull. I can remember, as clear as day, yelling out to the others, "He's made it, he's made it." I have never felt so relieved in all of my life.

'They were only twenty feet from the shoreline when a large crack told us they had hit one of the rocks.' He paused as he felt his throat muscle tighten, and fought to control himself. Taking a deep breath, he carried on.

'Dougie, Pip and Dave rushed straight into the sea and were waist deep before they reached the lifeboat that had broken free from the rock and lay stopped broadside on to the beach, wallowing sluggishly in the swell. They pulled it ashore and what I saw made my blood run cold.'

He stared unseeing out of the window, trembling with suppressed emotion. Nervously he took a packet of cigarettes from his jacket pocket and placed one between his twitching lips. Several silent moments passed before he replaced the packet and withdrew a box of matches.

'I have been a doctor for many a year,' he said with his Highland brogue becoming more noticeable with stress, 'and in that time I have seen some dreadful sights but what I saw that night is something that will haunt me for the rest of my days.' He looked back at the unresponsive window and with shaking hands struck a match, slowly raising it to the cigarette and dragging smoke forcefully into his lungs. He faced the other grieving faces around the table and tears flooded the tough old Scotsman's eyes as he recalled every detail, then continued in a strained voice: 'The boat was a wreck. Everything was smashed except for the light revolving its eerie blue brilliance over the shambles. Pip and Dave were leaning over the sponson staring inboard and I heard someone retching. There were two bodies lashed to the sponsons in the stern and two more on the deck either side of the console. Seated behind the broken steering wheel was young Bob here.' He hesitated, nodding in the direction of the lad. 'Even in the blue light I could see his face was a ghostly white and his eyes glazed and unblinking. His feet were firmly placed, one on each of the two bodies either side of him, but he didn't speak.'

He took another deep inhalation of cigarette smoke and blinked tears from his eyes. 'Then I heard Dougie yelling for someone to switch the blue flasher off and this seemed to snap me out of my horrendous daze and back into dreadful reality.' He licked his dry lips, lifting his whisky glass absentmindedly halfway to his mouth then returning it to the table, untasted.

'The two lads standing in the water were frantically untying the two bodies in the sternsheet by the light of their torches. Dougie climbed aboard the boat and gently but firmly helped young Bob from his seat, passing him over the side to me. Poor lad collapsed straight away, shock you know,' he explained. 'I laid him on the sand and was just about to tend him when I heard Pip's voice yelling excitedly that the two "bodies" in the stern were alive. By their clothing it was clear they were the two survivors from the trawler. Dougie had by this time shouted for my attention and, as I climbed aboard, I could see he was very agitated. He beckoned me to the body lying on the port side of the console and as I bent over it I saw with horror that it was Geoff, very obviously dead with severe head injuries. I automatically did a perfunctory examination before reluctantly leaving him to tend the others.'

Yet again, he stopped and dragged heavily on the little that was left of his cigarette.

'I turned to the "body" on the starboard side and was again shocked and stunned to see it was Jim but almost immediately, and to my great relief, the "body" stirred and struggled up into a sitting position, holding his head and neck in both arms and moaning in agony.

'By this time, the two ambulance men had joined us at the boat and were working like trojans to get everyone onto the beach and into the ambulance. They did a magnificent job,' he praised, 'and were absolutely soaked. I didn't get a chance to examine the two survivors who were whisked away into the ambulance by the driver and his mate. Dougie and I helped Jim ashore and sat him in the ambulance where I was very happy to find he had suffered no injuries that a few stitches and aspirin couldn't cure. Pip and Dave literally carried young Bob to the ambulance but I felt confident his was nothing other than exhaustion and shock from his ordeal.'

His thoughts became more orderly as he approached the completion of his story. 'Then, before I joined the ambulance for the journey to Langley Hospital, I reluctantly asked Dougie and the two other lads if they would remain with Geoff's body until I could make arrangements for collection.'

Leaning forward, his outstretched arm collected his drink from the table and lifted it to his mouth. The long ash of his neglected cigarette dropped off and splashed onto the floor. He shifted in his chair and hesitatingly continued. 'They were very brave, and their nod of assent didn't mask their feeling at such an awful duty, and I thanked God for the steadying presence of Dougie to sustain the two younger men.

'Once on the road, the driver radioed through our ETA to the hospital. He also asked for another ambulance to collect Geoff's body and requested his operations room to inform the Coastguard and police of the situation. And that's it,' he ended, abruptly and obviously relieved.

The Inspector had sat through the account without comment, totally absorbed in the doctor's story. Occasionally he had remembered to make notes of salient points but mostly he just listened, sharing the sorrow of the grieving crew. He clucked his tongue in sympathy, then, not knowing what else to say, said, 'Thank you gentlemen,' adding as an afterthought, 'I think that another drink is called for,' as he placed his finger on the bell push.

Chapter Thirteen

Doctor Stewart sat at his desk, head cradled in hands. His evening surgery had gratefully been quicker that usual which was a Godsend as his head was thumping like a steam hammer. Four weeks had passed since the preliminary hearing at The Jolly Taxpayer and during that time there had been endless official reports and papers to complete and sign and, of course, Geoff's heartbreaking funeral that had been attended by representatives from all the rescue services and local authorities.

Jim Taylor had fully recovered from his injury and taken to wearing a soft cap to hide the neat row of stitches like a zip down the centre of the shaven patch on the crown of his head. He had also been appointed Acting Coxswain until such time as Head Office reached their own decision.

Young Bob had been placed back on the active list, a much quieter and more mature person as a result of his experience, and the body of the missing fisherman had been recovered by the Search and Rescue helicopter from the Naval Air Station.

The one thing that hadn't been finalised was his own position as Station Secretary after his irresponsible authorisation of the fatal launching. When would he hear the dreaded decision? he wondered. Four weeks of worrying had taken a toll. No wonder he had a headache.

He reached out for his first cigarette of the evening and jumped as the telephone on his desk rang, his nerves jangling in concert with the bell. Snatching at the receiver he barked, 'Doctor Stewart!'

The calm, authoritative voice that answered made his heart leap.

'Good evening Doctor. John Godfrey. Sorry to disturb you so late in the day but may I pop in to see you in the morning?'

'Um-ah! Yes, ah of course,' stammered the flustered medic knowing full well that this was it. The fateful time of the Institute's judgement to be given by their appointed executioner. 'What time?' he queried.

'About eleven, if that's convenient,' said the disembodied voice of the Lifeboat Inspector.

'Make it ten if possible. I have an appointment later on,' lied the doctor endeavouring to reduce the waiting and suspense as much as possible.

'Yes, that's fine, see you then,' came the ominously quiet reply. 'Good-night.'

The line went dead with a click of finality and the doctor very slowly and gently replaced the receiver on its cradle. A long, sleepless night lay ahead of him.

By ten o'clock the next morning, he had been standing at his window for twenty minutes, looking anxiously through the spotless white lace curtains, his eyes darting backwards and forwards along the tree-lined village street.

'Damn the man for his punctuality,' he cursed, ramming his hands deeper into his trouser pockets, feeling they were hot and clammy. He dared not take them out for fear of the shaking he knew would start.

The sudden appearance of the red two-seater sports car outside his house startled him. He didn't need to see the white RNLI flag sticker in the top centre of its windscreen to recognise the Inspector's transport.

His heart pounded impossibly harder as he went to the front door and opened it before his visitor had even extricated himself from the low-slung car seat.

The Inspector strode purposefully up the short garden path, his hand held out to meet the doctor's welcoming handshake.

'Good morning, Doctor,' he greeted, but the worried Scot only nodded in reply, not trusting his voice, as he motioned with his free hand inviting the official to enter.

Accepting the silent gesture of his host's pointing palm, the Inspector settled himself into the large, well-cushioned armchair, declining the offer of a proffered whiskey bottle with a cheery 'No, thank you. Early yard-arm and all that,' as he opened his battered briefcase, withdrawing a sheaf of papers that attracted the doctor's eyes like a magnet.

'I do understand the trauma you've been through, Mac,' the Inspector began, in a friendly tone as his host lowered himself onto the very edge of a hard-backed chair opposite, 'so I'm sure you won't object if I get straight down to brass-tacks and read this to you.' He waved the report in his hand. 'It is a bit "official" I'm afraid.' Then he began.

'The Committee of Management, having examined the reports and circumstances of the Service carried out by Leemouth Lifeboat during the night of September 30th, and given full consideration to the actions taken by the Station Honorary Secretary, Doctor Ian Stewart MD, in authorising the launching of the 'Atlantic 21' lifeboat in conditions in excess of those considered to be the maximum suitable for that class, as stated in the Institution's Guidance Notes for Station Honorary Secretaries, ...'

The doctor tensed, waiting for the axe to fall.

'... has decided that, owing to the extenuating circumstances prevailing at the time, no further action is to be taken, other than to require the Divisional Inspector of Lifeboats to inform Doctor Stewart of its decision and to stress upon that person the advisability of observing the guidelines and recommendations made by the Institution from time to time regarding the authorisation of lifeboat launching.'

There was a clear audible whistle as the doctor exhaled his pent-up breath as he sat back in his chair, raising his eyes to the ceiling as the stress and tension drained from his face, to be replaced by a flush of relief. The removal of the oppressive burden made him feel light-headed and when he looked across to his visitor the room swam, making him blink his eyes until they steadied.

The Commander could not resist a smile of understanding and compassion for the likeable old Scot who, he knew without doubt, would take full heed of the subtle rebuke made in the Committee's findings.

'Congratulations, Mac,' he said warmly, extending his hand. 'I have been wanting to shake your hand and say that for a long time.'

The doctor accepted the open hand and shook it heartily.

'I am very, very grateful to you,' was his grave reply.

For a few moments the two men looked at each other with mutual respect and affection, then the Inspector said eagerly, 'Can we carry on with a few other items of a more pleasurable nature, Mac?'

Receiving a nod of agreement he fanned the wad of notes on his lap and selected one to be next in order of disclosure.

'The appointment of Mr James Taylor as Senior Helmsman is confirmed,' he read, then added by way of explanation, 'That's the new title for ILB coxswains.' Again he shuffled his papers in a manner that, to his host, appeared nervously excited.

'The last report that it is my duty to read to you this morning, Doctor,' he said with a broad grin, 'is one of the happiest duties that any Inspector has to fulfil and I take great pleasure, tinged of course with some sadness, in informing you that ...' he dropped his eyes and began to read, 'the following awards for bravery have been approved by the Committee of Management and will be confirmed to you, and the recipients, with citations, in due course, with details of the place and date of presentation.'

He stopped and, twitching his nostrils, inhaled a sharp breath.

'One,' he read. 'The Institution's Gold medal, posthumously awarded to Mr Geoffrey Ross.'

'Two,' he continued down the list. 'The Institution's Silver medal to crewman Robert Denning ...

'Three, the Institution's Bronze medal to crewman Mr James Taylor.'

He looked up and saw the delight on the doctor's face.

'To Head Launcher, Mr Douglas Fowler and crew-members Messrs. Phillip Langman and David Fulton, the Institution's framed "Letter of Thanks" on vellum.

'To ambulance men, Messrs. Peter Beeston and Frederick Cooke, Letters of Appreciation signed by the Director.

'And finally,' he said, 'you are at liberty to advise the recipients in advance of confirmation.'

He replaced the reports in his briefcase and withdrew an official looking envelope.

'I have been given this letter of condolence from the Director and Staff of the Institution and been instructed to present it to Mrs Ross in person.' He clicked his brief-case closed and placed it on the floor beside him. 'Well, that's it, Mac!'

He noticed a look of sadness returning to the granite-like features of the Hon. Secretary.

'Look old chap' he drawled, 'I understand what you are thinking, but you mustn't blame yourself, no one else does! Geoff accepted the consequences when he argued against your better judgement. I know that. The Institution knows that and so does everyone else! You couldn't have stopped him,' he said with finality.

After a long contemplation the doctor looked up. He had obviously endured a mental struggle and come to an acceptance of the situation, but his thoughts remained unspoken.

'Thank you, John,' he said at last. 'You're a good man. Shall we call on Mrs Ross together?'

Chapter Fourteen

It was a beautiful day. A few snowy white puffs of cotton-wool clouds hung almost motionless in the otherwise clear sky, giving an artist's setting for the ubiquitous wheeling gulls.

It was the first anniversary of Leemouth lifeboat's tragic journey of mercy and the crew were standing in two rows, one either side of the concrete apron on which the gleaming lifeboat sat, mounted on its launching trolley, smartly bedecked in flags and bunting for this special occasion.

At the head of each rank stood an erect figure wearing a shining medal suspended on its dark-blue ribbon from the right breast of his navy-blue jersey that bore the red-wool lettering RNLI.

Between the two ranks of lifeboat-men, the Reverend Grossly stood at a makeshift table covered with the white house-flag of the Lifeboat Institution. On it, the pages of his opened prayer-book flipped backwards and forwards in the light breeze as he mentally prepared himself for the start of a short Service of Remembrance for Geoff Ross and the lost fishing boat's skipper, that he was privileged to conduct.

Flanking him were the numerous dignitaries from the village, the County, and other rescue services including Ray Pearman of the Coast-guard, now in a wheelchair suffering from rheumatoid arthritis.

To his immediate right stood Mrs Ross, the slight black-suited young widow of the former coxswain, her head bowed hiding red-rimmed, grief-filled eyes from the hushed sympathetic crowd surrounding the lifeboat station who were patiently waiting for the Service to begin.

Around her shoulders the strong left arm of her son gave comfort. She twisted her head to see him, standing there with his father's medal proudly pinned to the lapel of his dark-suited jacket, his chin firmly tilted up. There was not a hint of a tear showing in his eyes to reveal the heaviness in his heart. He was being strong for his mother's sake, He was the man of the family now, yet his sorrow was that of a child, and it hurt.

Behind them, the two survivors of the *Bonnie Lass* stood in silent mourning. They had travelled to Leemouth the day before and were kindly accommodated at The Jolly Taxpayer, at the RNLI's invitation.

Last night they met with the lifeboat crew in the pub and tried to express to them their gratitude for saving their lives but the crew would have none of it. Under the circumstances it had been a good reunion and they had little memory of events after the pub 'officially' closed. Today they thought only of their lost skipper.

Opposite the slipway, standing on the breakwater amid the crowd of solemn onlookers, a young girl stretched her neck to get a better view. She cursed, unladylike, as a huge head and shoulders blocked her view forcing her to move sideways and push against the black-uniformed member of St John's Ambulance Brigade who graciously gave way and earned himself a grateful smile.

'Ah! There he is,' she exclaimed under her breath, as she caught sight of her be-medalled fiancé. 'My Bob,' she murmured lovingly.

Across the cobbled street, standing alone in the doorway of The Jolly Taxpayer like a Guardsman outside Buckingham Palace, PC 'Basher' Bates flexed his knees and wiggled his toes inside his size nines as he looked around at the throng of people covering the two breakwaters and the waterfront street, like ants. He had always enjoyed a good relationship with the lifeboat crew and tried to put in an attendance at the station whenever there was a 'shout.' His wife, as well as other women in the village, was keeping an unobtrusive eye on Geoff's widow, a likeable lass whom most of them had known since she was a young girl. He, of course, knew her well. In fact, during his fifteen years as village bobby he knew everyone, sometimes more than they knew. It was surprising what could be learned, and seen, walking his 'beat' at night. Last night for instance when the pub was still serving drinks hours after closing time. The drinkers couldn't all have been 'residents.' But they weren't doing any harm so he turned a blind eye, as he often did when seeing and hearing things he wasn't supposed to. He loved it here and had even refused promotion that would have meant his moving elsewhere in the County.

He ran a finger around the sweaty neckband of his high tunic collar – it was warm standing in the late summer sun. A smile creased the corners of his mouth as a vengeful gull splattered the black-suited back of the gold-chain wearing Leader of the County Council, a nasty vindictive man who unfortunately also sat as a member on the Police Watch Committee and considered himself above the Law. He raised his irreligious eyes to the blue sky and muttered to himself, 'Thank you, God, for that.'

A whisper went around the respectful assemblage as the Minister lifted his prayer-book, raising his head to gain their attention.

The stillness created an atmosphere of peace broken only by the caw-cawing of the sea-birds as they dive-bombed the surface of the harbour in their unceasing search for food under the watchful and covetous glare of their fellow gulls perched high up on weary looking chimneys and sagging roofs mottled with their droppings, vantage points for their scavenging eyes.

The high-pitched, undulating voice of the Minister echoed between the village buildings and around the harbour, swelling now and then with the sound of several hundred more as the ad hoc congregation joined in the hymn-singing and the final emotional words of the universal sea-man's anthem: 'Eternal Father strong to save'.

On the extreme edge of the crowd, almost at the end of the breakwater, a weatherbeaten face, full of sadness, sank neck-less into a rough fisher-man's jersey beneath which was beating a heart full of remorse. How had he become so bitter as to pour scorn on their boat? They were all good lads, especially young Geoff who had been with him in the crew of the old boat. And they had done a job for which they could rightly feel proud. Not their fault what the RNLI had done. Progress and modernisation they called it. Nevertheless, he felt ashamed, then char-acteristically blamed the Lifeboat Service for kicking him, and all the others, out of the crew when the old boat went. He'd only been fifty-seven for God's sake! He'd had every right to be bitter!

A hand dropped onto his shoulder and twisting his head, he saw the licensee of The Jolly Taxpayer who had been watching the anguished look on the old fisherman's face.

'Come on, Ernie, you miserable old bastard,' said the publican good-naturedly, 'I'll treat you to a pint when this lot's over.'

DISENCHANTMENT

Up until yesterday, I had been miserable, and depressed. What had promised to be an exciting, adventurous career had turned out to be mundane and boring.

Several months ago, as a Leading Wren, I had applied to become a 'Marwren', a Wren attached to the Royal Marines and wearing their coveted 'Globe and Laurels' cap badge.

I had been over-the-moon when accepted, and eagerly anticipated a more interesting life.

My first disappointment came when posted to Camp Blithe, Malta. This was a misnomer if ever there was one.

This so-called 'camp' consisted of eight large Nissen huts and a couple of small buildings situated on a barren headland, just about as far away from civilisation as possible, on such a small island.

Apart from a small 'guard' contingent of soldiers of the Maltese Artillery, the 'staff' composed of one Wren officer and a dozen 'Mar-wrens', all of whom had arrived within the last forty-eight hours.

No one knew what the 'camp' was used for. No one knew what we were supposed to do, or when we were supposed to do it. If the officer was aware, she didn't let us in on the secret, even though she was a 'nice type' – as far as officers go!

One of the Nissen huts was used by the soldiers, one by us girls, one by the officer (poor girl, all on her own in a big hut), one was the galley and mess-room, one was a store-room full of beds, blankets, lockers, tables and chairs, and the other three were empty.

A week passed. Seven long, monotonous days, with no duty other than to prepare two of the huts as living quarters, and one as a sort of lecture-room ... for whom?????

To add to our misery, we were not allowed to leave the camp – for security reasons, we were told. All very mysterious!

We 'girls' consisted of cooks, stewards, drivers, communication specialists and one cinema projectionist (?). Despite our varying trades, we blended together as a team, and as friends, but even so, a week in each other's company, with no entertainment, shore-leave or male company, stretched tolerance levels at times.

Yesterday, all this changed.

We were all mustered in the lecture room, sitting and wondering what it was all about when in marched our officer – actually smiling. It must be good news!

'Well, ladies,' she began, 'no doubt you have been concerned as to why we are here.' That was an understatement, but she had our attention.

The silence was solid. A falling feather would have been heard, as we stared, expectantly.

'We are here,' she continued, 'to receive, and cater for, a small unit of Royal Marines who will be using this camp as a training base for a forthcoming mission. I cannot say if their stay will be for days or weeks. The reason for the tight security is because these men are SBS.' She paused, looking around the sea of blank faces.

'For those of you who haven't heard of the SBS, they are an elite and highly secretive unit of the Royal Marines. No doubt you *will* have heard of the Army's SAS?' she queried, 'well, our boys are a notch better. I know, I have worked with them,' she added, with obvious pride.

Again, she scanned the faces, which now looked decidedly happier, and allowed herself a smile.

'Nevertheless, they are men,' she grinned, 'special men.'

Several eyes began to twinkle.

Adopting a more 'official' attitude, she continued, 'That's why certain rules will apply during their stay. These orders *must* be obeyed!'

She opened a small folder and placed it on the table, for effect. She knew the contents by heart. Licking her lips, she cleared her throat, 'My hut is divided in two halves. I will be in one end and the SBS Officer will have the other. Six SBS Marines will have one of the huts that you have furnished. Their four-man support team will occupy the other. The empty hut will become their Mess, and you will now understand why there are two ablution blocks. They will use the remaining hut as a lecture-room.'

She stopped as though gathering her thoughts. 'Your duties,' she said, 'which I shall detail in a moment, will be to cater for their well-being. They will require food at irregular times according to their training schedule. If my experience is anything to go by, they will return here exhausted, hungry and very tired. Our job is to be here for them, no matter what time of the day or night it is!' She looked down at her notes.

'Under no circumstances, is there to be any physical contact with them, other than in the course of duty. You will not – repeat not – attempt to discuss their mission. They are under orders to report you if you do.'

She paused again to shuffle her papers, and then read out our allocated duties.

I was delighted to learn that, not only was I to drive the coach to pick them up at the RAF aerodrome on arrival, but I would also act as 'operational assistant' to their officer. That meant that I would be the first to meet them *and* be involved during their stay. I had the cream job!

After repeating the order against personal involvement, she dismissed us, and we hurried back to our billet, excited at the thought of meeting these supermen.

Naturally, Vivian, one of the cooks, had met SBS men before. She had done everything before! If she was to be believed, she must have been in the Wrens for twenty years! Still, she was harmless, so we sat on our beds listening to her experiences which, if true, were probably greatly exaggerated. True or not, what she said really had our hormones working overtime.

She had cooked for them at their Poole base, a year or so ago, and had dated a couple of them. According to her, they were a blend of James Bond, Superman and an Australian beach lifeguard. Strong, muscular and very athletic. In fact, every woman's dream-man. I could hardly wait to see these fantastic men of mystery.

Next day, as ordered, I was at the RAF Station, impatiently waiting the arrival of their aircraft. I was all a-tingle as it landed and taxied to the apron where I had been instructed to wait.

Unloading began, on the other side of the plane from where I sat in my coach, but, after ten minutes or so, eagerness got the better of me. I got out and walked around the tail to where a group of Marines were off-loading equipment onto trolleys.

As I approached they greeted me with big grins. A heady experience after a week of celibacy.

Normally, I would have found these tanned, fit guys, very attractive, but today they were just ordinary Marines. All shapes and sizes. Probably, they were the support-team. I was keen to feast my eyes on the gorgeous hunks of our elite!

I walked up to one of them, a Corporal, unusually thin for a Marine. 'I've come to collect Naval Party 674,' I stated, using the unit's 'official' designation, with an air of superiority, 'do you know where they are?'

The Corporal looked at me with a toothy smile, then looked around at the others.

'That's us,' he replied, with a flick of his balding head.

My elation drained away like an ebbing tide.

Disillusioned and disappointed, I drove them to the camp. When the other girls saw them, their spirits plummeted too.

We weren't at all surprised to learn that the SBS motto was 'NOT BY STRENGTH, BY GUILE'.

Four days later, we awoke at 7 a.m., to find they had gone.

Quote from report made by Captain C. J. S. Craig CB. DSO RN Captain of HMS *Alacrity*, when inserting SBS team behind enemy lines during Falklands War, 1982.

'Our insertion team was just what I expected. When embarked I was not surprised to see that these men – the elite – were far from being ten feet tall: High competence often comes in innocuous packages.'

'JOINING'

(1948)

My head ached and I was freezing cold. I'd been travelling since six that morning, first by train from home to Bristol, then bus to Avonmouth where a quick turn-around put me back onto the bus for Bristol again to catch this train. I circled my head with eyes closed to ease the stiffness in my neck but the insides of my eyelids were like a night sky full of shooting stars, so I returned my gaze to the drab, dreary picture of industrial South Wales as it sped past my grime- and rain-streaked window. Hell!, I was cold.

The only other occupant of the unheated compartment sat huddled in an overcoat on the opposite seat. We hadn't spoken since boarding at Bristol an hour earlier. It seemed too much of an effort. I guessed he was a businessman of sorts, about middle age, very nondescript, not my sort. I would be glad when this journey was over. I was starving hungry and thirsty too.

My thoughts returned to the concern I was feeling as to what my next ship would be like. The Shipping Federation office usually gave a seaman some idea, when issuing him his joining instructions, but this time it was different. No one seemed to know anything about her; at least they weren't telling me!

I had just ended an enjoyable three-week spell of home leave after an eleven-month voyage on a tanker in the Far East. She'd been my third ship. The first was a cargo tramp, out via Suez and home through the Panama Canal, a nine-month round-the-world trip.

The second was a total contrast, as Bridge Boy on the liner *Queen Elizabeth*. Less said about that the better, but it was an experience.

Now, here I was, on a train going to join a ship no one had heard of.

'She's docked in South Wales,' the Federation man had said. 'Don't know anything about her but if you take her I will up-rate you to Senior Ordinary Seaman,' he offered.

This was too good to refuse. Only seventeen years old, with two years sea service, and promotion already! I had jumped at the chance. Now, in the cold semi-darkness of a miserable winter's afternoon, I didn't feel so enthusiastic, but consoled myself with the knowledge that, being

berthed where she was, she wouldn't be a passenger liner, thank goodness. I'd had my fill of them for a while.

The grey Welsh countryside began to change to the even greyer
outskirts of suburban life, as the train's speed decreased. Rows of uniform, slate-roofed houses parted to allow us through. It was like a black
and white photograph, no colour at all.

We were approaching my destination so, more to stretch my chilled
bones than anything, I rose and dragged my sea-bag down from the
netting above the seat and dumped it on the floor. I saw my companion
look up and raise his eyebrows, querying. 'Joining?' he asked.

A sarcastic retort sprang to my lips; I wasn't feeling very sociable,
then I realised that only a fellow Merchant Seaman would use such a
term.

'Yeah,' I replied, 'and you?'

'Yes.' His voice was cultured, what I would call a bit posh. '*San Verano*,
how about you?'

'*Emily Thorpe*,' I answered, hoping he would know of her.

He shook his head. 'Never heard of her, I'm afraid. What Company
is she?'

That was something else I didn't know. 'Haven't a clue.'

There was a few minutes' silence, then he spoke again. 'I shall be
getting a taxi to the docks from the station,' he said. 'You are very
welcome to join me if you wish?'

That brightened me up no end. I wasn't looking forward to humping
my gear all the way through the town and docks, and I certainly couldn't
afford a taxi so I accepted his offer gratefully.

The train pulled into the station and we walked together to the rank
of taxis queuing like bored housewives at the butchers, climbing into the
first one, me with my scruffy sea-bag and battered suitcase, he with his
smart and expensive luggage. 'Docks please,' he ordered.

The driver grunted at this interruption of his crossword puzzle and
noisily engaged gear – obviously it wasn't his taxi.

The journey was quite short and we soon drew up at the Docks gate,
halting at the imperiously raised hand of a uniformed policeman. My
friend wound down his window allowing a blast of cold air to enter.

'*San Verano*,' he informed the policeman who practically jumped to
attention with respect at the tone of voice, 'and this gentleman is for
Emily Thorpe, nodding his head in my direction. Cor! I'd never been called
a gentleman before.

The long arm of the Law gave me a quick glance, wrinkling his nose
before returning his attention to my companion.

'Very good, Sir. Thank you.' I could swear I heard his heels click
together.

I was mystified. Who was this man I was travelling with? He commands respect from Docks Police yet only travels third class on a train. What the Hell, he was paying.

Our driver pulled away, ruining another two gears in the process as we rattled along the quay, over railway lines and rain-filled pot-holes, dodging the forlorn cranes and top heavy gantries, while skilfully avoiding the stacks of oil drums, empty crates and piles of wood, all deliberately placed by bored dockies to catch unwary taxi drivers.

We passed ship after ship. Some rusty and work worn. Some covered in an unglamorous coating of coal dust. Most had dirty, threadbare Red Ensigns hanging limp and soaked from their flagstaffs. A few, very few, were smart, clean and newly painted.

One that came into this last category was the *San Verano* and I couldn't help but feel envious as we drew up alongside her gangway.

'This is as far as I go,' said my companion, handing a banknote to the driver as we stepped out of the taxi. 'Yours can't be much further up the dock,' he added, as he picked up his luggage and climbed the angled gangway to the ship, calling his best wishes to me over his shoulder, leaving me standing in a puddle, still wondering who and what he was.

Hoisting my sea-bag onto my shoulder, I took a firm grip on the case handle. The taxi driver gave me a sour look, knowing full well there would be no tip forthcoming, then slamming his door, he revved up and drove off, unsuccessfully trying to splash a pool of mud over my trousers. I wished him well should he reach the dock gates without exploding.

Shrugging my lumpy sea-bag into a more comfortable position I set off along the quay in the rapidly darkening gloom and steady drizzle, much of which was running down from my hatless head, soaking my shirt collar, and dripping from my bag-supporting hand into the sleeve of my coat.

Ahead of me were half a dozen ships. Although none of them appeared to be in the same class as *San Verano* they didn't look too bad and my spirits rose slightly, but not for long. Within minutes I was really wet and cold, getting more depressed as each ship came and went, with still no sign of *Emily Thorpe*, and it was now almost dark.

The last ship at the quayside was unlit and, as I approached, I peered eagerly for her name, desperate for her to be mine. Over her anchor there was a lighter patch on her black hull and I lengthened my stride. Now the patch became blurred letters that appeared to be just a single name. My heart sank. A few more steps and I knew the worst; she was the *Northman*.

Hell! What do I do now? ... I looked around bewildered, dreading the thought of a long trudge back to the dock gate.

I looked ahead in the direction I had been walking but there were no more ships, only an empty quay, with dejected cranes silhouetted against the black, heavy-clouded, night sky.

Then I saw a brief flash of light, or I thought I did, and decided to check it before heading back. Plodding on, I almost broke an ankle falling into a deep rain-filled rut.

Despite the effort of carrying my gear I was shivering. Both hands were frozen stiff and my nose felt like a block of ice. I'd have given anything for a tot of rum, or a mug of steaming tea, but I guessed the nearest pub or café was a mile away, back in town. I couldn't last out for that length of time. I had to find my ship.

I stumbled again, almost falling into a small dock that appeared in front of me at right angles to the main quayside. Vaguely, I could see a mast rising from it so, carefully approaching the edge, I looked down onto the vessel below.

She was an elderly coaster, about six hundred tons and two hundred feet long. Her only mast rose from between two hatches and from the 'all-aft' superstructure, a thin woodbine funnel stood tall from directly behind her wheelhouse.

Part of me was hoping that this old tub wasn't mine. The other part – the cold, wet, weary and hungry part – was fervently praying she was.

I turned and walked along the dock towards her after-end and there, painted on a lifebelt secured in its emergency rack on the front of the bridge wing, I saw her name. It was her, thank God. Any port in a storm.

Gratefully, I lowered my sea-bag and case onto the wet concrete dock-side, easing my stiff, aching arms and shoulders as I looked around for means of getting on board. There was an ordinary wooden ladder rising steeply from her boat-deck up to the quay, unlit, fragile and dangerous, and it took two very careful trips to get my gear aboard. I was thankful and relieved when it was done. The night was pitch black by now but I was beyond caring.

Leaving my baggage by her lifeboat I groped my way slowly towards her wheelhouse. All the cabin doors beneath it were locked so I felt around for, and found, the iron-rung ladder that led from the boat-deck down to the main deck. Climbing down, I worked my way aft, trying all the doors I could find – all locked. Then around the stern, skinning my shin on a valve sticking out from an ancient capstan.

'Anyone aboard?' I yelled, jumping at the sound of my own voice. The silence was scary.

I started to walk forward, along the outboard side, carefully probing with my feet for cleats, bollards and other fittings that clutter the decks of all ships. Then I saw a glimmer of light coming from an open door in front of me. With thumping heart I stepped towards it, and looked in.

It was the galley. A small, steel space, half filled by an old fashioned coal-burning cooking range from which a glow of fire shone from one of the round pot holes in the top. Beside it, slumped in a beach-type deckchair, was a man fast asleep with an open paperback book on his lap.

I knocked loudly on the iron half-door and cleared my throat. No effect. I called louder and louder, but it took a full-blooded yell before the figure showed any sign of life. Grunting and snorting, he eventually opened his eyes and stared at me. I started to explain who and what I was, when, suddenly, he came to life and belligerently snapped, 'Who the bloody hell are you?'

It took ten minutes of explaining before he accepted me for what I was, and another ten before he offered me a filthy, chipped mug of stewed tea into which he stirred several spoonfuls of condensed milk, leaving the spoon standing upright, unaided, in the mud-like liquid. It was nectar, and I gradually defrosted in front of the stove.

He was the AB, name of Ted. Everyone else was ashore. He had been ashore all day and only returned, with a skinful, to do his turn as ship-keeper. He became very talkative, wanting to know what I was doing signing-on a hell ship like the *Emily Thorpe*.

'What do you mean?' I asked, knowing full well she was far from being the sought-after flagship of the fleet.

'She's a black un,' he spat ... 'The old Man's bomb 'appy, the Mate's a useless drunk, and the crew are all DR men, like me.'

DR men, I knew, were seamen with a bad 'Decline to Report' record from a previous ship stamped in their Discharge Book which would, in effect, prevent them from ever getting employment on a decent ship.

'We're supposed to 'ave free ABs and a boy,' Ted continued, 'but all we got is me and that Geordie bastard,' Then he had another thought, 'and Ali of course.'

'Who is Ali?' came my obvious question.

'Ee's a Gyppo,' replied Ted, 'that's not 'is real name, only wot we calls 'im. 'Ee duzz anyfing and everyfing, from spud bashin' to engine greasin', and all the bloody Owners pay 'im is a boy's wage, even though e's nearly fifty, if 'ee's a day!' He paused to muster his thoughts, 'and I'll tell you sumfin else for nuffin', he continued, 'I don't like livin' in an open fo'c'sle wiv four stinking f ****** Ayrab firemen neither.'

This was the age-old war between deck and engine-room departments with a big dollop of racial prejudice thrown in, but I resisted the temptation to argue.

In the glorious heat of the galley my eyes were beginning to have a mind of their own. I desperately wanted sleep but Ted's interest was aroused.

'So, 'ow you cum to be 'ere then,' he asked, 'DR?'

'NO,' I snapped back, 'I was bloody well tricked.' It was all very clear to me now.

The fat-splattered, filthy glass-face of the clock fixed askew on the galley bulkhead, almost hid the hands underneath it, but I could just make out it was nearly nine o'clock and I was dead on my feet.

'Look, Ted,' I began, 'I'm absolutely knackered. I've been travelling all day. Any chance of something to eat before I get my head down?'

'Nuffin 'ot' he said, 'but there's some corned dog and bread in that locker there,' pointing a dirty, crooked, nicotine stained finger.

The bread was far from fresh but at least the corned beef came from a newly opened tin and I wolfed two man-sized sandwiches.

'Where's our accommodation, Ted?' I asked between mouthfuls.

'Forrard,' he grunted. 'You'd better take this torch 'cos there ain't no lightin' up there.'

I took the torch and turned to leave the galley.

'Got a match?' he enquired, 'there's an oil lamp 'ung up in the fo'c'sle you can light.'

I nodded and stepped out onto the deck. Obviously I wasn't going to get a helping hand from him.

The rain had stopped but it was colder than ever. With the aid of the torch I went back up to the boat-deck to retrieve my luggage. Not having three hands, I had to grope my way forward with the torch gripped between my teeth. It tasted foul.

Banging my way along the narrow space between the hatches and the bulwark, I negotiated the many obstacles, gathering a few more bruises on my battered shins.

Arriving at the fo'c'sle door, I threw my bags in and stepped over the coaming, torch in hand, its beam eerily illuminating the triangular compartment that, from the full beam of the ship, angled sharply to the ship's stem, a distance of some twenty feet.

Along the port side were four wooden bunks, two sets, two high, that were mirrored on the starboard side. Forward, two spurling-pipes came down through the deck-head into the cable locker below to ensure there'd be no sleep during anchor working. Between these, a round, iron, coal-burning 'bogie' stove stood uninvitingly cold and full of dead grey ash, its salt-stained flue pipe rising through the deck-head revealing the presence of a pretty bad leak.

Down the centre, built around two massive stanchions, a dirty wooden table was cluttered with the debris of an earlier meal. On each side of it, stood on the bare iron deck, were backless wooden bench seats, and against the after bulkhead a row of battered, rusty, tin lockers leaned wearily. The whole place was dank and stank of stale sweat, and urine.

Each bunk had a bundle of dark grey blankets that had seen better days – but rarely soap and water – and an uncased striped pillow. My nose rebelled. What a filthy hovel! I swung the torch around, looking for the oil lamp that I discovered hanging from a hook between the spurling-pipes. It lit easily, but gave barely a glimmer of light through the smoked-up glass. The wick had never been trimmed, not this decade at least, so it flickered and smoked like a factory chimney.

There was no sign of a toilet so I guessed that I was a member of the 'bucket and chuckit' brigade, an honour held by few in this day and age.

One of the upper starboard bunks had blankets folded reasonably tidily on its stained mattress, so I assumed it was a spare one.

Removing only my shoes, and damp outer clothes, I climbed into it. The smell was revolting but my tiredness won and I fell asleep almost immediately, my last thoughts being: tomorrow has got to be better.

IMMORTAL COMMAND

Part One

Angrily I rose from my high chair in the corner of the wheelhouse where, for the last forty-eight hours, I had been sitting waiting for the inevitable.

The faces of the officers, helmsmen, look-outs and signalmen on the bridge changed each time eight bells rang to announce the end of one watch and the beginning of another. Watch relieved watch, the hours passed; still I remained sitting there, the dutiful Master.

It seemed an age since the signal 'CONVOY TO SCATTER – HEAVY ENEMY WARSHIP IN SIGHT' had been received from our naval Escort Commander over on the far side of the convoy, and I'd immediately ordered 'full speed ahead and wheel hard-a-port' in an endeavour to put as many miles as possible between us and the murderous enemy ship.

During the following few hours several thunderous bangs and thumps had been heard in the far distance and it was obvious that the raider was reaping a grim harvest from our small, inadequate escort and fellow merchantmen.

Then all had become quiet.

The first twelve hours were the worst. Each shadow and breaking wave was the hunting battleship racing to our destruction, and the occasional seabird transformed itself into a searching aircraft. The majority of the crew found reason to be on deck volunteering their eyes as additional look-outs, but the sea remained empty. Not so the airwaves that were filled with the plaintive cries for help as ship after ship was found, shelled and sunk, by the voracious killer-ship.

As the hours passed, other enemies had to be fought: tiredness and complacency. Unfortunately I couldn't allow myself the luxury of retiring below to my cabin like the rest of the officers and crew. I remained sat on that damned hard bridge-chair fighting to keep my eyes open and mind alert, but I was fighting a losing battle as my head slumped deeper into the collar of my duffle coat.

As regular as clockwork, every two hours, a steward sustained my flagging energy with a steaming mug of cocoa, usually drunk scalding hot but occasionally left untouched on the shelf in front of me as I dozed off, to be removed, cold and congealed, two hours later by the peeved steward.

The tiredness left me after twenty-four hours and I seemed to get a second wind. No longer were my eyelids heavy and I sat straighter in the chair, but it was becoming increasingly difficult to maintain the crew in a high state of alertness. Most of them thought we had got away with it; we'd made our escape and were now hammering along at full speed away from our foe. A few, very few, knew that the enemy would still be seeking us with every means at his disposal. He would not be content until every ship in the convoy had been accounted for.

Compared with his speed of thirty plus knots, our modest fourteen made hopes of survival very slim. My problem was to keep the crew aware of this without causing panic. If we were going to end up in lifeboats, we would need all the strength and vitality we could muster, and the crew wouldn't rest if I threw too many scares into them. So, I had to sit there, waiting, ensuring that each set of watch-keepers were on their toes and that we were as ready as we could possibly be for whatever was to be our fate.

Lifeboats were checked and re-checked. Our meagre armament of one ancient four-inch gun and two Oerlikon machine-guns were manned and ready to match themselves against what could well be half a dozen eleven-inch guns. It was a sobering thought that we would be out-gunned by any one of the enemy's many secondary armament weapons.

I could hear the Second Mate talking softly to the helmsman behind me and it grated on my raw nerves until I eventually, and unfairly, shouted at them to stop their infernal cackling. A sullen silence reigned for the rest of the watch and this was just as bad, if not worse, than the whispering.

With stiff, heavy legs, I strode from the wheelhouse out onto the bleak windswept open bridge-wing where the lookout, thickly clad in several layers of coats, was conscientiously sweeping the horizon with binoculars, obviously aware of my presence. The fresh biting wind was a tonic as I rasped a hand across my chin, bristling with two days' growth of beard. I searched the horizon myself. The sea was a bit lumpy and the occasional extra high crest on the skyline took on all the fearsome appearance of a battleship's fighting top, causing my leaden heart to miss a few beats, but all seemed well.

Could I snatch a few minutes in my cabin to wash and shave? I asked myself. I would have to make sure not to sit down though, even for a moment; I'd never get up again.

Again my eyes swept the empty horizon, then I made my decision. I would go below, just for a wash, shave and change of clothing. It would do me the world of good.

'Just going to my cabin for a quick shave, Mr Davidson,' I called into the wheelhouse. 'I will ...' The sentence was never finished.

'Ship bearing red eight oh,' screamed the excited voice of the lookout.

'Hard-a-starboard!' I yelled to the helmsman as I stepped into the wheelhouse to snatch binoculars from the shelf in front of my chair.

The Second Mate barged his way unceremoniously passed me on his way out onto the bridge-wing where I joined him seconds later. We stood focusing our glasses on the ship out on our port quarter and what we saw frightened the living daylights out of us. She was massive. Even though still hull-down, her huge superstructure stuck up like a fort on the skyline.

'Steer zero five zero,' I called over my shoulder. That should put us just about stern-on to this evil looking warship rapidly closing on us. I couldn't take my eyes off her as she finally settled dead astern. She grew bigger and bigger until her bow wave became clear to the naked eye and we saw the flashing pinpricks of light coming from her bridge.

'Ship signalling STOP. DO NOT USE YOUR RADIO OR I WILL FIRE,' shouted our signalman in a high-pitched voice of fear. No doubts now as to her intentions. The Second Mate turned to me expectantly.

'Maintain course and speed,' I ordered with more bravado than I felt. 'Give the Radio Officer our position and tell him to send an RRRR signal.'

Obviously stunned, the Second Mate went to do my bidding and, as an afterthought, I added, 'Tell the gunners to open fire as soon as the enemy is within range.' Who the hell did I think I was, Nelson at Trafalgar? In all honesty I didn't know what else to say.

The Second Mate stopped, turned, and stared at me. Did he think I was mad?

'Did you hear me, Mr Davidson?' I snapped.

He nodded a speechless acknowledgement, exaggerated a swallow, then turned back into the wheelhouse.

The Bosun ran up the bridge ladder and looked at me enquiringly. He was a good man, very reliable and unflappable.

'Swing out the boats, Bosun, and get as many of the men as possible to their boat stations.' A curt nod of his head and he was gone. Probably my order had already been carried out.

Returning into the wheelhouse I took the engine-room telephone from its bracket on the after bulkhead. 'Engine room,' came the tinny voice from below.

'Captain here,' I said pompously. 'We have an enemy warship coming up astern of us. Get as many men as you can spare up on deck now and when I ring down "Finish with engines" get the rest up, pronto.'

'Aye, aye,' came the metallic reply which I recognised as that of the

Chief Engineer. I might have known he'd be down there at the first sign of trouble.

Out on the bridge-wing again, every detail of the Hun was clear. I could almost see the men on her bridge.

'Enemy signalling again, Sir,' reported our signalman, significantly using the word 'enemy' instead of the usual 'ship' '... STOP OR I WILL FIRE – LAST WARNING.'

'Is he within our range yet, Mr Davidson?' I asked, stupidly.

'No, Sir, nowhere near.' The look on his face was almost sympathetic.

'Well, tell the gunners that if she fires on us they are to fire back, in range or not,' I ordered. Now they all knew I was insane, yet surprisingly I still felt quite calm. I didn't honestly think they would fire on us. That sort of thing only happens to others. I had met many German seamen in my time and they were just like us, not murderers of innocent merchantmen. They wouldn't shoot, so showing a brave face could only calm my crew.

A red flash lit the other ship and someone screamed, 'She's fired.' Within seconds a sound like a rolling clap of thunder passed over us and a huge column of water rose from the sea ahead. They were only trying to scare us, I assured myself.

More flashes from the warship and I started counting. One, two, three, four. Then the whole world went mad. An eye-searing flash followed by an horrendous explosion turned the bridge into a red-hot mangled mess of iron, squeezing every drop of breath from my body. The deck reared up beneath my feet and flung me heavily against the bridge rail. I had no feeling anywhere but I knew that something, somewhere, was wrong. My eyes dropped as I tried to make out what was different. I was in a silent world of red mist that slowly cleared until I could make out the remains of Second Mate Davidson at my feet, and the red mass of tortured flesh and splintered bone where my shoulder and chest had been, moments before.

The last thing I can remember was a voice coming through the deathly silence, as though from far, far away. 'Oy, you – what are you doing?' ...

Part Two

Old 'Bogie' Knight ambled his way along the short stretch of muddy, wheel-rutted track that ran from the main road to the broken wooden gate on which, hung at a drunken angle, was a weather-worn notice telling everyone who had ventured thus far that it was the entrance to the premises of 'Percival Cloud. Shipbreaker'.

He walked slowly and carefully, as he had done for the last twenty years. Ever since the end of the war when the Navy decided that a rickety old three-badge AB with rheumatic joints was no longer a good advert in the King's uniform.

Warily he negotiated the pot-holes and crevices as he turned into the yard, making his way towards the old stone quay alongside which lay the broken, red-rusty remains, of once beautiful ships as they awaited the acetylene torches that would cut them up into manageable size lumps of scrap metal to feed the manufacturers of the nation's razor blades.

Like any seaman, he had been very depressed in such surroundings at first, to see so many fine ships in their final resting place. It was like working in a morgue, but beggars can't be choosers. Who wanted to employ a worn-out sailor? He'd been luckier than most to get this job as watchman. Didn't pay much but at least he was warm and dry most of the time.

His hut was positioned at one end of the quayside and he felt reasonably content with his lot as his thumb pressed down on the latch to open the wooden door. It wasn't very big, just room enough for a small table, a coal-burning stove and his ancient, threadbare old armchair that he would soon settle his aching bones into, just as soon as he could get the stove alight and burning.

Minutes later, with the stove glowing merrily, his knarled hands wrapped around a tin mug of tea brewed strong and sweet, Navy style, he stood gazing out of the smeared window. Nearest to his hut lay the dredger that had arrived just a week earlier. There were still signs of paint on her superstructure, and varnish on the bridge woodwork.

Compared with other wrecks in the yard she was in pristine condition.

Behind her, in various states of demolition, lay a dozen or more hulks, red-brown with rust. Some had been there for years. The Grand-daddy of them all was the old WW2 merchant ship, now a bare skeleton of her former self. She must have been a beauty in her day.

Someone once said she'd been used in a film back in the 1950s. Perhaps that's why she'd never been broken up. Since then she'd lain there, rotting away in the creek, her hull full of rubbish and mud washed in and out through the gaping holes in her sides by every tide.

He stared at her, trying to rebuild her in his mind's eye.

What sort of funnel had stood high and proud on her boat-deck? What colour had she been painted before the war came along and decreed that her dress be a coat of Admiralty grey? What had her name been? Perhaps the guvnor would know, or be able to find out from his books. He made a mental note to ask.

'Damn,' he swore as his eyes caught movement on what was left of her bridge. Opening his cuddy door he shambled along the quay.

Bloody vandals, he cursed. Kids nowadays ain't got nothing else to do but make a nuisance of themselves. He'd soon send them off with a flea in their ear. Still, he admitted, without them he wouldn't be needed. The thought made him happier.

As he got nearer the old ship he could see the figure standing motionless on the bridge-wing. It didn't look much like a kid. Can't be a thief, he thought, nothin' worth stealing. It certainly looked like a full-grown man.

He was now within thirty paces of her and still the figure hadn't moved. It was a man, stood like a statue, not moving at all, just staring down over the rotting bridge-rail onto the bare ribs of what had once been her busy foredeck.

Bogie's heart missed a couple of beats and his stomach boxed the compass. He was no hero and this bloke looked a bit weird. Perhaps if I shout, he said to himself hopefully, this guy will scarper.

He took a deep breath into his wheezy lungs and yelled as loud as he could. 'Oy, you. What are you doing?'

The figure didn't turn its head, or jump in surprise, or run away.

It just disappeared.

'THE CHANNELS'

I gripped the spokes of the wheel tightly as a shiver of excitement ran through me. We'd be docking tomorrow at the same port we had sailed from sixteen months ago; now that the voyage was nearly over it seemed to have passed so quickly. I guessed that the fact that she'd been a happy ship had a lot to do with it.

The trip had been a good one, too, with plenty of variety and interest. Out via Suez to Calcutta and Madras, then to Sydney to load for Japan. We'd hit a typhoon on that stretch, in the South China Sea, the roughest seas I'd ever seen, like mountains. The ship had stood on end at times. Still, she came through it all right, except for minor damage and a stoved-in lifeboat.

Then back to Melbourne, the rainy city, and across to Dunedin to top up our cargo for Buenos Aires via Cape Horn. Only the Mate and the Chief Engineer had been around the Horn before and we looked forward to the prospect with some trepidation. In fact, we had good weather all the way and the Horn itself was flat and calm – well almost, just a bit of a swell.

From there it was north to Panama and back into the Pacific where we spent some time. But now, back in the Atlantic, we were less than twenty-four hours from home.

'Watch your head,' snapped the officer of the watch.

I focused my eyes which had been staring blindly at the compass card. I was four degrees off course. I eased the spokes through my hands.

'Sorry, Third,' I apologised.

His answering grin told me that he understood. He knew my thoughts had wandered off, probably because he too was suffering, as we all were, from that age-old phenomenon known as 'the channels', which has afflicted seamen since ships were invented. It's a sort of mild hysteria one gets on the last days at sea before arriving home after a long voyage. It's a mixture of excitement, butterflies, a great thirst for a British pint, getting off the ship and, above all, the eagerness and anticipation of seeing loved ones. A really electrifying feeling that makes sleep impossible.

This time tomorrow I'll be home, I thought. Or more likely in my local, having forgotten all about the last year or so.

Five weeks' leave! What a wonderful thought!

I tried to concentrate on my job: keeping the ship on course. Normally in this sort of weather, she'd steer a line as straight as a ruler with almost no attention, just an occasional spoke this way or that. Tonight, with my mind all over the place, the lubber line was following suit and I chased it all round the compass rose.

Again the Third Mate looked over his shoulder. He had seen the ship's head roaming around the horizon and knew that if he were to look astern he would see our wake looking like a corkscrew.

This time he said nothing but the look was enough to warn me that a rocket would be forthcoming if I didn't buck up. A few more moments passed.

'Stayin' on for the next trip, Third?' I asked.

'No,' he replied over his shoulder. 'I'm doing a spell at nautical college then sitting my Mate's ticket. How about you?'

'Five weeks blind drunk then ship out on the first ship I'm offered.'

He laughed, knowing I wasn't much of a drinking man.

In the silence that followed I again enjoyed the intoxicating thrill of 'the channels' running through me. I twisted my head round to see the clock on the bulkhead behind me. Five to twelve – five minutes to go to my relief. The time seemed to go quickly as my mind ran through the presents I'd bought for friends and family. Had I forgotten anybody? Too late now, even if I had.

The Third Mate caught my eye and nodded towards the clock. I turned again and was surprised to see it was midnight. Taking hold of the bell rope with its fancy ropework I rang eight bells and my relief appeared magically at the last double stroke.

'All yours,' I offered. 'Course 042.'

We changed places and he looked into the binnacle.

'Cheers,' he answered, unenthusiastically looking forward to his two hour trick. '042.'

'Wheel relieved, Third. Course 042,' I called as I left the wheelhouse and stepped out onto the bridge wing where the night air smelt so fresh after the stuffiness of the wheelhouse.

I stood for a few moments looking for'd and thinking that home was not too far away over that dark horizon. Another delightful wave of 'the channels' swept though me and I slid down the bridge ladder with only my hands on the rails. Trotting and jumping like a three year old I ran along the boat-deck and down onto the main deck. I passed two massive hatches which would soon be disgorging our cargo and then up the ladder to the poop-deck, where surprisingly two of the lads were sitting dangerously casual on the stern rail.

'Whassamatter,' I enquired. 'Can't sleep?'

'Nah,' said one of the dim figures. 'Just finished me dhobeying.'

I couldn't think of a smart answer to that so I left them waving their glowing cigarettes and entered the deckhouse, sliding down the ladder into the dark interior of the crew accommodation. Everyone seemed to be awake.

'Fifteen two, fifteen four, and a pair's six,' chanted the voice of one of the crib players sitting at the table in the mess-room as he put his cards down in front of him, face up.

'Bloody back peg up, that's me,' complained his opponent. 'One more each and we'll be level.'

Beyond them, one industrious member of the crew was putting the finishing touches to his ham-fisted needlework as he closed a rent in his denims with big 'homeward-bound' stitches.

Either side of him sat the intelligentsia, one avidly reading a Western paperback while the other solved a mystery thriller by reading the back page first.

A quick count showed that not one man was in his cabin. Most unusual for watch-keepers at this time of night; a sure sign of 'the channels'!

Pouring myself a mug of stewed tea from the dixie on the mess table, always available at watch change-over, I spooned in a lavish helping of condensed milk and went to my cabin. Like the others, I wasn't the least bit sleepy. I was too excited as I dragged my half-packed suitcase from off my bunk and placed it on the deck. I'd finish packing in the morning.

Switching on the bunk light and dowsing the main deck-head one, I climbed into my bunk and puffed up my pillow. Perhaps I can finish off my book before we get in, I thought, then I can leave it for the next seamen who occupies this cabin.

Up on the bridge the Second Mate raised his powerful night glasses and peered expectantly ahead through the rigging of the foremast. Yes, there it was, a small momentary lightening of the sky. He smiled at this proof of his good navigation and felt a thrill of pleasure. Self-satisfaction or 'the channels'? He pondered the thought.

Within minutes a shrill ring of the bridge 'phone shattered the stillness of the wheelhouse. He twisted the receiver from its bracket on the bulkhead.

'Bridge,' he said.

'Loom of light just a point on the starboard bow,' reported the tinny voice of the lookout at his lonely post right for'rd on the fo'c'sle.

'Very well,' acknowledged the officer. He replaced the 'phone.

Home at last.

MASQUERADE

I felt uncharacteristically angry as I belted the innocent, stubbornly resisting nut with a heavy wrench. 'Bloody Army!'

This morning, I had parked my van, as usual and as ordered, behind one of the historic buildings of the Military Academy and walked carefree towards the boiler-room to continue my job of overhauling the three big boilers.

Winning this lucrative contract had done wonders for the prestige of my small welding and maintenance, business, as well as making it financially secure for the foreseeable future.

Usually, I was a happy-go-lucky sort of bloke who, at thirty, was beginning to enjoy the fruits of years of hard graft. My ginger moustache and long, unruly mop of tangled red hair earned me the inevitable nickname of 'Brillo' from my many friends.

Wriggling under the large-bore water pipes to reach a slightly leaking flange, I tried to reason with my anger.

When I started this job I had been requested, politely, to respect the sanctity of the parade-ground, or whatever it was called. It was, they said, holy ground to the Army, upon which no one, other than officers of the staff and the RSM, was allowed to walk. Fair enough!

Each day I walked its perimeter road, careful not to offend, but this morning, because it was chilly and I wanted to reach the warmth of the boiler-house, I had unwittingly cut across the corner of their hallowed ground.

Less than halfway over I was stopped abruptly as a voice, seemingly close to my ear, bellowed, 'That man there ... Stop!!!'

I turned to see a figure twenty yards away strutting arrogantly towards me, highly polished boots crunching into the gravel and crashing to a halt within an inch of my tatty work-shoes.

Eyes glared at me from under a mirror-like, nose-touching peak of a chequered cap sat squarely on a florid face, mostly covered by a walrus moustache. Its uniform was immaculate. Everything was pressed, spotless and glittering. One arm carried a huge badge of some heraldic design on its sleeve while the other gripped a pace-stick in the armpit at exactly ninety degrees to the horizontal with fingers precisely aligned along its length.

A hole appeared among the hair covering its mouth and from it came decibels equal to a space-ship's launching.

'Wot har you doin' on my parade-ground, you 'orrible little man?' screamed the voice as the face looked up to me.

I stood still, shocked, open-mouthed and nearly jumping to attention.

Without waiting for my reply it continued, 'Get out of my sight you hexcuse for a 'uman being or Hi shall 'ave your guts for garters.'

He stood rock-still as I moved hurriedly away to my boiler-room sanctuary where my brain recovered from the shock and began to re-function.

What the hell was I doing, running away from him? I was a civvy, for Christ's sake! I fumed at this affront to my dignity.

Slowly I came off the boil, then heard the boiler-room door open and a young officer stepped in, peering into the gloom as his eyes accustomed themselves after the bright daylight outside.

'Oh NO!' I said to myself, 'not another rollicking!'

'Anyone there?' called the up-market voice.

I crawled out, wiping oily hands on a piece of rag.

'Good morning,' came his greeting as he saw me. 'I'm the Duty Officer. Everything O.K?'

I scowled at him. 'No, it's bloody well not,' and related this morning's happening.

'Don't worry yourself about him,' smiled this cheerful officer. 'That's RSM Rosemary. He is always like that. It's his job. He is third only to God and the CO, within the Academy, and sometimes even *they* are frightened of him. It's his way.' He paused, 'I think it is a means of covering his insecurity at having such an embarrassing name for a man in his position. He's known as "Rosie" of course and, like most powerful men, he has to intimidate people by shouting.'

My anger subsided a little more.

'Yes, but it's not very nice being shouted at like that,' I complained.

'No,' he answered, 'I can understand that, and you are entitled to make a formal complaint but, in all honesty, nothing would, or could, be done.'

He leaned towards me with a twinkle in his eye. 'Would you like a little unofficial advice?'

I nodded affirmatively.

'If he does it again,' he continued, 'look him straight in the eye and quietly give him this reply, but please don't tell anyone it came from me.'

I listened carefully. I liked his suggestion and it was obvious I wasn't the only one wanting to get my own back so, on my last morning at the Academy, when I had finished the job, I deliberately walked across the corner of the parade ground.

He had probably been in hiding every day waiting for me to transgress.

I awaited the expected scream, and wasn't disappointed.

'Stand still, that man!' came the shrieking command as he crunched his way to where I stood, unafraid.

'Hi told you before,' he bellowed bull-like as we nearly kissed Eskimo style. 'Keep orf my parade ground!'

I couldn't bend forward, we were too close, so in a calm, conspiratorial whisper, I apologised.

'Sorry RSM. I wasn't thinking … Oh, by the way, I'm not an 'orrible little man. I'm an officer in the 22nd.'

Behind his twitching moustache, his apoplectic face became even redder. Probably for the first time in his life he was speechless.

As I walked unhurriedly away towards my van, across his sacred soil, I wondered what his thoughts were at this moment, as he pondered his confrontation with a covert officer of the famous, or infamous depending on one's opinion, SAS.

Reaching the corner of a building, out of his sight, I ran to my van chuckling child-like, and drove away, fast.

INVITATION?

The lorry wheels crunched on gravel, as our driver nonchalantly steered us along the tree-lined driveway, which now looked in need of urgent attention after three years of military misuse and neglect.

It had been a long journey from our base, and I felt cold and miserable, sat alongside the driver, hunching my neck, tortoise-like, down into the comforting warmth of my greatcoat collar.

'My four lads must be feeling even worse,' I thought sympathetically. Only someone who had sat on hard, inflexible, wooden bench seats, in the draughty back of a three-ton lorry, for hours on end, in mid-winter, could empathise with them. In comparison, I travelled in relative luxury, on an upholstered seat, feeling the warmth from the engine casing next to my leg. Oh, the privilege of rank!

We had just been cleared through the entrance gate of our destination, by deceptively low-key security guards. Deceptive because they were dressed in civilian clothes, looking less smart than they would normally have been in their white webbing and red caps of the Military Police, as they checked our documentation and thoroughly examined the vehicle.

My Marines in the back were probably bewildered by the scrutiny from these 'civvies' but they were not aware – as I was – that we had just entered a top-secret training facility for operatives from MI5, MI6, SOE, and other civilian and military covert units.

No, we weren't trainee spies! We were a small team of Royal Marines arriving for a short course of special demolition techniques. So special that they could only be taught at this establishment.

As we bumped over the pot-holed surface of the road, I cautiously raised my head, just enough to peer over the rim of my collar, in a reluctant effort to appease my curiosity. Between the trees and bushes, I could see people furtively dashing hither and thither. Then a loud bang, which made me jump, made me swivel my head to the right, where I glimpsed a small group in a clearing, who appeared to be enjoying a free-for-all fight.

'Cor! Look at that, Sir!' exclaimed my driver, nodding his head forward, as if heading a ball.

We had emerged from the canopy of trees onto a large, circular, gravelled area surrounding a central group of stone statues standing in a dry, green-slime covered bowl that was once a magnificent fountain. On the far side stood a huge, imposing, castle-like building, whose tall arched windows peered from ivy-covered walls.

Grey-stone steps, edged by weeds and grass, led up to iron-bound wooden doors, guarded by moss-covered, life-size, nude stone statues, and a couple of overalled armed sentries.

Leaving my lads to unload the lorry, I pushed open the impressive doors and entered the cathedral-like reception hall. Even without its peacetime trappings, it was breathtaking. The centrepiece was a magnificent grand staircase, now carpet-less, rising in a left handed curve and edged by delicately carved handrails – now sadly chipped and knocked.

The grandeur of this palatial hall was shattered by the numerous bodies, all in uniform overalls, going about their duties.

'Ha! Lieutenant Hall!' greeted one of the ubiquitous overalls, as he approached with open hand outstretched, having obviously recognised my uniform. 'I am the Duty Officer. Welcome to Bloddington!'

Not knowing his rank, I shook hands tentatively, returned his greeting, and requested my requirements to get my four men, and the driver, settled in, then to enjoy a large gin in the Officers' Mess, if he would kindly point me in the right direction?

'Sorry, old chap,' he answered. 'this is a government establishment, not military. We're all the same here. No rank. Everyone eats and drinks together.' He smiled as he turned away. 'I'll show your quarters, then you will need to get out of uniform and into the coveralls that you will find on your bed.'

Climbing the staircase, and along a corridor lined with doors, he opened one marked A–11 and ushered me into a room containing six beds, each with a side cabinet and wardrobe.

'This is for you and your chaps,' he said. 'The driver will stay in the transit block. I will look after him.' I nodded my thanks as he continued, 'All meal-times are on the notice-board downstairs. Sit where you like, but tell your chaps that there is a strict rule here. No one talks about who they are, or what they do. The bar is open at 7 p.m.'

Turning to leave the room, he called back over his shoulder to advise me that we would be 'called-for' at 9 a.m. the following morning by our Instructor.

'This is a novelty,' I thought as I retraced my steps downstairs to collect my lads. They were delighted at the news but, at that stage, I couldn't answer their question, as they laughingly enquired, was it promotion for them, or demotion for me? Personally, I could not have cared less. I wasn't a snob and our unit was very informal anyhow.

Back in the room, unpacking my gear and donning the overalls, I noticed a square patch on the wall above my bed. It looked like a power-point that had been papered over. I didn't think any more of it at that time.

After a good meal, we gravitated to the bar to meet our fellow trainees, socially. A less likely looking bunch of spies would be hard to find. Mostly men, but quite a number of women, they looked more like bank managers and secretaries, than secret agents. They were quiet, introverted, and unassuming people who immediately earned my utmost admiration and respect.

During conversation, I learned that 'Bloddington' – or Bloddington Hall to give it its correct name – was, in peacetime, an internationally famous, and very exclusive, school for daughters of the very rich and famous, with term fees well in excess of my annual pay!

Many of the pupils had been 'Lady This' or 'The Right Honourable That', and not a few had been Royalty.

Later, after a convivial evening, I lay on my bed, head cradled in my hands, gazing up at the ornate ceiling, wondering how many nubile young females had done the same, dreaming of a Knight in shining armour riding to their rescue. Where were they now?

My eyes drifted to the patch on the wall, and curiosity got the better of me, as I teased off a corner of paper and carefully peeled the patch away. It wasn't a power point. It was a reminder of the Hall's previous role as a School for Young Ladies, and I decided not to enlighten my Marines of its existence for fear of arousing their animal instincts. Nevertheless, I was very tempted, and had to suppress the yearning to check for a response.

It was a bell-push and under it was the provocative instruction: 'Press to call for a Mistress'.

ROUND PLUG, SQUARE HOLE

Corporal Penwith, MM Royal Marines, and a member of the elite SBS, was really cheesed-off. What the hell was he doing here, standing in a corridor of the army's Middle East Headquarters of the SAS, guarding a door behind which SAS officers were holding a top-level briefing – probably about their next book, he thought sarcastically.

He hadn't asked to be seconded to this unit any more than he had 'volunteered' for this guard duty.

Like most Royal Marines he had little respect for 'the regiment' as the SAS themselves liked to be called. His own unit was more covert than theirs and far less known, mainly because we prefer it that way, he supposed, as he recalled seeing the rows of library shelves full of their crap stories of missions for which they had been deluged with medals, even when they botched the job.

He was irritable, hot, sweaty and pissed-off, standing like a prune in an airless passageway. Why, he wondered, had they chosen the only Royal Marine in the unit for this duty. Couldn't they trust their own troopers?

He recalled the anxiety his unit felt when required to work alongside the SAS who, in his opinion, had watched too many war films, believing in their own 'superman' image.

His unit much preferred to operate alone but, if they had to work with anyone they would choose an ordinary County Regiment. He personally had a great regard for the everyday PBI, the poor bloody infantry, whose reliability and steadfastness wasn't ruined by Gung-Ho medal seekers.

He paused in his reminiscences as the door at the far end of the corridor opened letting in an unwelcome blast of hot desert air and a travel-worn figure whose dust-covered uniform and 'cherry-berry' beret identified him as a Colonel in the Parachute Regiment.

'Ha,' he thought surprisingly, because the Paras and the Marines were friendly rivals, 'a real soldier.' He sprang respectfully to attention, saluting.

'Good morning, Corporal,' greeted the weary officer, equally surprised to see a Royal Marine in an SAS base, as he returned the salute.

'Good morning, Sir. Can I help you?'

'Yes please, Corporal,' he replied with humour, 'what I need most is a shower.'

'Right, Sir,' came the poker-faced response as the Marine pointed to the door he was guarding. 'You've come to the right place. Would you like "C" troop or "D" troop?'

SLIP OF THE TONGUE

Shoulders hunched, I shrank my head, tortoise-like, down into the up-turned collar of my overcoat, in a vain attempt to protect my newly shorn head and neck from the bitter blasts of wintry wind that scythed over the bleak waters of Greenock Docks.

Low clouds raced heavily across the sky making a contrasting dark back-cloth to the white tops of the wind-driven waves that streaked the dirty River Clyde.

Head down, studying my boots, I struggled along the deserted cobbled quayside, making my way back to the haven of my ship, after a visit to a barber's shop where the sadistic wielder of blunt sheep-shears had misinterpreted my wish for a 'trim'. The result was a hairstyle suitable to be seen only on the green baize of a billiard table.

My anger at this desecration of my curly locks was held in check solely by the fact that he was a six foot tall brute, whereas I was a puny fifteen year old.

I hoped he shaved with an open razor, and that the next time he cut himself it wouldn't be too fatal!

The sight of my ship, appearing out of the morning gloom, alongside the quay a few hundred yards ahead of me, lifted my spirits.

Her drab, grey painted hull, exuded a warm welcome compared to the freezing, windswept, depressing environment of 'sunny' Greenock.

She was my first ship. I had joined her a few months ago, straight from school, delighted at last to be at sea but, like most boys of my age, disappointed at having missed out on the war by just a few weeks. Nevertheless, I was proud to be in her crew, even as a lowly Boy Seaman, as I climbed the steep gangway onto her deck, eagerly anticipating the warm fug of the crew mess-room.

'Hello Shrimp!' came my greeting from Stan, one of the ABs, who then burst out laughing as he spotted my bristly bonce. His gleeful hilarity attracted the attention of our Welsh Bosun who, poking his head into the mess-room, looked unsmilingly at me and said, 'Thought you were going for a haircut?' His straight face didn't even crack as he turned and left.

No wonder he was known as Di the Death!

I put my frozen hands on the red-hot radiator and waited patiently for Stan's mirth to subside. I didn't think it funny. Eventually, after several uncontrolled bursts of giggling each time he looked at my head, he wiped the tears from his eyes and nose, and quietened down.

'We had some news while you were ashore getting your perm,' he smirked, almost spluttering with laughter again at his humour. 'We're sailing this afternoon.'

'Oh yeah!' came my expected response. 'Where to?'

'Aultbea,' he said, 'to load some Naval stuff.'

'Oh! Good,' I replied knowledgeably. Then, after a pause, added, 'Where's that?'

He looked at me with the pitying look of someone who has just learned something that you don't know. 'Bloody Russia, init!'

Memories of Russian convoys, seen on newsreel at the cinema, battling their way through storms and frozen seas, their decks thick with ice and snow, came flooding into my head. Heroically, I was now to face these same dangerous hardships.

I dashed to my cabin. I had an hour to write home and tell them the news that I knew would be passed on to my mates who were always eager to hear what I was doing. I'd be the envy of them all, as they went about their mundane humdrum jobs.

Modestly exaggerating how awful and perilous a Russian run would be in mid-winter, I told my folks not to worry – I would probably survive such horrors – but I stressed they should let my friends know, just in case.

We sailed in a blizzard, but I consoled myself that it was nothing compared with what we would be getting later as we approached the Arctic Sea.

Leaving the confines of the River Clyde, we were soon pounding into quite heavy seas. It was freezing on deck so, as soon as we dropped the Pilot – who took our mail ashore for us – I hurried below.

Being a Boy Seaman, and therefore a day-worker, I didn't stand watches like the others, and after a lonely evening reading in a deserted mess-room, I turned in for a good night's sleep, fearful of what lay ahead in the next week or so.

Next morning, wakened by a watch-keeper, I looked out of the port-hole. Nothing but cold grey sea and murky drizzle. At least the sea was calm.

After scoffing a thick sausage sandwich for breakfast I began my routine morning chores, cleaning the mess-room and ablutions, careful not to waken the off-watch men snoring in their pits.

During the mid-morning, as I was preparing a big urn full of tea for the watch-keepers, I was surprised to hear a loud rumble and roar that I recognised as our anchor being dropped. Curious, I went up on deck to find Stan, who had just returned aft from the foc's'le head, standing looking out over an expanse of water. We were almost surrounded by land!

'Where are we?' I asked incredulously.

'Loch Ewe,' came his laconic reply.

I looked at the nearby land and saw a group of buildings on our port bow. Stan pointed to them. 'That's Aultbea over there,' he said.

'How come?' I queried in surprise. 'We only left Scotland yesterday!'

He turned to look at me with a frown on his face. 'This is still Scotland,' he snapped.

'But you told me we were going to Russia,' I said in total confusion.

The frown on his face changed to a smile of understanding as he placed a hand on my shoulder. He looked at me, then after a pause, said, 'No, you big pillock. I said we were going to Aultbea in Ross-shire.'

FOR QUEEN AND COUNTRY

I didn't enjoy the trip ashore, from the troopship to the invasion beach, in the tiny landing craft. It wasn't seasickness, the sea was calm. It was being packed tight, shoulder to shoulder, with thirty other troopers, smelling their fear, and feeling my own.

Ahead of us, although fortunately we couldn't see because of the high ramp that formed the bow of the craft, was an open beach covered in smoke, fires and explosions.

We were all scared, but worst of all was the young officer at the front who would be first off. He was in a blue funk, and who could blame him? Luckily, our training and discipline held our fear in check. We were here to do a job, fear or no fear.

'Stand by!' croaked the officer, and a few seconds later we gratefully felt the craft crunch onto the beach. None of us enjoyed being sitting ducks on a boat at sea and we were eager to get off into our military element.

As the bow ramp dropped, we charged forward, to be met by a hail of machine-gun fire that shredded the leading ranks, including the officer. Stumbling over their bodies, I leapt ashore in sheer panic and splashed through ankle-deep water onto a beach littered with bodies of the first wave of our assault troops.

Already, men of my section were falling either side of me, cut down by murderous fire from the concealed defenders, whose weapons covered every inch of the landing area.

It was bloody slaughter.

The few of us that reached the dubious shelter of sand dunes at the back of the beach were greeted by mortar bombs, and targeted by snipers.

I was in a state of numbed shock as I threw myself into a shallow scrape, squirming to embed myself deeper in the soft sand. Face down, I lay terrified, expecting any minute to feel a bullet smash into my body.

Explosions shook the ground. Bullets whined inches above me. The frightening, awesome, ripping sound of automatic weapons filled the air. The agonised screams of wounded men. The shouting of incoherent orders.

The sounds of battle.

From somewhere nearby, a sobbing, muffled cry of 'Mummy, Mummy.'

Half my face was burrowed in the sand. Opening my uppermost eye I saw a number of ants busying themselves within an inch of my nose and, incongruously, this had a calming effect on my shattered nerves.

I raised my head a fraction of an inch. To the right, a small mound of sand blocked my view, but I was certain the sobbing voice was just beyond it. Carefully, I turned to look the other way. As far as my eye could see, the beach was covered with sprawled, lifeless bodies.

At the water's edge, uniformed rag-dolls were being washed around, face down in the red-stained wavelets, and beyond them a dozen or more landing craft lay wrecked and burning.

Out at sea, naval ships were firing their great guns, but nowhere could I see more troops approaching. Had the raid been called off? Were we, that were ashore, being abandoned?

Ten yards away, and much to my relief, I saw movement in a shallow depression in the sand and recognised Corporal Hall, my Section Leader. At least I wasn't alone.

He was obviously alive and seemed to be trying to shout across to me, but no sound came from his mouth.

My whole world had gone silent. No gunfire, no bangs, no noise at all.

Everything seemed in slow motion, like a dream. To my horror, I realised I had gone deaf.

I dropped my head back into the sand in dreadful despair then, as quickly as it had gone, my hearing returned, and the noise of war hit me like a bomb blast.

Despite my relief, I was on the verge of panic so I concentrated my attention on the ants in an effort to compose myself.

I was still alive, I told myself. Death only happened to others. I would survive this somehow. I would not be a coward. I was a soldier and this was what I'd been trained – and paid – to do.

Gradually I regained control of myself and began to take stock of the situation.

Cautiously, I raised my head, then quickly ducked as a bullet smacked into the rim of my sand-scrape, showering me with grit and gravel.

'Missed me – ya bastard!' I shouted irrationally.

Again, I inched my head up and was comforted to see 'Henry' Hall still in the same position. He looked over to me, smiled, and yelled several words, but all I could make out was 'GO.'

He sprang to his feet, waving and pointing forward with his arm, like John Wayne ordering a charge of the Seventh Cavalry, but he had hardly taken a step before being thrown violently back several yards to land spread-eagled on his back, his face and chest a raw mass of redness.

Unthinking, I raised myself up on hands and knees, to charge forward in a blind rage of vengeance.

I didn't feel the two bullets enter my head. Neither did I see several ants drown in the blood draining into the sand from my slumped, lifeless body.

TALES OF THE SNUG

There are only two pubs in the village. One, the Black Swan, known as the 'Mucky Duck', is a spit-and-sawdust place mainly used by airmen from the nearby RAF Station and the less discriminating members of the small community. For a start, the landlord was a foreigner – from London!

The other is the King Richard, fondly called the 'Royal Dick'. It is an eighteenth-century coaching inn with original walls of solid stone and flaking brickwork, and low oak-beamed ceilings coloured almost black by the stains of nicotine.

Inside, a large, open, log-burning fire blazes and crackles a warming welcome to customers coming in from the bitterly cold January weather. Len, the landlord, a big built ex-RAF Flight Sergeant with rosy complexion, reigns supreme and alone, behind a row of gleaming brass beer-pump handles standing, like a rank of Guardsmen, along the highly polished bar on which the life expectancy of a splash of beer, or speck of dust, could be counted in seconds.

From under the hanging rows of silver-plated tankards, the jovial 'mine-host' dispensed the local brew to his thirsty customers, three of whom almost filled the small public bar, next to which, separated only by a pillar, a large and very old table, scarred and chipped from many decades of use and misuse, stood in an alcove surrounded on three sides by cushioned bench-seats.

Ancient prints of the village, mostly in damaged gold-leaf frames, hung at varying angles from rustic nails driven deep into cement-washed walls.

This was 'The Snug'. By inveterate tradition the sacrosanct reserve of the local Panjandrum. God help any intruder, no matter how unintentional or innocent their action, for they would be driven to a hasty departure by the silent, unflinching and frosty glares from the current incumbents. Unless, of course, they were extremely thick-skinned and insensitive, like a certain Air Force officer.

It had been a typical winter evening. The usual group sat around the table listening to each other's oft repeated reminiscences, mostly true but frequently exaggerated, as they caressed their glasses of ale, peering at each other through the haze of tobacco smoke that fogged the unventilated room.

There was the unfortunately named John Thomas, kindly nicknamed 'JohnTom', a lifelong farmer who had, reputedly, never been out of the

County. Still active at 82, he ran his small farm, rundown over recent years, with his 40-year-old widowed grandson.

Alongside him sat Captain James Blackler, a retired merchant ship-master with a vast memory – or imagination – from which he recounted stories of years of wide-world travel, again and again and again.

Then there was the 60-year-old former Colonel, Percy Thorpe. Actually he had only been a Major in the Signals Corps, a secret widely known by all the villagers. Perhaps that is why he spoke very little of his Army career. Nevertheless he was a good sort, and a patient listener.

Another ex-Serviceman, Commander Coulden-Pollock, known through all his Service life as 'Golden Bollocks', was another gifted raconteur. Full of humour, his tales of life in the Royal Navy, never aimed at besting or belittling others, were guaranteed to keep smiles on the faces of his friends.

Lastly, but certainly not least, was the youngest of them all. Seriously wounded two years ago during the evacuation of troops from the beaches of Dunkirk, 50-year-old Chief Petty Officer 'Lucy' Lockett had been medi-cally discharged from the Navy to exist on a meagre pension that, luckily, he was able to supplement from the roadside sale of flowers and vege-tables from his extensive garden. His irrepressible ebullience, and often coarse stories of lower-deck Naval life, were sure to bring everyone back down to earth when arrogance or pomposity crept into conversations. In fact, he had just ended an unlikely recollection of an incident when he had ordered a young, and very scared, boy seaman, to let him know as soon as the Inspecting Admiral stepped on board. On seeing the officer arrive, the lad and gone up to him and said, 'Excuse me, Sir, are you the Admiral?' The amused officer affirmed that he was, to which the youngster replied, 'I'd watch it if I were you, Sir. The Chief's looking for you!'

The laughter on the group's faces became frozen as a uniformed RAF officer approached their sacred table, placing a hand on the back of an empty chair.

'Good evening, gentlemen, anyone sitting here?' he enquired as he drew up the chair and sat down without waiting for their answer.

In shock and astonishment they each shook his proffered hand, noting the ribbons of the DFC and AFC on his tunic beneath Pilot's wings, as he nonchalantly introduced himself. 'Squadron Leader Buckingham, David. From RAF Aldinghurst, just up the road.' He looked at each man and smiled disarmingly. 'Thought I'd get to know the local people.'

Len, the landlord, anticipating an upturn in trade at least, or a heated argument at most, hovered expectantly across his gleaming bar over-looking 'the snug', trying successfully to catch the RAF man's eye.

'Will you allow me to buy each of you a drink?' offered the Squadron Leader.

'I knows what they all drink, Sor!' interrupted Len, pre-empting the possibility of a refusal as he turned to his pumps, grinning at the disquiet of his regulars and pleased that the cause was an officer of his own Service.

Several drinks later, all at the Air Force man's expense, the village doyens were warming to him as they listened avidly to his tales of air combat over France and during the Battle of Britain. At their insistence, he related the circumstances leading to the awards of his decorations, and the wounds that led to his subsequent grounding.

They were delighted to be hearing new, fresh stories and anecdotes of a Service they knew little about.

As the evening progressed, the frown on Len's forehead became more intense as he earwigged on the airman's reminiscences. Something was wrong, and his concern increased as each tale unfolded. Eventually his mind was made up and he went to the telephone.

It took ten minutes for the occupants of 'the Snug' to finish their drinks after Len had struck the ship's bell on the wall between the empty spirit optics and called 'Time Gentlemen, please!' and another ten before they completed their slightly inebriated, farewells and left the premises.

Outside, waiting by his bicycle propped against an unlit street lamp standard, the local Police Constable stood, cold and miserable in his cape, talking to two overcoated servicemen. He was not in the best of moods, being called out at this time of night after a long, tiring day visiting the other villages and hamlets on his beat, but his Inspector had left him no option. At least the Raff had responded equally as quickly, he consoled himself as the door of the pub opened and the Squadron Leader emerged from behind the black-out curtain.

'Excuse me, Sir,' called the policeman as he approached the airman. 'Could I see your ID please?'

The surprised Squadron Leader tapped the breast pocket and side pockets of his tunic under his open greatcoat. After double-checking each he said, 'Sorry, Officer, seems I've left it in my billet. Can I bring it to your Station in the morning?'

The Constable turned and beckoned to the two servicemen behind him.

'RAF Police, Sir,' they said showing their ID. 'We must ask you to accompany us to RAF Aldinghurst.'

Several weeks later, the following report appeared in the County newspaper.

Rupert Middlemass, a forty year old butcher from Tenbury, near Aldinghurst, was charged at Tenbury County Court today, under the War Emergency (Uniform) Regulations, with the offence of impersonating a commissioned officer in HM Forces, wearing the uniform of a commissioned officer in HM Forces, and wearing medal ribbons of awards and decorations to which he was not entitled.

The Court heard that Mr Leonard Price, landlord of the King Richard Inn at Little Harmsworth, himself a former RAF Non-Commissioned Officer, became suspicious when Middlemass entered the Inn wearing medal ribbons on his tunic that he, Mr Price, noted were in the wrong order of precedence. His suspicions became further aroused on hearing Middlemass relate stories of air combat that were incorrect in technical detail. He became convinced the man was a spy and called the police.

Following investigation by the RAF and Civil Police it was clear that Middlemass was not involved in espionage or covert operations of any description.

Pleading guilty, Middlemass admitted he had been foolish. He had only done it for a laugh, he said.

Finding him Guilty, the Judge, Mr Appleton QC, said, 'You are a very stupid man who has caused a lot of trouble and concern.' He was sentenced to eighteen months imprisonment.

NOT BY STRENGTH, BY GUILE

'You're a jammy bastard', grumbled Roy as he watched his mate take the back peg from the crib board and replace it twenty-four holes in front of what had been his leading peg. 'That's the third twenty-four hand you've pegged this game!'

Norm grinned in self-satisfaction as he contemplated the remaining nine holes he needed to win yet another game.

'Give in?' he offered.

Neither man even noticed the slow rolling motion of the Royal Fleet Auxiliary ship as it wallowed in its designated area of the South Atlantic, fulfilling its role of being a floating NAAFI and BP petrol station for the Fleet.

Everything on board was a hive of activity as warship after warship came alongside, in a continuous stream, to fill their rapidly emptying fuel tanks, to top-up with food, water and, above all, their dwindling ammunitions stock, before returning to support the ground troops battling against forces so recently considered friendly, on the cold, bleak, inhospitable Falkland Islands, just over the horizon.

Everyone on the huge supply ship, from cabin-boy to Captain, was busy. Everyone that is, except for Norm and Roy idly passing their time at the crib board in the almost empty 40 foot container secured to the ship's deck, supplied and sparsely furnished as the 'home' for the ten members of the Royal Marines Special Boats Squadron and their small support and admin staff.

There was plenty of room now in the dimly lit container, already christened the 'gloom-room'. Six days ago, two four-man teams had flown off to relieve those that had been put on the Islands weeks ago, shortly after the Argies had invaded. These guys had been helo'd back to the ship for a four-day rest and had stunk to high heaven after living rough for so long.

As a source of information and 'intelligence' their covert operations had been of invaluable help to the planners of subsequent actions by our troops so, in typical Service manner, they were rewarded by being re-inserted again yesterday. Back to the God forsaken bog-land that they had hoped never to see again. Oh! For the life on the ocean wave!

Being the only two remaining operational SCs, Roy and Norm were becoming more pissed-off as each day passed. Their mates were seeing all the action whereas all they had done was clean and fumigate the container! 'Why?' they asked themselves. They were both Corporals and SC2 rates. They were among the most experienced and skilled Swimmer Canoeists in the Corps. They were used to being 'first-in' not 'left-out'.

Luckily (or unluckily) for them, they were not privy to the thinking of the upper echelon planners who were soon to alter their peaceful boredom.

'Come in, don't knock,' they shouted in unison, in answer to the loud banging on the metal door that reverberated around the container like a bass drum in a gnat's ear.

With a grinding screech the heavy door swung open to reveal a seaman standing, legs astride, holding a double-handed wrench. His unshaven jaw jutted forward aggressively.

'Your Boss wants you two in his cabin,' he grunted, then turned away, leaving the door wide open.

They looked at each other and Norm shrugged his shoulders. 'His Master's Voice!'

Walking aft along a deck that compared favourably with an assault course, covered in a maze of pipes and securing wires, they stepped over the coaming of the door leading into the Bridge superstructure and entered a long passageway. The third cabin on the left had a thick-pencilled notice pinned to its door informing all that the occupant was CAPTAIN CHAIN. ROYAL MARINES, under which some wag had stuck another note, as yet unseen, 'Known to his friends as DAISY.'

They knocked, leaving the second note undisturbed.

'Come,' came the imperious command.

The Boss was a rugged six-footer, tough as old nails, but a gentleman to boot. His face lit up as he saw his two Corporals.

'You're a couple of happy looking buggers I must say,' he laughed. 'Feeling a bit left out, are we?'

They nodded, but kept silent. The Boss knew how they were feeling.

'Well. Don't be too despondent,' the officer continued. 'I've got some-thing for you that may cheer you up.'

He looked at his two NCOs as they unconsciously sat up straighter in their chairs. All of a sudden he had their attention.

'For some time now, the powers that be, have been concerned that the Argies have been using a code that our experts cannot crack. They believe they are using a coding machine similar to the ENIGMA that the Jerries used in WW2. You've no doubt heard of that?'

The Corporals nodded assent.

'Our people have now learned of the whereabouts of such a machine, which they have code-named DELPHIC, and have asked if we could get it for them,' the Captain continued, 'but there are problems.'

He paused, seeing the eager anticipation of the faces opposite.

'Firstly, and this is the good news, it's at a signal station a mile or so inland from the coast, so it should be a relatively soft target. Secondly, and this is the bad news, the coast in question is on the Argentine mainland. Thirdly, and this is the jackpot, the "spooks" don't want the Argies to know that we have got it – if we get it.'

He looked up and raised his eyebrows, waiting the expected questions, but they didn't come. Instead, Roy asked, 'You have a plan of course, Sir.' A statement, not a question.

The officer smiled. He knew his men; they were a canny pair, ideal for this job.

'Yes,' he answered. 'I've been working on it and have been in touch with the "spooks" who have sent me maps and a replica of the DELPHIC machine, but not even an Argie would recognise it because it has been made to look as though it has been destroyed by fire and explosion.'

He stooped under the desk and lifted a mangled model onto his desk-top.

'Clever buggers, aren't they?'

Roy and Norm leaned forward to examine it. 'And?' asked Roy.

'The plan is to pinch the real one, leave this one in its place then create an explosion,' the Captain explained. 'Hopefully, this will dupe the Argies into believing their secret is still safe and will give us the advantage of deciphering their coded signals.'

He sat back and steepled his fingers beneath his chin.

'You two will be leaving this evening by helicopter to rendezvous with a sub south of the Falklands. The sub will take you to a position several miles off the Argentine mainland opposite the signal station where you will be floated off in canoes.' He stopped and raised a finger to pre-empt their question. 'I have two SC3s being flown over to us this afternoon from No. 1 SBS on *Fearnough*. They will be your canoe crews and will take you as close to the shoreline as you consider suitable and safe. The canoes will then lay-off while you two swim ashore with waterproof inflatable bags containing this model,' he pointed to the 'thing' on his desk, 'and your personal weapons, explosives, etc. Once ashore, you hide your bags and dry-suits then make your way to the signal station which, with care, should take you an hour at most. Circumstances will control your actions from then on. We have been given no "gen" on the whereabouts of the machine in the Station, but an educated guess is that it would be in the Operations Room, wherever that may be. There is no "intelligence" given on numbers of personnel there but the "spooks" say that it is unlikely to be heavily guarded being on the mainland and a low-priority target.'

He stopped and wiggled his stiffening shoulders, then continued, 'You should land on the shore at about 2300 local time. The canoes will wait at the inshore RV until 0530. If you have not returned by then it will be presumed you have decided to extend your holiday ashore and the canoes will return to the sub. The sub will keep a submerged visual watch at the off-shore RV. It will not surface until the recognition signal from the canoes is seen. At 0700 the sub will leave, owing to the approach of daylight, with or without canoes and swimmers … An alternative RV for the next three consecutive nights is included in your orders.'

He took a deep breath and gave the NCOs a quizzical look.

'That's it, lads,' he said. 'Go back to your grots and study your order packs, then come back to see me in an hour with any comments or recommendations you may have. That will give us time to make any changes and give you time to get some scran and kip before you get off.'

Back in their accommodation the Corporals spread the maps and their orders over the table, carefully reading each section and analysing the pros and cons, trying to fault each action and considering alternatives. Finally, Roy sat back and clasped his hands behind his neck. 'Looks like the Boss has thought of everything, don't it?' he said.

Norm pursed his lips, placed his elbows on the table and cupped his chin in his hands. 'Yeah, but he would, wouldn't he!'

'So we go along with it, as is?' asked Roy.

Norm nodded. 'Glad he's getting us the SC3s for the canoes instead of some dim sandscratcher.'

Their return visit to Captain Chain's office, where both notices were still stuck on the door, lasted just long enough to clarify one or two minor points. The officer emphasised the need to avoid any killing if possible, saying, 'If you have to knock anyone off, do it in a manner to make it look as if they were killed by the explosion. No gunshot wounds. The whole idea is that it looks like an accidental explosion has occurred.'

He shook both men by the hand and wished them luck. 'Not that you will need it with your experience,' he added with a smile.

Six hours later, watered, fed and rested, the Corporals, with their equipment and two marine canoeists, lifted off from the deck of the RFA ship in a helicopter, bound for the mid-ocean rendezvous with the submarine whose Captain was, at that very moment, reading his own operational orders for the mission, with his First Lieutenant.

'Rather them than me,' was his only comment.

Despite the pitch-black night, the Sea King appeared to have no difficulty in locating the submarine. Hovering low over the black, sinister hull, it lowered the Marines, with their canoes and equipment, down onto the boat's casing where they were met, and ushered quickly below, by the crew in a well-rehearsed routine.

In the forward torpedo space, the four Marines, befriended by inquisitive submariners, checked their canoes and equipment for the umpteenth time while being plied with thick, sweet, hot cocoa, Navy style.

The boat's First Lieutenant came to allay his fears at having the explosives on board. He was not amused when Norman reminded him that what they had was nothing compared with what was in the heads of the torpedoes. At least this gave the lads a giggle – after the officer had left of course.

Twenty-four hours later, after unsuccessful attempts at sleeping, the Marines were woken, with more cocoa, by a Leading Hand and told the boat would be on station and surfacing in thirty minutes.

The First Lieutenant honoured them with another visit to emphasise the need for a fast disembarkation.

'We are in enemy territorial waters you know,' he said unnecessarily.

'Most grateful, Sir,' replied Roy in a carefully worded wind-up, not lost on the officer.

The submarine had hardly broken surface before the crew had bundled the loaded canoes up through the hatch and placed them across the casing, closely followed by the Marines who quickly stepped into them and fastened the body aprons as the submariners leapt back below, slamming the hatches close behind them as the boat dived.

As soon as the sea washed over the submerging casing the Marines paddled furiously away to the side to avoid being caught under the boat's jumper stay.

It was all over in seconds and, as the Marines paused after a dozen or so frantic strokes, the boat was already disappearing beneath the sea.

Arranging themselves comfortably, the two crews began to paddle, soon settling into a rhythmic stroke that they would easily keep up for the four-mile journey to the mainland. Ahead, there was nothing but black emptiness, but on their port bow a well lit town, probably three or more miles away, gave them a good bearing and saved the chore of continuous staring at the dim light of the luminous compass.

They paddled on, each with his own thoughts, until they could discern the whiteness of small wavelets breaking on the beach in front of them. A tall building, silhouetted against the slightly less dark skyline, gave them a fix they needed. Their course and steering had been good. They were spot on.

'We'll swim in from here,' hissed Roy, looking at Norm for agreement and easing himself out of his seat and over the side into the cool water with hardly a splash. Each crewman handed his swimmer his fins and inflated bag that was then deflated until barely buoyant to minimise being seen.

Pushing his bag in front of him, each swimmer made for the beach, his finned feet working smoothly, causing hardly a ripple. The last fifty yards or so was covered dead slow as their eyes scanned the beach for signs of movement.

When they touched bottom they lay silent for several minutes with the wavelets breaking over them until they were satisfied there was no reception committee. Norm pointed to the right where, a short distance away, a ridge of black rock came down to the water's edge. Both swimmers backed off a few feet from the shoreline and edged towards the rocks. Exiting there would avoid leaving tell-tale footprints on the sandy beach.

Among the rocks they stripped off their fins and dry-suits and felt the cool air on their bodies. Unzipping the waterproof bags, they took out the explosives and DELPHIC model, each in its own Bergen backpack which also contained survival packs, pencil torches, night vision glasses, and their personal weapons.

Hiding the suits, fins and bags in a crevice, they strapped sheathed fighting knives to their leg, hoisted Bergen onto backs and belted a holstered 9mm Beretta pistol around their waist. Roy gave an enquiring thumbs-up signal to which Norm gave an affirmative response. Then, taking a final check on a compass bearing, they set off cautiously for their objective, less than a mile away.

It took twenty minutes to reach the first of their way points, a junction on a very minor lane that the two relieved NCOs were pleased to get to. So far, so good.

They had not seen a soul during this first part of the journey and they fervently hoped it would stay that way. After all, who in their right mind, would expect to meet two enemy soldiers on their homeland, thousands of miles away from the battlefield?

Pausing only to adjust their compass setting onto a new course, they passed through a hedge and made their way cross-country in the black moonless night, occasionally being startled by the screeching and panic fluttering of an agitated bird, disturbed by their passing.

The second way point, a dilapidated wooden bridge over a river, appeared out of the stygian darkness. Delighted that their navigation was so good the two men exchanged grins before cautiously skirting the bridge. They had no need to cross it, or the river that curved to the right, away from them. Their course was straight ahead on the same compass bearing, to their destination now less than a quarter of an hour's march away.

For the first ten minutes they maintained their careful, steady pace, then, nearing their target, they slowed to a vigilant crawl, inching forward step by wary step, until Roy – who was leading – took a sharp intake of breath and stopped, pointing to where, outlined against the cloudless night sky, the signal station emerged out of the gloom, less than fifty yards ahead.

Side by side the two dropped to their knees, silently inspecting the objective through night vision glasses. They later described it as looking like a WW2 emergency air traffic control tower. The ground floor was a concrete building about twenty feet square with windows and a door. On the side, what appeared to be an open wooden stairway led up to a smaller block, roughly fifteen feet square, also with windows and a door, surrounded by hand-rails to create a veranda. Above this block, a mass of aerials and masts reached up to touch the stars. It was eerie, ghostly. Not a light could be seen or a sound heard.

For ten minutes the Marines remained silent and motionless, observing the tower and surrounding area with the powerful night vision glasses. When they felt assured that there were no sentries, they rose to their feet and watchfully crept forward, ready to drop at the slightest sound.

Logically, in their minds, the upper block would be the Operations Room and the lower one the accommodation. If there was anyone at home, the Ops Room would most likely be manned by one or two operators and be the most obvious place from where the alarm could be raised. Whereas, hopefully, down below would only contain sleeping bodies.

Roy touched Norm on his shoulder and pointed his forefinger upwards. Norm nodded agreement and hesitantly stepped onto the lower step of the stairway, gradually applying his weight to avoid any creaking until he could try the next step. Noiselessly he reached the top, then Roy followed, equally as silent, until they stood side by side with drawn pistols. The windows appeared to be covered with curtaining, or something, so they inched their way around to the door. Blast! – No keyhole to peer through. Norm placed his hand on the cool round door-knob, gently pulling it towards him and gradually turning it, fearful of creating a noise. Soundlessly, a fraction at a time, he opened the door. The inside was lit only by the LED lights and dials on the humming transmitters and receivers around the room, and a bright desk lamp that shone down on the solitary operator whose head was resting sideways on an open paperback book, his snoring indicating he was fast asleep. It was clearly not a busy station.

Roy glided across the floor and, holding his pistol by its short barrel, smashed its butt onto the sleeping man's temple. If he survived he would be unable to explain anything.

Meanwhile, Norm had located the DELPHIC, quite openly positioned on the desk-top, and placed it carefully in his Bergen with any books and papers that looked important enough to take. The wreck model was put in its place. The luminous dial of his wristwatch showed 0010 hrs.

Quickly they placed the explosives and detonators, with twenty-minute fuses, where they would not easily be seen should anyone come looking before the explosion. Then they made their way out of the room and down the stairs, still very careful not to awaken anyone who might be asleep in the lower block.

Having a good knowledge of their way back, and the unlikelihood of meeting anyone, they quickened their pace without throwing caution completely to the wind. They were about half way when Roy checked his watch and, as he did so, a massive flash lit the sky behind them, making them jump. Almost immediately, a violent explosion followed, bursting against their ear-drums, as the signal station roof was blasted high into the air.

Pausing only to shake hands, they hurried on, but it was nearly one o'clock by the time they reached the rocks and retrieved the bags and dry-suits. In haste, they filled the bags with the Bergens and personal weapons before zipping them sealed and re-inflating them with small 6-inch cylinders of compressed air.

Helping each other into dry-suits, they waded knee-deep into the sea and pushed their feet into swim fins. With several hundred yards to go to the RV they swam strongly with little thought of caution. In any other circumstances it would be a very pleasant swim. The water was cool and calm, a beautiful night, but in their minds was the thought that, not far away, men had probably just died as a result of their action.

Their anxiety was relieved, and their spirits boosted, when they sighted the two canoes paddling purposefully towards them, bows showing white moustaches as they thrust through the placid sea.

White teeth grinned from a blackened face of the Marine canoeist as he 'back-paddled' to a stop alongside Roy. 'Everything okay, Corp?' he asked.

'Yeah,' came the whispered reply, 'Piece of cake.'

'It's been bleedin' cold out here waiting for you while you've been ashore enjoying yourselves,' continued the paddler. 'Have fun, did you?'

'Bollocks,' grunted Roy, passing up his inflated bag and fins, then heaving himself up across the bow and awkwardly sliding into his seat.

From across the few feet separating the two canoes came Norm's tired voice.

'Home, James – chop, chop.'

A POLICEMAN'S LOT

The clock on the mantelpiece struck nine tinny bells, well rings really, as I stretched my feet towards the glowing coal fire, enjoying a last few precious moments of warmth and laziness. It was so comfortable laid back in my battered armchair with threadbare cushions seemingly wrapped around me. I wasn't looking forward to pounding a beat for the next eight hours when I could be in my cosy bed, cuddled into my Missus.

'Time to go and protect the great British public, sweetheart,' I yawned, looking across at my wife sitting in a matching armchair opposite me reading a paperback novel.

One last luxuriant stretch then I sat up, chin resting in cupped hands, unwilling to move further. 'I just realised,' I said, 'it's ten years since the war ended.'

She looked up from her book, giving me an enigmatic smile. 'Would you like another hot drink before you go, love?'

'No, better not,' I declined, 'I'll be weeing all night.'

She grinned and returned to the world that I had interrupted, in which a young, handsome, virile millionaire was just about to seduce a gloriously beautiful girl in the magnificent bedroom of his stately apartment overlooking the spectacular yacht-filled harbour of Monaco.

Reluctantly, I eased myself out of the clinging chair and flexed my knees, an old habit of policemen, then forced my protesting legs to carry me upstairs to the cold, unwelcoming bedroom. Pulling aside the heavy curtain I looked out onto the bleak, dark, deserted road, lit only by the dim glow from well-spaced streetlights. Why hadn't I joined the police in Malta, or Palestine, or anywhere warmer than here?

At least, I consoled myself, it wasn't windy or raining tonight. Just bloody cold!

Taking off my house clothes I put on pyjama trousers and tucked the bottoms into my socks – they were wonderful 'keep warmers'. Then shirt, uniform trousers and tunic completed my constabulary ensemble except, of course, for a pair of 4-cylinder, 100 h.p. Rolls-Royce, rubber soled boots that I was only allowed to put on as I went out of the house.

Downstairs again, I added the armour that protected me from the knives and bullets of the violent public. A pocket-book with integral pencil, in which everything had to be recorded, went into the right breast pocket of my tunic. A silver whistle and chain that draped across from a centre button into the left breast pocket (supposedly) to keep my right hand free to draw my murderous truncheon from its long pocket, sewn inside the right trouser leg, from where its leather wrist-strap poked out like the butt on a cowboy's holstered six-gun. A pair of heavy handcuffs placed uncomfortably in a back trouser pocket from where it was impossible to extract them one-handed if trying to restrain an uncooperative subject of the Crown.

Finally, but by no means least, a life-saving packet of 'Fisherman's Friends'. Now I was ready to face the (often) inimical citizens of our proud city.

'You going to be warm enough, love?' asked Julie, tearing herself away from her Mediterranean hedonistic dreaming, as I threw a heavy uniform cape around my shoulders and secured the 'lion-head' throat hooks.

'Yeah, snug as a bug!' I lied as I kissed her, then settled my helmet square on my head with chin-strap resting on the front of my chin. 'You going to bed soon?'

Her lovely head of hair nodded as I went into the hallway where my boots stood waiting on the door-mat like the footwear of an invisible sentry.

At first, the bitter outdoor temperature took my breath away but I soon warmed up as I peddled my sturdy 'Raleigh All-steel' push bike on the ten minute journey to the 'Nick' where I was to parade at 9.45 for the night-shift.

'Right, you lot,' welcomed the shift Sergeant as we lined up for his perfunctory inspection. 'Here's your beat cards and stolen car list.' He dealt them out with the deftness of a casino croupier. 'Whoever's got 4 beat, keep an eye on 35, Cromarty Road. They're away and want us to check on it now and again.' He paused, looking down at his clipboard. 'Oh!, and make sure you inspect your properties. There's been a spate of break-ins lately. Okay, dismiss!'

I looked at my beat card. No. 3 beat. Good, that's interesting enough. Mainly residential, there was a main road running through it with the usual mixture of shops, pubs, cafés, etc.

I had a 'point' at 11 p.m. at the telephone kiosk on the corner of Derby Road, and one at 12.15 at the Police Box in Commercial Road. (These were blue painted telephone boxes, boldly marked POLICE, on a stand which had a blue beacon light on the top. By pulling open the small hatch door of the box, the user would speak directly to the HQ switch-board operator, and if HQ wanted the beat officer they would switch on the blue flashing light.)

My mid-shift meal break at the Station was 1.45 to 2.30, with 'points' at 3.45 outside the Odeon cinema and 5 a.m. at Derby Road telephone kiosk again.

These 'points' served two main purposes: to ensure the beat officer covered his 'patch' correctly, and to have a rendezvous place where the shift Sergeant or Inspector could meet or make contact with him, should they wish to do so. Remember, these were the days before personal radios were even thought of.

To miss a 'point' without good reason was a serious disciplinary offence.

A quick glance at the Station notice board (nothing new) and a look at my 'Stolen cars' list (only six numbers listed), then Constable 'Doggy' Barker, PC 242 'B' Division, exited the 'Nick' to inflict his awesome, authoritative presence on the innocent public.

A fast stroll across No. 2 beat (don't want any trouble on someone else's patch) brought me to my own patrol area.

Pubs and cinema were beginning to discharge their customers out onto the Commercial Road so I varied between standing, unseen, in a shadowy doorway and pro-actively pounding the pavement or standing openly as a deterrent to any would-be transgressors of the Queen's peace ... All was well.

A few lads who had sniffed the barmaid's apron reacted well when I bid them 'goodnight' as they went on their joyful, but peaceful way, and at 10.55 I was at my first 'point'. No one turned up, neither did the kiosk phone ring so, at 11.05, after noting the 'point' in my pocket-book, I continued my patrol around the, by now, quiet residential streets.

At 12.15 I made my second 'point', also unvisited, then went up and down Commercial Road 'shaking hands with doorknobs' to ensure the locked security of commercial premises.

At around 1 a.m. I heard a short, sharp noise like a stone being thrown against a brick wall. It appeared to come from an unlit alleyway between two shops that I was just passing and it made me jump. My heart rate stepped up a few notches. Cautiously I entered the dark passageway, feeling carefully with my feet for any dustbins or anything that would give away my presence. I deliberately refrained from using my torch for the same reason.

After a short distance, just the length of the building and its small back yard, the alleyway became a 'T' junction, left and right, passing behind the back of the buildings. I stopped there for several minutes, hardly daring to breathe, trying to pierce the blackness, straining ears for the slightest sound ... Nothing.

Slowly I edged to the right but this quickly became a dead-end with a locked door. Retracing my steps, I made my way along the left hand passage. This was longer, but again a dead-end ... Still nothing.

'Bloody cats,' I thought, and was about to walk back to the road when a blinding light came from an uncurtained ground-floor window only twenty feet away beyond a five foot high wall. I stood motionless, feeling like an aircraft caught in a searchlight beam.

The light had been switched on by a woman, in her late twenties I guessed. For several seconds she fussed around with this and that, then quickly stripped off her clothes and lay uncovered on a bed. Almost immediately a man entered and he too undressed. Then the light went off and I gratefully got out, back onto the road. It was all over in less than two minutes and I was very relieved. I'm no 'peeping-tom' but I could well imagine the repercussions back at the Station had I been seen.

By the time I returned to the 'Nick' for my meal break my heart rate had returned to normal. It was a scare I never wanted to repeat.

I had hardly settled down at the dining room table, and fed the first forkful of steak and kidney pud into my mouth, when in came the Sergeant.

'Oy! Barker,' he shouted unnecessarily, 'the Inspector wants to see you in his office – NOW!'

My heart leapt and blood pumped through me like an express train. In my dying seconds, my life raced before me.

'Come in,' commanded the voice in response to my timid tap on the door.

There sat the Guvnor, judge, jury and executioner, with two silver pips on each shoulder.

'Ha, Barker!' he greeted, motioning me to sit on the chair in front of his desk. 'How's things?'

After two false starts I managed to croak, 'Fine, thank you, Sir.'

'Good,' he replied, 'that's what I like to hear.'

He held out his hand, palm up. 'Let me see your pocket-book.'

Dutifully I handed it over and he ominously opened it at the last entry. 'Mmmm,' he murmured, 'anything happen on 3 beat tonight?'

'No, Sir,' I croaked again.

He glared at me with eyes like gimlets. 'I see you've made no entries other than your "points",' he said, indicating my pocket-book. 'Do I take it there were no other reportable incidents?'

The look on his face, and the tone of his voice, told me I had been rumbled so, with a shaking voice, I related the happening in the alleyway.

He listened without comment.

When I had finished there was a long deathly silence. I could see his brain cells ticking over. Was it the sack or some other disciplinary punishment?

'You do realise you are a hundred per cent bloody idiot, don't you?' he snapped.

I nodded, eyes downcast in embarrassment.

'Look at me when I'm speaking to you,' he ordered ... I complied.

'You were seen, and reported, by someone whose house backs onto the alleyway. What on earth were you thinking of?'

Without thought I answered honestly, 'I was scared of being seen, Sir.'

Another long pause.

'The only redeeming feature in all this is that you've been honest and admitted it,' continued the Inspector. 'I consider your action to have been extremely stupid, but without intent. I shall see this person who reported you sometime today, explain the circumstances, and say I have dealt with it. From you ...' he said, pointing a warning finger, 'I want no more stupidity. Now get out!'

I left hurriedly, gratefully, and very relieved, gently closing the door behind me, thereby not seeing the smile that crept across the Inspector's face.

The rest of my dinner, though cold, tasted wonderful.

Was it coincidence that I was never again given 3 beat?

Two months later, I was offered, and accepted, a probationary period with the Vice Squad as an Aide. Actually the job was only being a 'goffer' to the Squad officers. To do all the dirty jobs they didn't fancy doing themselves, such as sitting in a gents toilet for hours on end trying to catch importuning homosexuals. Not very pleasant but certainly a change from shift work and pounding a beat. It was nice working in 'civvies' as well as, hopefully, being another rung on the promotion ladder.

Late one evening the Squad Sergeant took me in an unmarked Ford car to a house where the occupant had given permission for us to use his back bedroom to keep observation on premises at the rear of his place that was believed to be being used for 'improper' purposes.

I was left there with a camera and binoculars and told to keep 'obbo' from 11 p.m. until 3 a.m. for the next three or four nights. The old chap who owned the house kept me supplied with tea and coffee every hour or so, under strict instructions not to turn on any lights. He also kept watch for me during my frequent visits to the loo and entertained me with tales about 'when I was in the Navy'. It all helped pass the time.

Careful not to ask questions that might upset the Squad officers, I weedled out of him the story of the house we were watching. He had spent hours, he said, over the last few months, sat in this very window watching the antics 'over the back'. Almost every night he had seen the woman 'entertain' different men and 'Yes' he had enjoyed it until a couple of nights ago when he had seen money change hands, and the woman slapped.

Then the hypocritical old git decided he should inform the police!

Nothing happened that first night. Not a sausage! Sod's Law in practice.

The next night, about midnight, I was sat talking to the old 'salt' when the downstairs bedroom light in the house opposite flicked on, making me jump. I snatched up the camera and through the viewfinder saw a woman and a man in the room. He grabbed her and began to almost rip her clothes off. It was obvious she wasn't objecting.

Remembering that my main purpose was, if possible, to get a photo of money changing hands, I stopped clicking the shutter, to save film.

Picking up the binoculars, I continued my spying, feeling very voyeuristic, and a little excited. It was then that I had a clear, close-up look at her face and got the shock of my life. She was the same woman I had seen from the alleyway a couple of months ago!

Much to the disappointment of my host, the light quickly went out and as soon as I regained my night vision I scanned the area. My suspicions were proved right. There was the alleyway and the backs of Commercial Road buildings. It was the same house!

I was soon convinced that this old lecher sat beside me was the one who had reported me!

An hour or so later, the light came back on again. We watched, camera at the ready, as the guy quickly dressed, and I was able to get several shots of him handing her money as she remained lying on the bed.

Mission successful. I was chuffed. The Squad would be pleased with my efforts, and the result.

Using the old chap's phone I called the Station and was told to get back there as soon as I could.

Thanking the old chap for his hospitality, I was about to go out of the front door when he stopped me.

'Do you know who that "bird" is?' he asked.

I shook my head. 'No mate, haven't a clue.'

He looked at me with the triumphant smile of someone who knows something you don't.

'She's the wife of one of your blokes,' he grinned.

All of a sudden it was apparent why I had been given the job.

THE BOSUN'S 'CALL'

Snug in its purpose-built boat house, the royal blue and orange hull of the lifeboat sat poised, paint-work spotless and brass-work gleaming, waiting only for its crew and a hammer blow to knock away the restraining shackle and chain to release it down the long slipway into the calm waters of the small harbour.

The *Maude Johnson*, named by a millionaire in memory of his late wife, was one of the RNLI's latest class of lifeboat, capable of twenty-five knots. She was the heart of the small community and the main topic of conversation. Without exception, everyone in the village was involved with her in some way, either as sea-going crew, shore-helper, fund raiser or just a supporter.

On the cobbled quayside, the unofficial headquarters of the Lifeboat Committee was an olde worlde pub, 'The Safe Return'. Inside, the aged stone walls were covered with photographs and newspaper cuttings, in battered frames, of local lifeboats and crews, past and present, depicting many of their dramatic rescues.

Upstairs, over the one and only bar, in the low-ceilinged 'social room' the Committee sat around an ancient dark-wood table in the smog-like atmosphere of tobacco smoke, contemplating the papers on the table before them and their half empty beer mugs as they discussed the reason for this extraordinary meeting.

In the Chair was the Station Honorary Secretary, Doctor Ian McCullam, a dour Scot whose broad accent belied the fact he had been the village GP for over twenty years.

Next to him sat retired Army Colonel Thomas Hitchings, the Honorary Treasurer. A man of few words, his main purpose in life was the accuracy of his account books and golf. Not necessarily in that order.

There was Danny, a former crew member, now serving as Deputy Launching Authority to Doctor 'Mac'. Injuries to his back, sustained in a building accident, forced his reluctant retirement from the crew.

And Helen Spray, forty-year-old spinster of the parish, the prolific and tireless Chairperson of the Fund-raising Committee. A heroine of the Treasurer, whose coffers she kept full, she was seldom seen without a collection box in her hands as she toured the surrounding towns and villages, collecting money and organising fund-raising events.

Last, but not least, the unassuming thirty-five year old Les Harris, postman, window cleaner, and part-time Harbour Master. He was also the lifeboat coxswain, as had been his father and his grandfather. His family home contained many medals and framed certificates awarded to the Harris men-folk for life-saving bravery over many decades, dating back to when most local men were fishermen and the lifeboat was manned by these stalwarts, rowing with heavy ash oars.

'He's going to be a great loss,' murmured Doctor Mac, referring to the recent death of the Committee President, Rear Admiral Boothway. CB, DSO, RN Rtd, who had been their leader, guide and mentor, since leaving the Navy and buying a retirement cottage on the outskirts of the village.

Heads nodded in agreement. The purpose of the meeting was to discuss their President's last wish, that his ashes be scattered at sea from the lifeboat.

'The cremation is on Thursday,' continued the Hon. Secretary, 'and Mrs Boothway suggests we could take the ashes out on the following Thursday.' He paused then looked up at the members. 'Naturally she wants them in the house for a few days,' he explained. 'How do you feel about that, Les?'

The Coxswain lifted his beer mug and took a long swig before replacing it gently back onto the table.

'Oy don't think it's right to take the lads away from their jobs on a weekday,' he answered in his broad West Country brogue. 'Whoy don't we do it on Sunday, after all that's the Holy day, innit?'

'Perhaps you are right, Les,' the Doctor replied. 'I will nip downstairs and ring Mrs Boothway, see what she thinks.'

Scraping his chair back he rose wearily and left the room, leaving the door open and allowing a refreshing draught of fresh air to come in.

'I think you are right, Les,' said the softly spoken Treasurer.

'Me too,' agreed Danny. 'It's best.'

Helen Spray just nodded and gave a loud 'Mmmm.'

The level in the beer mugs, and in Helen Spray's whisky glass, had lowered considerably by the time Doctor Mac climbed back up the stairs and re-entered the room, dumping himself heavily into his chair.

'That's fine,' he said, giving them a small smile. 'She's all for a week on Sunday.'

For the next thirty minutes, beer mugs and glass recharged, they talked details. Who would do what. Timing. Sequence of events. Who would go out on the boat, etc.

With all arrangements agreed, they were just about to close the meeting when Danny had a brainwave. 'Don't sailors like them little whistles blown when they'm buried at sea?'

'You means Bosun's Pipes, Danny,' said Les knowledgeably.

'They are called Bosun's calls actually,' corrected the Colonel softly.

Danny stuck to his guns. 'They'm still whistles!'

'I think it is a grand suggestion,' exclaimed the Doctor. 'Do we know anyone who has one and knows how to blow it?' He looked around his Committee, enquiringly.

'I'll ask around' offered Les as they finished their drinks.

The following afternoon, down in the little harbour, Les was checking the few boats alongside the quay in his role as Harbour Master, not at all surprised to see there were no newcomers.

The harbour had gradually declined in importance over the last ten years, since its heyday as a fishing port. Now only an occasional private boat or yacht called in. There were few facilities to attract the yachting fraternity.

'Hi, Les,' came a voice behind him.

He turned to see the heavy figure of 'Spider' Webb, one of his lifeboat crew, ambling towards him.

'Allo m'dear,' he greeted.

They sat together side by side on the low quayside wall talking, as always, about lifeboat matters.

'You were in the Navy, weren't you, Spider?' asked Les.

Spider nodded. 'Yeah! Why?'

'Do you know about them Bosun's Pipe things?'

Spider turned to face him, almost pityingly. 'Christ, Yeah, I spent years listening to they bloody things at sea, didn't I?'

The Coxswain explained his reason for asking. 'Do you know anyone who's got one – and can blow it?'

Spider didn't hesitate. 'I got one,' he said. 'Used to blow it for fun, 'spect I still can.'

'Great,' grinned Les, relieved that his quest was answered so quickly.

Spider shook his head. 'Don't know what the burial "call" is though,' he muttered almost to himself. 'Fact is, I don't remember hardly any of 'em.'

'Don't matter,' came back Les. 'Blow anyfink. No one'll know the difference.'

Sunday morning, the *Maude Johnson* had been launched down the slipway and was now secured, dressed overall with bunting signal flags, along-side the grey-stone quay that was the landing dock in the harbour's fishing days. Her crew stood ready to welcome the chosen few of the burial party, the most important being Mrs Boothway carrying the urn containing her husband's ashes.

Outside the harbour, about a hundred feet from the breakwater that was crowded with several dozen people gathered to watch the ceremony, the lifeboat's engines were stopped. She rolled gently in the calm sea as the on-board party gathered at the boat's stern where the RNLI flag hung limply at half-mast.

The local vicar, the Reverend Allways, who was also the Chaplain to the lifeboat, gave a short eulogy and prayer followed by the hymn 'Eternal Father strong to save', sung lustily by the crew.

Mrs Boothway stepped to the stern rail and, leaning over, emptied the contents of the urn into the sea, her eyes tearful as Spider blew his 'call'.

On the breakwater, the solemn crowd reverently bowed their heads as the words of the sailor's hymn and the haunting shrill of the Bosun's pipe were heard across the intervening water.

At the back, respectfully apart from the villagers, two middle-aged men off a visiting yacht stood watching the ceremony in curious silence. Then, as they slowly walked back along the breakwater, one said to the other, 'That was a very moving, wasn't it, Richard?'

'Yes,' replied his companion. 'First time I've seen anything like it.'

In deep thought, they neared their boat moored peacefully alongside the ancient quayside, nudging gently against its fenders.

'The Bosun's Pipe was a nice touch, wasn't it?' suggested the first man.

'Yes, it was, Donald' came the puzzled reply, 'but if I remember rightly the "call" he piped was "Hands to dinner"!'

TIGHT SITUATION

Danny felt a right prat, sat on the edge of his bed holding a pair of women's tights in front of his face and rolling them up with his fingers. Lifting his left leg from the floor he pushed his toes into the foot of the tights, easing the nylon back over his heel, around his ankle and up over his calf.

Putting his foot back onto the floor he did a repeat performance with his right foot, then stood up with the tights bunched behind his knees. Bending forward, he pushed his thumbs inside the material and, with fingers on the outside, gently pulled the tights up around his thighs, careful not to hole the nylon with his clumsy fingers.

Standing upright, he wriggled the tights up over his hips and bottom, as he had watched his girlfriend do a thousand times, ensuring the crotch was a comfortable fit and not drooping halfway down to his knees.

He was quite chuffed to have successfully put them on without making holes or ladders. In fact, it was quite sensual to feel the silky nylon against his skin. He had always loved to touch his girl's legs when they were sheathed in nylon tights or stockings and now he could understand how sexy she felt wearing them.

His thoughts were rudely interrupted by hoots and whistles coming from the other men sharing the hut.

'You look gorgeous, Danny.'

'Put your skirt back on, sweety-pie.'

'Cor! I could really fancy you!'

He looked up, grinning. What he saw would have turned a sex maniac into a Trappist monk! It was a horrible sight. He was surrounded by fat legs, skinny legs, hairy legs and bloody awful knobbly knees, all clad in women's tights. It was revolting.

'Christ almighty,' he responded, 'if I thought I'd end up with a bunch of queers like you lot I'd have joined the Raff.'

'Don't knock it, Danny boy,' laughed 'Wing-nut' (so named because of his protruding ears), 'you look very nice, my love!'

'Yeah, 's'right,' added Butch Cassidy the eldest member of the group. 'You're a bleedin' sight better looking than Teressa at the 'Donkey's Flip-Flop' (the navy's name for the notorious gay pub called the Horse-shoe).

'Never mind me. Have you any idea what *you* lot look like?' queried

Danny, trying hard to keep a straight face. 'I've seen sexier sights in a geriatric ward.'

'Oh yeah!' quirked a voice behind him, 'which one were you in?'

At that moment, the door of the separated room at the end of the hut opened and a figure, dressed in combat coveralls, emerged to stand hands on hips, glaring at them.

'What on earth are you lot fannying about for?' shouted Corporal 'Mickey' Rooney as he surveyed the motley group. 'When I told you to pinch a pair of your girlfriend's tights it was to help keep you warm up here in the Arctic, not to turn you into a bunch of raving poofs!' He shook his head in amazement. 'Now, for Christ's sake grow up and get your "combats" on. The Rupert [1] will be here in a minute and if he sees you like this he'll do his nut!' He turned back into his room then, before closing the door, poked his head back out again. 'Oh! By the way, I'll turn the heating down as soon as the Rupert's gone – that'll give you about fifteen minutes to get kitted up.'

'Charming bastard,' someone muttered as each vision of gruesome loveliness disappeared into their coveralls.

The heat inside the hut was maintained at between 18 and 20 degrees Centigrade; a vast difference to the outside where, even at best, readings would be well below zero. Today they were lucky. It was only minus ten in the quiet windless outdoors. Such a rarity would be short-lived and the chill-factor of icy Arctic winds would soon cause the temperature to plummet, at least another ten degrees.

Without protective clothing, no man could survive such intense cold so, in addition to wearing non-issue nylon tights next to the skin, each man would don woollen thermal long-johns, fleecy 'teddy-bear' suits, heavy twill combat coveralls, and a long, hooded, fur-lined parka jacket. Thermal socks, Arctic boots and gloves, eye goggles and scarves completed their attire.

To dress like this in a warm hut would cause heavy sweating that would soak undergarments. This could be very unpleasant, possibly fatal, in the extreme cold outside. Hence the reason for lowering the heating in the hut.

Within minutes, three men dressed in parka jackets entered the hut. They wore no badges of rank. Only the separated crown of the badge on the leader's green beret indicated he was an officer.

Captain Hugh Taylor, Royal Marines, raised a hand and motioned the men to sit down as they leapt to attention.

'Relax lads,' he said. 'Gather round. This is an informal meeting.'

He looked at Danny, then dropped his eyes to the space alongside

---

1. Rupert is the other-ranks name for an officer. Often derogatory.

where Danny sat on his bed. 'May I?' he asked, then sat down without waiting for an invite.

'Welcome to Norway and the Royal Marines Arctic Warfare and Survival School,' he began. 'My name is Taylor and these two gentlemen are Sergeants Bates and Webb. We will be your instructors. You are all trained soldiers and qualified SCs[2] so you will not be shouted at like raw recruits, or told to jump up and down by numbers, or given punishment press-ups. You are highly skilled men in your trade and our job is to add to those skills. But, for your own sakes, do exactly as you are instructed. This is a very dangerous environment. The first part of the course is basic arctic training, followed by Arctic survival and finally Arctic warfare. Remember, you not only have to live and survive in these conditions, you also have to fight! Socially, we have no distractions to offer you. No Wrens,[3] or sheep.' He paused for the expected sniggers – and got them. 'We are about 250 miles inside the Arctic Circle and the nearest town is Narvik, about 100 miles to the south west. There is a small village 10 miles away but the inhabitants are reindeer farmers and they don't have a pub so obviously we do not run a liberty boat. You will have to make do with our meagre camp facilities. Finally, I hope you will enjoy the course. I am sure you won't!'

He rose to his feet, gesturing for the lads to remain seated, then left the hut with the two sergeants.

'Prat,' whispered Wingnut, 'typical bloody Rupert.'

'I heard that,' called the Corporal. 'You are the Prat – as always. For your information Captain Taylor came up through the ranks. He was a Sergeant M.L.[4] and they don't come much tougher than that. So shut it!' He glanced around the hut, 'Outside, fully booted and spurred in twenty minutes,' he ordered.

At the appointed time, the Marines were lined up outside the hut standing on the hard packed snow, looking quite massive in multi-layered clothing and with heavy Bergen packs on their backs, all covered by a white smock.

Green berets peeked out from under fur parka hoods and rosy cheeks were already feeling pinched in the bitter rising wind.

They stood waiting, SA80 weapons, covered with white material where possible, slung across their chests, and skis held upright in mittened hands.

---

2. SC. A Special Qualification of SWIMMER-CANOEIST of the Royal Marines elite Special Boats Squadron. (SBS).

3. Wrens. Derived from WRNS, The Women's Royal Naval Service.

4. ML. A Special Qualification of MOUNTAIN LEADER of the Royal Marines elite Mountain & Arctic Warfare Cadre.

In his own good time, one of the Sergeant Instructors appeared, dressed identically. He walked along the lined and looked each man up and down.

'I 'ear you've been acting like a bunch of queers in your Missus' tights,' he greeted. 'Well, let me assure you that the only thing you'll get up your arse here – is my boot!'

'Welcome home – nothing changes,' came a muttered comment from the far end of the line.

CHARITY WORK

The waters of Portsmouth's historic harbour were whipped into white crested wavelets by the cold, northerly breeze driving down from the overlooking slopes of Portsdown Hill whose normally green back-drop to the city now looked grey and dismal under the heavy, overcast sky.

Huge Admiralty mooring buoys leaned lazily away from the fast ebbing tide, pulling against their retaining anchor cables as the seas rushed against their weather sides splashing halfway up to where ubi-quitous seagulls perched facing the wind, immobile except for an occasional head movement as they scanned each passing piece of flotsam in the hope of it being their next snack.

The masts of Nelson's flagship, forlorn in its cold, empty stone basin, and those of HMS *Warrior*, her sister tourist attraction berthed a few hundred yards away, reached up to almost touch the base of the black boulders of cumulus clouds blanketing the City and Naval Base.

Small passenger ferries, fussily pushing their bow waves ahead of them, plied their way across the harbour, thankful that the summer-time hordes of yachtsmen were safely out of their way tucked up in a marina, or high and dry in their winter berths.

A few, very few, warships lay, almost apologetically, alongside the sombre jetties of the dockyard, their white ensigns giving the only splash of colour to the funereal scene.

As regular as clockwork, huge cross-Channel ferries, as aesthetic as blocks of flats, thundered through the harbour dwarfing even the largest naval aircraft carrier that infrequently honoured the city.

On the Gosport side of the harbour, berthed at Priddy's Hard, a grey painted Admiralty Fleet tanker lay silently and apparently lifeless as I made my way towards her, along the concrete jetty lined with large diameter pipes that terminated at the seaward end with gigantic valves and wheels.

Turtle-like, I shrank my neckless head deep into the collar of my greatcoat trying, unsuccessfully, to avoid the worst of the bitter winter wind doing its best to blow me off the jetty's side. My greying hair trailed downwind like the cotton 'tell-tails' yachtsmen tie to their shrouds to indicate wind direction. My frozen nose ran like a hose-pipe washing through a ship's hawse, glowing red in fair imitation of a centrally placed port sidelight but, even so, the distinctive smell of fuel oil prevailed and brought back vivid memories of my own tanker days, long since past.

Thrust deep in a pocket, one gloved hand felt warm and snug compared with the other which stiffly grasped the handle of a small briefcase that the wind knocked annoyingly against my leg.

The ship's centre-castle superstructure loomed larger and larger, towering above me as I neared her gangway where a uniformed seaman was stationed. As I approached, he stepped forward.

'Captain Thorpe, Sir?' he asked brightly having been standing sheltered in the ship's lee during his wait.

I nodded in response, not trusting the reaction of my frozen lips.

'This way please, Sir,' he said over his shoulder as he led me up the gangway onto the ship. 'I've been told to take you to the ship's office, if you will follow me.'

I was glad of his guidance. In my days these ships were only half the size and there was no such thing as a 'ship's office'.

Along a maze of alleyways, up several flights of stairs known as companionways when I was at sea, I was eventually delivered outside of a door on which the brass plate said was my destination.

The seaman knocked, then stood aside respectfully as he opened it.

'Captain Thorpe, Sir', he reported to the officer who was in the process of rising from his desk-chair, two rings on his sleeve indicating his rank of Second Officer.

'Good morning, Sir,' came his cheery welcome as he took my coat. 'My name is Hutchinson and I'm the Navigation Officer.'

I returned his handshake as he continued. 'The Captain is engaged at the moment with a Dockyard official but he would like to meet you if you would kindly wait a few minutes?' His voice inflection rose at the end making his statement into a question.

In answer to my nod of assent he went on to inform me that the Captain would ring down to him as soon as he was free.

I looked around, wondering if I was really in a ship. It looked more like the busy administration office of a large successful business concern with computers everywhere. Everything was immaculate, as was to be expected of a ship of the Royal Fleet Auxiliary Service. They always were a 'pusser' fleet, even years ago when I was in the Service. Admiralty owned, they were manned by officers and men of the merchant navy but run on naval lines with none of the easy-going life-style of a merchantman.

Officers tended to start as Cadets and remain in the RFA for all their sea-going careers. Ratings too were frequently long-serving 'company men' prepared to accept the stricter discipline of quasi-service life in exchange for job security. Very few 'one-trippers' served in their ranks.

The wall telephone jangled into life, waking me from my reminiscence as the Officer snatched it from its hook.

'Ship's office. Pilot speaking.' He listened for a few moments then said, 'Aye aye Sir,' looking at me.

'Captain Hood can see you now, Sir,' he advised as he edged past me into the doorway. 'If you will follow me, please?'

Along more alleyways, up more stairs, to the Captain's quarters where the young officer knocked reverently on the door.

'Enter,' came the command.

I had been expecting to see a grizzled, weather-beaten, old mariner but the man walking towards me with outstretched hand was relatively young, about mid-thirties or forty I would guess, looking more like a dapper businessman than a Master Mariner and Captain of a 20,000 ton Fleet tanker.

His greeting was warm. His offer of a drink even warmer. The sun wasn't over the yardarm yet but the cold weather made it legal, so I accepted gratefully, noting my large measure as compared with his small one – but there, I guess he had to drink with each of his frequent guests. I wondered if he was given an allowance? I never was.

Well trained in social graces, he steered the conversation towards me and my sea-time, showing sincere interest in the difference between commanding an RFA vessel in my day to what it was like now.

We spent an enjoyable half an hour discussing the merits and demerits of the Service, then he asked if I would like a tour of the bridge. I said of course I would, very much, so he pushed one of the many buttons on his telephone base unit.

'Send one of the Cadets to my cabin, please,' he instructed the receiver.

'I am sorry I can't accompany you personally,' he apologised, 'but unfortunately I have a couple of naval officers due shortly who, with their vast three years of experience, will probably tell me how I should do my job. Ah! well, the trials of life,' he sighed as a knock on the door was heard.

My new guide was a young lad, probably eighteen or nineteen years old, immaculate in his Cadet's uniform, very respectful and polite as he introduced himself as Cadet Bellingham. He was rather amazed and taken aback when I asked his Christian name.

'Ralph, Sir,' he said.

'OK, Ralph, lead on,' I commanded laughingly.

It was my turn to be amazed when we arrived on the bridge. It wasn't a ship's bridge at all. It was a vast communications centre. Computers and electronic gadgets were everywhere. LED lights twinkled from a dozen sources. I was totally out of my depth. I couldn't even tune my TV set at home. I was used to a bridge being completely silent shared only with a helmsman at his wheel, a couple of engine-room telegraphs and a highly technical battery of telephones and voice pipes.

There was no silence here, just one continuous electronic hum of automated machinery doing the mariner's job for him.

'Where's the wheel and telegraphs?' I enquired, knowing how silly my question must seem.

The young man looked at me sympathetically.

'The telegraphs are those two levers there,' he pointed, 'and we have no wheel as such, as we are tiller steering.'

Images of a team of exhausted men, pushing and pulling at a wooden tiller fixed to the rudder-head, came to mind but dispelled as he continued to tell me that the steering tiller was a small lever, a few inches high, on the central console, that a helmsman joggled from side to side with his forefinger and thumb.

'Of course, at sea, we are usually under automatic pilot,' he stated.

... Of course. I should have known(?) ...

He then explained the navigational aids. No sextants, no paper charts, no parallel rules. Everything was electronically displayed. Even the 'chart' was like an horizontal TV screen!

'As you know, Sir,' he went on. 'this is the Loran and this is our satellite positioning indicator' ... Of course I knew. (What the hell was he talking about!)

The puzzling, baffling tour left me with a distinct feeling that I would not like to be at sea in this day and age. One didn't need to be a seaman, an electronic engineer would suffice. With my education I would never progress beyond being a cadet! My guide seemed to have more knowledge in his little finger than I ever had in my head.

I thanked the young lad for his effort as he returned me to the Ship's Office, feeling sure he was shaking his head and wondering how duffers like me ever took a ship from one place to another.

A very welcome cup of strong coffee was given me by the Second Officer as I explained my bewilderment.

'Don't worry yourself, Sir,' he answered, 'my Dad's your age and a Master Mariner. He feels exactly the same as you every time he comes aboard to visit me.' He lifted his cup and sipped his hot drink.

'I have often thought,' he continued, 'how we would get on if our electrical source failed completely? Those of us that can still use a sextant, and work out a position, are so rusty through lack of practice we would probably end up putting the ship in the middle of Trafalgar Square, whereas the likes of you and my Dad wouldn't turn a hair!'

I suppose what he said made sense but I gained no satisfaction from hearing it. Still, that's progress and when these young men reach my age they will probably be equally as confused and baffled by the state-of-the-art at that time.

'Now, Sir,' he said, 'I expect you want to get down to the purpose of your visit?'

I wasn't really. I'd be happy to stay in the office all day rather than face the walk back along the cold, endless jetty.

He went to the wall safe and, unlocking it, withdrew a box and handed it to me.

I split the seal and emptied the contents onto the table, resealing the box before returning it for his safe-keeping.

Several minutes later, shrugging myself back into my greatcoat and buttoning it up to the neck, I handed the young officer his receipt, shaking his hand and expressing my thanks before being led back to the gangway by my earlier uniformed seaman.

I had thoroughly enjoyed my visit and was now looking forward to getting home and out of this awful weather. My only consolation was in knowing that my briefcase now contained the contents of the ship's collection box and I had another £92.50 towards RNLI funds.

MOON DREAMS

The night was warm, beautiful and balmy. Perfect for poets and lovers, and ideal for standing on the open bridge-wing of my ship, relaxing and enjoying the cooling breeze that ruffled the short sleeves of my cotton shirt as she thrust her sharp stem through the black velvet ocean streaked by a sparkling lane of shimmering lights pointing towards the fat faced man-in-the-moon, his angelic aura glowing in the cloudless sky.

Dreamily, I laid my forearms on the varnished bridge rail, staring ahead into the dark cavern of the night, looking down onto the foredeck illuminated by shafts of light from the saloon portholes beneath the bridge, watching the bow gently rise and fall in majestic harmony with the long Pacific swell.

She was a lovely ship. Her sharp flared bow and curvaceous sheer gave her an attractive appearance to seamen and passengers alike. Sleek and streamlined with all her functional necessities made attractive by inspired design. Her role, primarily to carry cargo, allowed for a small number of adventurous passengers who preferred to unwind in the tranquil atmosphere of a working ship rather than aboard one of the gaudy cruise liners with their brash high-class holiday camp environment.

The spotless paintwork of her white superstructure contrasted agreeably with the plain buff coloured funnel standing tall among the gaggle of cowl necked ventilators, lifeboats and skylights.

Derricks on the masts and sampson-posts stood sentinel over the tarpaulin covered hatches under which lay our precious cargo of Canadian grain.

Above me, the ever vigilant radar scanner revolved lazily, sending its probing emissions far beyond the visible skyline as the mast and rigging swayed gracefully across the star studded sky like the weary pendulum of a grandfather clock. The masthead light, occluded from where I stood, was a spectral halo of gossamer white mist.

What a way to earn a living! Each of our dozen passengers was paying the equivalent of my annual salary just for the pleasure of being on this voyage. They should be up here now, enjoying the tranquillity of this blissful Pacific night, instead of drinking and playing cards in the smoke-laden atmosphere of the lounge below.

Automatically, my eyes swept the unreachable horizon seen only as one shade lighter than the black surrounding sea. No problems out there. We had miles of water beneath our keel and hundreds to the nearest land. No wonder the Officer-of-the-Watch was unconcerned. I looked to my left. Yes, there he was, leaning against the radar console inside the wheelhouse. Probably dozing off I shouldn't wonder, or dreaming of his latest female conquest. Oh! For the joys of youth! Nevertheless, I'd have to keep my eyes on him. No doubt he was thinking the same about me!

Behind him, standing idly beside the wheel, bored out of his skull, stood the duty Quartermaster, his face eerily lit by the dim binnacle light, his eyes staring unfocused at the hypnotically clicking gyro compass, his mind probably far away. What a demoralising job, just standing for two hours at a time, watching the automatic helmsman doing its work. No doubt his job would soon be under scrutiny by the 'Owners' in their never ending quest for cost cutting and manning reductions. It was all very worrying.

The automatic, electronic, computerised systems are taking over. Ships are being built with engines controlled from the bridge resulting in vast numbers of engineers becoming redundant.

Navigation is already computerised, with sextants becoming almost instruments for pleasure and a means of keeping a Navigator's skill alive.

Ships are having their position electronically plotted, and digitally displayed, on purpose-made charts that look more like television screens.

What happened to parallel rules and dividers?

In all probability my job would also go, eventually, and unmanned ships would sail the seas controlled by a computer in an office somewhere.

The thought was most depressing on such a glorious night so I forcibly pushed it to the back of my mind and again felt the refreshing night breeze blowing through my hair.

Below me, to my right, the green ethereal glow of the starboard steaming light shone its warning to other non-existing ships, casting ghostly rays onto the white foaming sea that swept along the ship's side in a hectic rush to join the churning maelstrom of the propeller's wash and form a bubbling wake astern of us, a temporary mark of our passing.

I tried to concentrate my thoughts on tomorrow's work. Like a housewife at home there is always something that needs doing but, I decided, now was not the time to be thinking of that so I let my thoughts wander back to my home and family in Hampshire. Was my wife looking after the lawn? Did she manage to get the shed roof repaired?

Hopefully there would be mail waiting for us in Japan and these questions answered. I must remember to renew the piping of my garden tap during my next leave.

I swept the undefined line separating the sea from the sky once more, first with my naked eyes and then with binoculars, for ships that would have been located ages ago by our lofty radar scanner.

Three more days would see us in Japan with our valuable cargo and twelve, hopefully happy, passengers, so I made a mental note to check with the Mate in the morning regarding arrangements for crew mail and shore leave.

Tiredly, I looked at my watch but the luminous dial was too faint to see so, lifting my hand to face level, I twisted my wrist to and fro until a glimmer of light from other sources combined to enable me to see the hands ... Five minutes to midnight.

I paced the bridge wing for the umpteenth time. Six steps out, turn, six steps back, turn, six steps out, turn, six steps back. Backwards and forwards, endlessly.

How did Admiral Lord Nelson feel as he paced the quarter-deck on HMS *Victory*, looking for'ard along the cannon-lined gun-deck watching his bare-footed seamen scrambling among the spider's web of rigging and billowing clouds of sails as they prepared the ship to meet the King's enemies, knowing full well that within days, maybe hours, many of them would be a bloody mangled corpse ripped apart by shot, sword or vicious wood splinters blasted from their own ship.

What of his thirteen-year-old Midshipmen, trembling in fear of the forthcoming battle, holding the belted dirks they wore in place of an officer's sword that would be too large for them to carry or handle? Would they fight like men or cower among the coils of rope? Would he capture an enemy vessel and become rich, or die, drowned in an unforgiving sea, sliced open by a Frenchie's sword or smashed to a pulp by cannon shot? ...

Again, my eyes swept the indistinct sky-line ... nothing. Radar would show us if there were any other vessel within twenty miles but nevertheless the Law of the Sea, and common sense, requires input from the human eyeball. Radar isn't infallible. It doesn't 'see' everything.

With this thought, I once more drifted into a dream world. How would it feel to command a giant ocean liner, to pace a bridge wing longer that our foredeck, then retire below to the First Class restaurant for a sumptuous meal in the company of Lords and Ladies, film stars, the *nouveaux riches* and other high fliers to whom I had given the ultimate accolade of dining with me at the Captain's table.

After an hour or so of boring, uninteresting small talk I would most likely feel weary from having eaten my fill and downing several glasses of wine suitably diluted, on my orders, by my personal Steward who, at a pre-arranged signal, would dutifully inform me that I was required on the bridge, allowing me to make my excuses and get away from the onerous social duty imposed upon me by financially guided

'Owners'. I was a seaman, not an entertainer, but even I had to follow orders.

Duty done, I would probably go for a stroll along the promenade deck to cleanse my lungs with good, clean, fresh, salt air and receive respectful admiration and salutations from the sun-worshipping passengers lounging in their deck chairs enjoying, in most cases, a holiday of a lifetime, being cosseted and pampered by obsequious stewards who, if truth be know, have thoughts only for the size of their end-of-voyage tips.

Hearing a faint voice bragging, 'I've just spoken to the Captain!' I reach my staterooms under the bridge; I gratefully kick off my shoes and remove my choking bow-tie and starched shirt before ringing the wheel-house to ensure all was well with my ship. Then slip into a smoking jacket, thoughtfully laid out by my steward, pour myself a large but weak whisky and soda, light one of my favourite cigars kindly presented to me by a member of Indian royalty, and stretch out on the settee, feet up on the upholstered arm, to enjoy a couple of hours peace and relaxation before returning to face another round of socialising while my Staff Captain and Officers continued to run the ship for me.

Never mind the film stars, the millionaires, the Royalty. On this ship I was The Man, the main attraction, God!

Blinking myself back to reality I pushed away from the cap-rail just as 'eight-bells' rang to announce midnight, the start of a new day, and the beginning of the Middle Watch.

Soft footsteps crept up the bridge ladder behind me and a shadowy figure, still half asleep, groped cautiously towards me in the darkness with unacclimatised eyes.

'A beautiful night, Andrew,' I greeted in cheerful and annoying recognition. 'A really lovely one and an empty sea,' I added. 'Goodnight.'

I turned away as he grunted a response and walked towards the wheelhouse. Stepping through the doorway I could see young Mr Alexander, the Third Officer, in whispered conversation with his relief, Second Officer Stewart. I strode across the wheelhouse towards them, saw them look in my direction and stiffen. I had their attention.

'Starboard Look-out relieved, Sir,' I reported.

'GOING HOME'

I felt really tired. It had been a long, weary day and I was looking forward to going home for a bath, a hot meal, and getting into the lee of bum island with my Missus – not necessarily in that order!

My cab was now first in the queue at the taxi rank near the railway station. One more fare and that would be it for the day.

Ten minutes passed. It was unusually quiet for an early evening and I was just dozing off when an urgent tap on the window made me jump.

'Are you free?' enquired the voice of the young lady peering in.

I put my arm out of the window and opened the door to the back seat, nodding in reply. She climbed in and sat demurely with a small bag clasped tightly on her lap.

'Brentworth Road please. Number 27,' she called, leaning forward unnecessarily.

'Bloody Hell,' I thought, 'that's twenty minutes away. Bang goes my early night.'

I tried to engage her in the usual taxi-driver's small talk and banter but she seemed reluctant to respond so, after an awkward few moments, I left her to her own thoughts. Perhaps she was either very shy or having a bad day – and we all have them from time to time. At least it left me free to concentrate on getting through the heavy evening traffic.

Luckily we were only held up twice. Once by a policeman who was questioning the intelligence of a motorist trying, and failing, to do a U-turn in the main shopping street, and once by temporary traffic lights at roadworks that were stuck at red and overcome by a big truck driver who eventually lost patience and ignored them. We all followed him.

Entering Brentworth Road I slowed to see the numbers and cruised to a halt outside Number 27.

Turning to open the back door I was shocked and astounded to see the back seat was empty. Where had she gone? I hadn't seen or heard her get out! It must have been during one of the hold-ups. Surely I would have noticed. I must be going daft, but not daft enough to forego my fare!

I got out and went up the short pathway to Number 27 and knocked hard on the heavy wooden door. There was no answer so I treated myself to a few choice Anglo-Saxon expletives.

At least my Missus had a laugh at my expense when I told her.

Next day, returning from a fare, I found myself a few streets away from Brentworth Road so, bloody-mindedly, decided to try again.

My knock was answered almost immediately by a middle-aged woman who looked as though she hadn't slept for a month. Her dull eyes stared lifelessly at me as though I were a man from Mars.

'Morning,' I greeted as cheerfully as I could muster. 'Does a young lady about twenty-ish live here please?'

'Why?' came the answer from bloodless lips that hardly moved.

'Well,' I explained. 'I picked up this young lady yesterday evening outside the railway station to bring her to this address but she got out without paying her fare.'

The heavy eyes glazed over and the pale face became like marble.

'What time was that?' the voice croaked.

'Just on six,' I replied.

She just stared right through me and I felt very embarrassed. What had I said that was so wrong?

After several seconds that seemed like minutes, the lips twitched.

'My daughter was knocked down and killed outside of the railway station at six o'clock last Thursday evening – exactly a week ago yesterday. You must be mistaken!'

With that she quietly shut the door, leaving me dumbfounded.

I have never believed in ghosts ... I do now!

'AMENTIA'

Chapter One

'This is the life for me,' I said to myself for the umpteenth time as I lay stretched out on the canvas-covered cockpit seat of my twenty-five foot sloop-rigged sailing cruiser, my left arm idly resting along the gunwale and my right draped over the tiller that quivered from the vibration of the rudder cutting through the gentle turbulence of the wake trailing astern.

Even under full sail, the light sou'westerly breeze was barely enough to cause a white moustache under the bow where the stem cut through the ruffled surface of the south Irish Sea, the Patent log spinning astern on its long twisting line, clocking our speed at a little over four knots.

From an almost cloudless sky the early morning sun beat down on my bare legs and chest – only recently revealed to the world after the removal of several layers of warm clothing – easing away the chill from my bones after a long night-watch as I eagerly awaited the appearance of my solitary crew member whom I had shaken awake thirty minutes earlier. I was looking forward, in tired anticipation, to crawling into my bunk for a much needed few hours sleep.

Heavy eyelids told me it was going to be a toss-up as to which would be my priority, hunger or tiredness, but the mouth-watering smell of frying bacon, wafting up from the galley below, convinced me that sleep would have to wait – just for a few moments at least.

Then my crew climbed the few steps up from the cabin and stood in the cockpit, taking my breath away. She was a vision of loveliness, dressed only in a waist length T-shirt and the briefest of thong-style knickers, as she expertly balanced herself against the gentle roll and pitch of the boat, a mug of steaming tea in one hand and a plate of bacon sandwiches – oozing with tomato sauce, just as I like it – in the other.

'Good morning,' she smiled, tossing long blonde hair from her eyes with a swooping motion of her head. God, she looked desirable, even in my tired state.

It was hard to realise that it was only a few days ago when I had first set eyes on her.

130

I had gone ashore from my boat, moored to a bobbing buoy in Falmouth harbour, for a last hot meal and a few pints. A treat to celebrate my last evening in England for several weeks before setting off to Ireland on a cruise that I had long dreamed of.

I had had my meal and was standing in a crowded pub in the High Street, squashed by a throng of thirst-quenching revellers against a table at which two young ladies sat enjoying their glasses of wine.

The oak-beamed bar was thick with cigarette smoke that irritated my nostrils and I had already made up my mind to escape out into the fresh air as soon as I finished my beer. I didn't smoke myself and the pungent tang of nicotine made me nauseous.

I put my beer glass down on the ladies' table, belatedly asking, 'Do you mind?' and was rewarded by a nod of assent and a beautiful smile from the one who I now saw was an absolutely stunning blonde.

Taking a handkerchief from my trouser pocket I tried, in vain, to blow the tobacco fumes from my nose, then reached out for my glass. As I lifted it I noticed, too late, that it had a beer mat stuck to the bottom and, to my horror, it dropped off hitting the blonde's wine glass – luckily half empty – knocking it over and spilling the contents across the table. Both ladies jumped to their feet, scraping their chairs back across the floor in panic but luckily, for me at least, the wine ran from the table straight onto the floor without dripping into their laps.

I flushed with embarrassment and stammered an apology as the brunette gave me a withering glare of the sort usually reserved for something slimy and horrid. With my already soiled hanky I mopped the wine from the table top, watched by a hundred pairs of condemning eyes, and offered to replace the spilt drink. The blonde placed her hand lightly on my forearm and gave another of her bewitching smiles. She was so beautiful.

'Please don't worry,' she whispered huskily, 'it was only an accident.'

I gave her a grateful look before turning to fight my way to the bar to replace her wine, but again she placed a restraining hand on my arm to stop me.

'No, please, I don't want another drink.' She looked at me with her big blue eyes. 'I was just about to leave anyhow.'

She stooped low over her friend and said something that gained me yet another dirty look from the seated brunette, then turned to me saying, 'Let's get out of here shall we?'

Outside, the cool evening fresh air smelt wonderful and we both laughed as we took deep exaggerated breaths together.

'Wasn't it awful in there?' she said, pulling a face. 'I'm so glad you did what you did. I was looking for an excuse to get away.'

'You're right,' I agreed. 'I can't put up with tobacco smoke for very long, it makes me feel bad.'

I looked down at her lovely face and, plucking up courage, asked if she would like to go for a walk.

'Let's,' she answered without hesitation, tucking her arm through mine and cuddling close like a lover. 'My name's Helen.'

We walked for an hour or so, slowly through the narrow streets full of evening strollers – many champing on their take-away pasties, or fish and chips – up the winding road to the ancient Castle that stood mysterious and gloomy in the fading light, high on the hill overlooking everything for miles around, getting to know each other more with each step. I felt a very strong attraction towards her especially when my nose became clear of the sickening nicotine and I could smell the exciting perfume she was wearing. Her closeness was very evocative.

We found an empty bench-seat at the side of the footpath that circled the Castle and sat close together overlooking the calm, moonlit waters of Falmouth Bay. The feel of her thigh pressed against mine made me very aroused and, as I put my arm around her shoulder, she snuggled into me. I could feel myself trembling like a schoolboy and wondered if she noticed it, as I kissed her gently. Her lips were so soft and moist and there was no resistance as I slowly and carefully placed my hand on her thigh. The warmth of her leg through the thin material of her summer dress sent me into orbit and she responded passionately as I kissed her hard and urgently.

Still there was no resistance from her as my hand slid under her dress and up her smooth bare thigh. Her heavy breathing matched mine but, as I became bolder, she stiffened.

'No, not tonight,' she panted breathlessly. 'Not the first time.' She kissed me hard to ease my obvious disappointment. 'Sorry darling, perhaps next time?'

Reluctant to agree, I had no option and withdrew my hand, to be rewarded by her grateful, and presumably relieved, smile.

As we sat, arms around each other gazing out over the twinkling sea, I told her of my forthcoming trip across to Ireland.

'Oh! how wonderful, I'd love to do that,' she cried. 'I've done quite a lot of sailing with my brother, but only on day trips.'

'Pack a bag and come with me?' I joked, thinking I should be so lucky. The thought that she would accept never entered my mind.

'Can I?' she asked excitedly. 'I could if you'd have me.'

I hadn't even considered having a companion before. I much preferred to sail alone with no one else to be responsible for. To do my own thing without concern for anyone else, but one look at this beautiful, gorgeous creature beside me brought about a rapid change of mind.

'Tell you what,' I replied with a pounding, hopeful heart. 'I'll be sailing tomorrow afternoon and will be away for two, maybe three, weeks. You think about it overnight and if you still want to come be at the Town Quay by ten in the morning. If I see you there I'll come ashore and pick you up. Fair enough?'

'Oh! I shall be there, have no doubt,' she answered, all starry eyed. 'And you'll not be sorry – I promise!'

Chapter Two

I hardly slept a wink that night, tossing and turning in my bunk. Listening to the tapping of the taut halyards against the aluminium mast and the gurgling of tide water bubbling past the hull within inches of my face. Thinking and dreaming of having her all to myself for a couple of weeks, my mind working overtime.

I tried, unsuccessfully, to prepare myself for a massive disappointment should she not turn up but all I could think of was the feel of her hot, passionate body, the smell of her femininity and the overpowering yearning to possess her. I knew I would be shattered if she changed her mind. I'd never felt this way about a woman before – ever.

Next morning, all agitated and excited, I was sat on the dew-covered cabin top at 9.30, scanning the Town Quay through binoculars. By ten to ten there was still no sign of her. I had to do something. I couldn't just sit waiting any longer. If I rowed over to the quay now it would be ten o'clock by the time I got there so, throwing oars and rowlocks into my eight foot dinghy, I jumped in after them. One last look told me she still hadn't arrived and with a heart getting heavier by the minute I started to row.

I was over halfway when, unable to stand the strain of uncertainty any longer, I glanced over my shoulder and saw her walking onto the Town Quay carrying a hold-all and small suitcase. My heart leapt with joy and with renewed energy I sped the remaining distance, bringing the dinghy alongside the rough stone quayside like a high-speed launch.

Excitedly, I jumped ashore and took her in my arms, still holding the dinghy painter in my hand. She was flushed and breathless as we hugged, oblivious to the amused looks from passers-by. I told her I hadn't slept all night.

'Me neither, I could hardly wait for this morning,' she replied. 'You haven't changed your mind about taking me have you?'

I shook my head emphatically with a big, stupid grin on my face. She hugged me tighter. 'I regret so much, having said "No" to you last night,' she whispered apologetically. 'I wanted you so much too, does that sound terribly wanton?'

I assured her it didn't. It sounded wonderful!

Rowing back to the boat I told her I would put her on board then return ashore for fresh milk and bread, and a daily paper, while she settled herself in. This shopping trip only took me a little over half an hour, but it seemed like ages.

Arriving back, I climbed aboard, secured the dinghy and looked down into the cabin. Helen had discovered that the cabin table dropped down to the level of the cushioned locker seats surrounding three of its sides to convert it into a double bed and was lying spread-eagled on it, holding her hands out towards me in invitation, completely naked.

Such presumption on her part annoyed me intensely, especially so early in the morning, and it took me the next two hours, in her arms on the bed, to instil in her that, on this boat, I was the Captain. I gave the orders. She only had to obey. She would do as I say, not the other way around. This was shipboard discipline.

'Yes Sir,' she laughed as she rolled off my exhausted body.

We slipped from the buoy two hours later than planned, missing vital hours of ebb tide, and sailed out through the Heads, nostalgically looking up at the old Castle high on our starboard side before turning westward towards Land's End ... Conditions were perfect.

Close-hauled in a steady sou'westerly breeze, about Force 3 or 4, we made good progress, nodding our bows in a long swell that was probably the aftermath of an earlier storm somewhere far out in mid-Atlantic.

My crew was perfect too, and proved herself to be a good sailor.

Basically, we split into two twelve-hour watches with me doing the night watch from 10 p.m. to 10 a.m. This was far better than sailing single-handed with the worry, in busy waters, of relying on the self-steering gear to snatch a few hours sleep.

In fact though, apart from periods of off-watch sleep, we managed to spend much of our time together, using the self-steering only when an empty sea allowed us the pleasure of a few precious moments below.

Twenty-four hours later, with the Scilly Isles several miles away on our starboard side, we altered course to the nor-west bringing the wind onto our port beam and adding a little to the rolling motion of the boat. It was still excellent sailing weather and it seemed as though we were the only people in the world. Surprisingly, in such a busy sea-lane, we only caught an occasional sight of distant ships way out on the horizon. None came near us so Helen was able to spend much of her time enjoying the hot sunshine, sun-bathing naked on the cabin top, much to my sexual discomfort. Still, there was always the self-steering gear!

Now, on the morning of our third day at sea, she was standing in the cockpit handing me tea and bacon sandwiches.

'Bit overdressed this morning, aren't we, darling?' I grinned suggestively at her short T-shirt and brief knickers.

'Thought you'd be too tired to notice, Captain,' she mocked, 'I can always take them off if you wish.'

'Nah,' I joked, 'I'd rather have me a bacon sahnny and some sleep.'

'Wanna bet?' she answered with a smile as she pulled the Tee-shirt off over her head.

The bacon sandwiches were cold by the time I ate them, and the tea lukewarm, but what the hell, worse things happen at sea.

'We should be seeing the Irish coast in a few hours, sweetheart, so keep your eyes open,' I called out over my shoulder as my weak knees carried me down the steps into the cabin and welcoming bed. 'Hopefully we should be in and tied-up by teatime, if the wind holds.'

A minute later I was asleep.

Chapter Three

It took a few sleep-sodden moments for my mind to register the hand on my shoulder shaking me awake from the depths of unconsciousness, and the sultry voice of a sea-nymph calling me to her ample bosom. 'Wakey wakey, darling.'

I levered my eyes open, slowly and painfully, one at a time, and blearily saw the fish-tailed mermaid disappearing up the cabin steps, calling that the coast was in sight.

'What bloody coast?' I frowned to myself, as my brain kick-started itself into what could vaguely be described as sluggish activity, reluctantly dragging my leaden body off the bed to crawl wearily up the four mountainous steps out onto the deck.

'Where?' I grunted irritably as I squinted aft, past the beautiful goddess sat smiling at the helm.

'That way, Rip Van Winkle,' said the golden voice, pointing forward.

Slowly, to prevent my eyeballs shooting out of my skull, I turned my head. 'Christ,' I blasphemed as I saw the undulating hills less than two miles ahead. 'We're almost there. Why didn't you call me earlier?'

'Not necessary,' she grinned insolently. 'You needed sleep and I can cope.'

I went back below, woke myself with a face full of cold water, then returned to the cockpit where my ill-disciplined crew handed me a cup of hot tea, sweetened with a kiss.

We were rapidly approaching the small harbour when she suddenly pointed ahead saying, 'Look at that!' I looked as ordered.

From out of the harbour a topsail schooner, under full sail, was coming in our direction, her canvas billowing in the breeze.

'Cor!' I whispered in awe, 'what a beautiful sight. I haven't seen one of them for ages – can't be many left afloat.'

'She's magnificent,' said my astonished crew. 'I've never seen one before.'

With a white, curling, bone-in-her-teeth, the tops'l schooner swept past less than a hundred yards on our port side, momentarily taking the wind from our sails, her crew waving in response to our salutes.

'They must have been having some sort of pageant,' I said, 'did you see her crew were all dressed up like old-time seamen?'

'Wasn't it wonderful?' she nodded. 'Wish I'd had my camera.'

With only a half a mile to go I cranked our small diesel engine into life. The smelly, thumping piston shattering the peaceful tranquillity of our world as I wound in the roller-reefing foresail then dropped the main, securing it temporarily with sail-ties until we had time to make a neat harbour-stow.

Our destination was a small fishing port that comprised two ancient, seaweed-covered, stone breakwater moles. The south one, longer than the north, had a miniature rusty lighthouse, eight feet tall, on its seaward end and the two embraced a silted-up harbour that would probably dry out at low water. It looked deserted.

As we motored serenely through the entrance, we could see two small fishing smacks alongside the south mole and from the amount of red-painted, barnacle-covered hull they were showing it was obvious they were still sitting on the bottom.

In the centre of the harbour, three trot-lines of moorings were occupied by a miscellaneous gaggle of open-boats, launches and dinghies. At the seaward end of each of these trots were large spherical buoys, once yellow coloured but now covered in a coat of seabird droppings, on which could faintly be seen the word 'Visitors' above a waterline of thick, slimy seaweed.

We looked up at the 'lighthouse' as a head appeared calling in a rich Irish brogue, 'Hook anto one av de tree yella buoys fer an 'our or so Mister, den dare will be enough wahter fer ye to git alangsoide in front av de fishing boots.'

I waved an acknowledgement and did as instructed. No doubt he was the Harbour Master and would be calling for his dues before long.

The buoy we chose was guarded by a huge gull that stood motionless, glaring at us with beady eyes as we slowly motored towards it. Only at the last second, with the buoy right under our bow and Helen reaching to pass a line through the guano covered ring-bolt, did it flap angrily away, annoyed at our intrusion, cawing like a politician at question time in the House.

The hour or so spent there enabled us to put our mains'l into a neat 'harbour-stow', fit the sail cover and get everything down below ship-shape and Bristol fashion.

At our starboard yard-arm hung the Irish National tri-colour courtesy flag and on the port side a yellow quarantine flag requested 'free practique' from Customs. I wasn't too sure if this was a legal requirement for Ireland or not, but decided to play safe. In either case, no one took any notice of it.

We gave it ninety minutes, to be on the safe side, before slipping from the buoy to go alongside, allowing the return of the irate gull to its private perch. By this time our deck would be level with the quayside and I had given Helen strict instructions on how she was to jump ashore and secure our mooring lines; all of which she studiously and disdainfully ignored as though to tell me to teach her Grandmother to suck eggs. Her expertise was not to be put to the test however.

As we approached the quay, with Helen poised ready to leap into action like a Nelsonian boarding party, an aged woman appeared from one of the fishing smacks and held out her arms to indicate she would take our lines, which she did effortlessly.

While we were still busy securing our boat alongside, the woman walked away without uttering a word. Not wanting to be ungracious I called out after her, 'Thank you very much, madam.'

My call was ignored.

Our new, temporary home, was a small village. A very small village of not more than a few dozen terraced houses lining the cobbled road that appeared from out of a wooded area.

Fronting the harbour stood a row of ancient, rough-stone, slate-roofed buildings, gloomy and depressing even on this lovely summer evening.

Outside of one, a weather-beaten sign hung on an equally rusting bracket, telling anyone who cared to decipher it that this was 'The Captain's Return', the village's one and only pub, entered by a squeaky, iron-bound ill-fitting door, that served better as ventilation than insulation. We made a bee-line for it.

Inside, our enquiry as to whether accommodation, hot baths and hot meals were available, was answered by the huge stooping landlord who was busy cleaning and polishing behind the row of beer pumps in the low-ceilinged, cold and draughty bar, empty of customers at this early hour.

He informed us that 'We don't do dat Soir', in a strong Irish accent that could be cut with a knife, adding mystifyingly, 'an' da Post Office shop is closed.'

Back on board a few minutes later, very disappointed, we made the best of things. Instead of an eagerly awaited pub-style, home-cooked meal and a soak in a hot bath, we had to satisfy ourselves with tinned braised steak and potatoes, followed by a strip wash from a plastic bowl.

My crew – being a woman – wanted to dress up and look feminine (how could she fail?) for our run ashore, in the hope that there would be some sort of life-form later in the evening, so she spent an hour fixing her nails, hair and make-up, then five minutes putting on a short flared summer dress over very little else, making me as horny as hell just looking at her.

The atmosphere as we entered the pub bar a while later, was electric. The customers were all male, mostly elderly, with a sprinkling of middle-aged, so we rightly guessed that the native females were prohibited from this masculine bastion, and female visitors a rarity.

This much was obvious as a dozen pair of eyes devoured the sight of Helen. Mind you, I couldn't blame them. She looked ravishing – and knew it – as she deliberately chose to sit where she was in full view of everyone.

Apart from the popping of eyes out of sockets, the dropping of jaws, and the sharp intakes of breath, you could have heard a feather drop. I could see why as I turned to join her from the bar where I had ordered the obligatory Guinness for me and lemonade for her. She was sat crossed legged with the hem of her short dress half way up her thigh showing more bare thigh than the locals had probably seen since last Christmas!

I placed the drinks on the table and went to sit opposite her.

'Don't sit there, darling,' she hissed, 'come and sit beside me.'

I did as I was told, then realised from the sighs of relief from the other customers that, had I sat opposite her, I would have blocked their view.

'You randy little bitch,' I laughingly whispered in her ear. 'You'll be flashing your knickers next.'

'So what?' she grinned back, 'you're not jealous are you?'

'No, I'm not!' I answered, 'but you do realise that in the last few minutes you've been mentally stripped and raped by every man here.'

'Ooo-lovely,' she cooed, and had the grace to blush.

As the evening progressed and the novelty began to wane, her 'audience' fractionally lost interest. Much to her disappointment.

Going to the bar for more drinks I asked the landlord how often the topsail schooner called in at the harbour.

'Wat schooner wud dat be, Soir?' he frowned.

I was a little taken aback by this. Surely no one could miss seeing or hearing about such a rare and beautiful square-rigger. 'The one that sailed from here this afternoon just as I was arriving.'

His frown deepened and he leaned forward, his hands spread on the bar top. 'Sure and we 'aven't 'ad such a boat in since the last tradin' schooners, back in the 1920s, Soir. You must be mistaken.'

'I'm not mistaken, you Irish git!' I burst out angrily, momentarily losing my cool and attracting the attention of the other customers. 'I saw it as plain as I see you – and so did my lady companion over there,' I said nodding over my shoulder to where Helen sat at the window table.

'Over where, Soir?' queried the perplexed landlord.

I pointed towards her. 'There, damn you,' I snarled, 'and you have the nerve to suggest *I* am blind!'

Snatching the two drinks from the bar top I returned to my seat, very irate, and told Helen of the landlord's insolent remarks. Her only reaction was to tell me not to worry about such trifles, but it took me a while to cool down.

Behind the bar, his forehead still deeply furrowed with concern, the landlord lifted the phone from its loosely nailed wall bracket and dialled the number of Doctor Roger Allen, the village GP and his very good friend.

Fifteen minutes later the latch on the front door of the bar clicked open and a relieved landlord saw the doctor enter, in shirt sleeves. Together they went into a huddle at the far end of the bar, elbows on the polished top, heads close together, conspiratorially.

'Tell me about it, Thomas,' invited the medical man.

'Well, tis like thas, Doc,' the landlord began in a broad West-country accent. 'You sees that old chap sittin' ower thar.' He nodded towards the window table and the doctor turned to look. ''Ee's bin sat thar all evenin' talking to 'imself, an each time 'e comes to the bar 'e orders a pint for 'imself and a glass of lemonade. No 'arm in tha' o'course but 'ees 'ad five pints now and the five lemonades are still on tha table, untouched!' He paused to gather his thoughts, then continued. ''ee tells I 'ees got a yacht in tha 'arbour but thar ain't no strange boats in. 'e tells I 'ees done a three day trip from Falmouth to 'ere but tha knows Falmouth's only just around tha corner, 'alf 'our's sailin' away.' Another pause as he looked furtively around. 'Than 'ee gooz on about 'is lady companion but as thee can see thar ain't no one wiv 'im. 'e talks to 'imself all the time. Next, 'e says 'e saw a tops'l schooner sail out of 'ere jast as 'e were arrivin' but tha knows we ain't 'ad one of them in 'ere for well over 'alf a century – anyway thar's too much silt for one to get in now even if 'e'd wan'ed to. Then, to cap it all, 'e calls I a bloody Irishman. Me!' he hissed with indignant pride. 'Me, born an' bred in tha village an' ain't bin outside of Cornwall in all me life, 'cept for me Army time.' He blew out his cheeks and took a deep breath. 'One las' thing that's queer is that 'e calls 'imself Doctor Smith, but I sees 'is plastic card when 'e laid 'is open wallet on the bar, and that said Martin Shepherd!'

Doctor Allen pondered his thoughts for several moments then raised himself up off his elbows. 'You did right to call me, Thomas,' he said to the anxious landlord. 'May I use your phone please? Then I'll go over and talk with the old fellow.'

Chapter Four

Back at my table, with Helen, I was still quietly seething. The bloody cheek of the man to insinuate I was imagining things. Helen didn't help either. She was getting fed up with the lack of attention directed her way.

'What do you say we get away tomorrow instead of staying in this God forsaken hole?' I suggested, and she came alive.

'Oh! yes please,' she pleaded. 'I don't like it here. I want to go where I can have a hot bath and a decent meal.'

'No problem,' I promised, 'there's plenty of places within a day's sail. How about trying Youghal?'

'You what?' she asked, but before I could reply a man in shirt-sleeves came to the table.

'Doctor Smith?' he enquired, in an educated English voice and offering his hand. 'My name is Roger Allen, I'm the local GP. So pleased to meet you.'

I grunted a response. I didn't really want the company of a third party but he seemed friendly enough and I didn't wish to appear churlish so I shook his hand and invited him to join us.

'Is yours a medical Doctorate?' he asked, and seemed delighted when I affirmed it was. 'It's so nice to meet and talk with a fellow MD. We don't get many visiting our little village.'

I felt like telling him that I could well understand why, but instead introduced him to Helen whom he appeared genuinely pleased to meet.

He listened, interestedly, as I told him of our trip across the Irish Sea from Falmouth and of our unfriendly welcome here. He was a good listener. After a while, he leaned across the table and whispered, 'I wonder if I could ask a favour of you, Doctor Smith?'

I nodded agreement and he continued. 'I have a very difficult case on my hands at the moment. The patient is in the local hospital and to be perfectly honest I would be most grateful if you could help me with a second opinion? I have a car outside that will take us there now, if you would be so kind.'

'I'd be pleased to give whatever help I can, Doctor Allen,' I assured him, rising to my feet and instructing Helen to return aboard to await my return.

Outside, the waiting Constable opened the car door and gave a smart salute as we climbed into the back seat.

Chapter Five

'Evenin' Tamas,' greeted the rosy cheeked fisherman as he shouldered his way through the wooden door and strode heavily towards the bar, slamming his gnarled hand, as big as a polar bear's paw, on the polished top.

'Evenin', Willum,' answered the landlord, already pulling a pint of best bitter for his regular customer; "ad a good day?'

'No. I yaint,' came the grunted reply as the huge paw wrapped itself around the proffered glass of foaming brew that disappeared in half a dozen deep thirsty gulps, his tongue sweeping his lips like a windscreen-wiper.

'Needed tha',' said William, dragging the sleeve of his jacket across his mouth, and handing the empty glass back for the refill.

Thomas, waiting in anticipation, pulled the pump lever, careful to minimise the 'head', then passed the glass back across the bar. William held it up to eye level, against the light, and gazed through it with affection before lowering it to his lips gently, slowly sipping the nectar, relishing every drop.

'All'ays enjoy the secon' pint best,' he murmured to no one in particular. It was a phrase he used every evening as he stood silently and absentmindedly inspecting the rows of bottles, optics and memorabilia on the wall behind the bar. The landlord knew better than to intrude on the faraway thoughts of this hardworking fisherman, unwinding at the end of a gruelling day. He would talk, if and when he was ready.

'Did 'e ever 'ear anymore of tha' looney tha' were in 'ere a few weeks ago Tamas?' asked William, after a long pause

'Oo ar,' replied the landlord knowledgeably, pleased to have someone to talk to. 'Doctor Allen and the Poliss took 'im to Camborne 'ospital. Fer observation thay said. But 'e got worse overnight an' by naxt mornin' ee were raving mad so thay 'ad 'im locked up in tha mental ward. Apparently 'e weren't a doctor at all. 'E were a chiropodist from Plymouth.'

'Oh yea,' grunted William, not knowing what a chiropodist was, 'how did thay get on on Sa'erday?'

'How did who get on?' asked the landlord.

'Plymouth Argyle o'course,' snapped Willum.

'Oh, thay lost diden um.'

SENTENCE OF DEATH

Chapter One

The windowless Courtroom with its pale-panelled walls was as cheerful as a welcoming morgue. Lighting from the inter-ceiling reflectors illuminated the room without shadow, adding to the cadaverous complexions of the assembled people who were already slightly chilled from the efforts of an over-zealous air conditioning system. Only the imitation oak panelling of the imposing justices 'bench' relieved the cold austerity trying, unsuccessfully, to copy the ambience of a pre-20th century Court of Justice.

Gaudily, a massive crest of the United European States Ministry of Justice hung like a guillotine blade from the wall above the Honourable Lordship's plush velvet-covered 'throne'.

It was an atmosphere obviously designed to send arrows of fear into the hearts of anyone not involved in the fraternity of a legal profession that still tried to retain the mysticism and awesome authority of the Court, despite the demands of the European Civil Rights Act passed at the turn of the century to ensure 'justice without fear'.

This was the year of our Lord 2019 and the Act was doing me no good at all; I was scared stiff and trembling as I stood rigidly to attention before the God-like figure who was about to pass sentence upon me.

Throughout my trial I had been honest and open with my responses to the prosecutors in the hope that, by doing so, it would earn me some degree of consideration and leniency when the inevitable sentence was decided. Nevertheless, I was dreading the punishment in store for me. The thought of prison was terrifying – anything but that – yet I knew in my heart that anything less was about as likely as summer snow in the Sahara. My only hope lay in some little-known legislation that allowed the sentence of a qualified Master Mariner to be served afloat.

My solicitor, his face patterned with deep wrinkles, had tried to explain this to me although he was clearly not too conversant with the actual details himself. Still, it was hope. Whatever was entailed I would accept, if it meant keeping me out of prison.

I looked up as his Lordship, a desolate cadaverous-looking man, shuffled the papers before him, digging my nails into sweating palms, hoping no one could hear my heart pounding, ten to the dozen.

'Gordon David Thorpe' growled the gowned Judge staring down from his high 'bench' overlooking the lesser mortals, and me in particular, as he lamented the demise of the judicial wig that would have covered his balding pate ... 'You have been found guilty as charged, of False Accounting under Section Eleven of the Community Offences Regulations, 2010.'

His several layers of chins collapsed onto his chest as he endeavoured to peer down at me over the top of pince-nez precariously balanced on the end of his bulbous nose, as if I were something obnoxious.

'It was my intention to pass a custodial sentence upon you to be served in a State prison,' he continued, like an old-time Town-crier making a Royal proclamation. 'You may however, because of your maritime qualifications, choose to accept an alternative sentence under the "Confined Sea-service Regulations" 2011, the details of which your solicitor has, no doubts, explained to you.' He raised a querying eyebrow in my direction ... 'What is your choice?'

On the receiving end of his laser-like, censorial stare, I felt stunned and ashamed.

I had gone to sea, straight from school, in 1990, as a fresh-faced cadet at the tender age of sixteen, when the British Merchant Navy was a fleet – albeit small – of fully manned ships. In 2001 I gained my Ship Manager's certificate and five years later was appointed to my first command, the nuclear powered passenger ship *Sea Queen* on the commuter link between Tilbury and Rotterdam. I had a promising career ahead of me.

Three months ago, in desperation, I made false entries in a monetary register and diverted 26,000 Euros into my own personal account to pay the cost of laser surgery to remove my mother's brain tumour, her death being the only alternative.

To my horror, a spot-scan audit discovered my falsehood and I was called to the office of my employer and arrested by State police. My poor mother, deprived of the life-saving operation, died ten days later.

Now, after thirty years at sea, my career was shattered and I was a convicted criminal.

I cleared my throat and answered in a voice thick with emotion and humility. 'I accept your sentence of sea-service my Lord.'

The Judge sat back in his high-backed chair with a self-satisfied sigh, steepling his fingers to touch his concertina'd chins. His tongue appeared snake-like to moisten his lips in anticipation of the numerous gins that would follow his forthcoming round of golf with the Chief Constable later that afternoon. Then, leaning forward on ermine-clad elbows, he pierced my forehead with arrows of disgust and gave his imperious verdict.

'You will be taken from this Court and placed into the custody of the State Maritime Police until such time as you have completed a minimum of three voyages. You will then remain in their custody until your release has been considered and approved by the Court of Rehabilitation.' He nodded, self-righteously, in the direction of the SMP Inspector standing alongside me. 'Take the prisoner away,' he commanded.

I stepped back and to the side, stunned but relieved that I would not be incarcerated in some window-barred jail. The broad-shouldered, immaculately dressed SMP officer took hold of my elbow firmly as though seeking a pressure-point and led me down a narrow flight of carpeted stairs to the floor below the Courtroom.

Passing along a short corridor lined by four cells, two either side, we entered a room – brilliantly lit by concealed lighting – that was humming, almost vibrating, with an electronic buzz.

Several SMP officers were sitting, with electric ears clamped over their heads like the ear-muffs of Arctic skiers, huddled over consoles of knobs, surrounded by flashing pin-pricks of LED lights, their eyes scanning banks of what appeared to be CCTV screens, occasionally speaking softly into mouth-microphones an inch from their scarcely moving lips.

The Inspector pointed to a straight-backed wooden chair in front of an empty metal table and indicated I should sit down.

'Sorry, old chap,' he commiserated. 'Know just how you must be feeling. I used to be a ship manager myself before I joined this lot.' He jabbed a finger at his uniform cap placed on the table between us as he drew up a chair for himself.

'There but for the grace of God, etc,' he continued in his clipped staccato style of speech, as he opened a large cabinet beside him and took out a slim watch-like instrument.

'This is your tag,' he explained, holding it out between his hands towards me, like a butcher offering a choice cut of beef for inspection. 'It goes around your wrist and stays there until your sentence is complete and you are released. It is not removable and continually monitors your health and movements twenty-four hours a day. You will have complete freedom of movement within specified areas but should you move outside them we will be alerted. We can also spot-check your location at any time.' He looked at me, his eyes full of false sympathy – he should have been an actor. 'It's better than having prison warders and being behind bars,' he muttered testily, taking hold of my left arm and swabbing the wrist with a pad soaked with an ice-cold substance. 'How the hell would you know?' I thought belligerently.

He looped the tag over my hand and clamped it, quite tightly, around my wrist with a long narrow key that quite illogically made me think of a branding iron.

'You will get used to it,' he promised. 'It's totally waterproof and absolutely indestructible. But, a friendly word of warning; if we *are* alerted or you aren't where you should be when we spot-check you, it means another round-trip is added to your sentence with no right of appeal.'

He examined his handiwork then released my hand.

'What happens to me now?' I queried, trembling like a frozen jelly.

Scuffling his chair backwards he stood and reached for a heavy book from the top of the cabinet and placed it on the table, moving his cap to one side.

Settling himself back on the chair, he opened it and made an entry.

'You will stay here tonight, old chap,' he said condescendingly. 'Tomorrow, first thing, you will have a medical that won't make any difference to your sentence unless you've something really drastic wrong with you, in which case it will be prison instead of a life on the ocean wave.' A fleeting smile crossed his face as he enjoyed his own humour.

'There's nothing wrong with me,' I said emphatically.

He nodded his acceptance of my medical diagnosis. 'Okay,' he said, then continued. 'After that you will go by train to the offices of the Occidental Oil Company in London – escorted by one of my officers of course – for a couple of days training at their special school where they will explain what you can expect during your time on the COBVs ... Then you'll be off to Bantry Bay in Southern Ireland to join your vessel ...' A faraway look gleamed in his eyes and I guessed he hadn't been away from the sea for very long. 'In any other circumstances I could almost envy you.'

'That's great,' I retorted sourly. 'I do know where Bantry Bay is ... and what's a COBV?'

His eyebrows lifted to kiss his hairline and a look of surprise pursed his lips. 'Didn't your solicitor tell you – anything?'

'Yeah,' I snapped back sarcastically. 'He said I was guilty and should take my medicine like a man.'

'Jesus!' he blasphemed in astonishment then, after a moment's consideration, asked, 'Would you like me to explain it?'

I nodded, 'Please.'

Much to my amazement he took a packet of cigarettes from his breast pocket and studiously selected one as if it was different from the others. Placing it between his lips he lit it with an old-fashioned lighter and inhaled deeply.

I watched with interest. He must be one of the very few nicotine addicts left now that the filthy habit was banned almost everywhere and they had been priced beyond the pocket of most people.

He sat back in his chair, crossing his legs, blowing out smoke like a dragon and fanning it away from me with his hand.

'COBVs,' he began pontifically, 'known generally as Cobbs, are Computerised Oil-Bulk Vessels. I believe there are two or three of them, about 500,000 ton dead-weight each. They transport crude oil from the Arabian Gulf, via the Cape of Good Hope, to the European terminal at Bantry Bay. Each voyage takes a couple of months. They are computerised throughout and you will be the only person on board so it's like a big, luxurious, and very comfortable, prison. They will tell you all the details, and what you will be required to do, when you get to the training place. That's it in a nutshell.'

I was flabbergasted. 'You mean I will be in command of a 500,000 tonner all by myself?'

'No ... you don't get it, do you,' he answered patiently, as a statement, not a question. 'The computer is in command. You are there only to keep an eye on things. Don't worry, it will all be explained before you go on board.'

I blew my cheeks out ... 'I bloody well hope so!'

My accommodation that night was surprisingly comfortable, seeing as I had been expecting a cold, draughty cell. The shiny-metal sliding entry door led into a warmly decorated room furnished almost to hotel standard and I found it hard to believe it was built to accommodate convicted felons who didn't normally rate having Sat-link entertainment units and en-suite toilet facilities. (I later learned that there were two standards of 'confinement rooms'. Mine was the better, the others were cells.)

The sleeping cubicle was very inviting, even better than the one I had on *Sea Queen*. I couldn't resist trying it out. Removing my outer coverall suit I sat on the edge of the three-quarter size bed and kicked off my shoes. Then, swinging my legs up, slowly lowered myself onto the self-moulding mattress with a sigh ... almost contented.

I lay there for several minutes trying to compose myself, and re-living the trauma of the last weeks and days. The panel of labelled sensors above my head stared down invitingly at me and I couldn't resist reaching up to touch them. The cubicle light went out and a barely perceptible vibration from the mattress ran delightfully through my weary body like a gentle massage. So soothing, so relaxing. Within seconds I was fast asleep.

Chapter Two

The opening hum of the sliding door woke me. The lights went on and the mattress died. A young, acne-faced uniformed man entered bearing a serving cabinet that he placed on the table with relief. He had obviously carried it some distance.

'Breakfast,' he announced. 'It's 0700 and you'll be collected at 0800.'

I raised my head from the pillow to thank him but he was already passing out through the door.

Memory came back to me like an electric shock as I realised where I was. My stomach turned cartwheels. What the hell did my future hold? ... What a stupid fool I had been to think I could have got away with what I did, even for such a good reason. Mum would probably have died anyhow, or been a cabbage for the rest of her life. Now I knew what fear of the unknown felt like, and I was scared. I must try to be positive and look on my immediate future with a spirit of adventure. Pretend I was joining a new ship in the usual way. If I don't I shall be a nervous wreck in no time flat. Yes, that's what I must do – pretend.

I sat up, squinting at the blurred face of my watch, and it hit me like a wet sock ... I had been asleep for nearly twenty hours!!! ... Christ, I must have been shattered. No wonder I felt starving. My stomach was sending panic signals saying my inner man needed satisfying.

I sat at the table in front of the serving cabinet that stopped its whispering hum as I opened its door.

Breakfast consisted of a fare normally associated with a good class hotel, not a prison. Fresh grapefruit, a tasty muesli, a container of delicious hot hash and, best of all, a flask of sweet coffee ... heaven. I had always had a fondness for coffee. Over the years it had become rarer and rarer through the actions of the anti-caffeine brigade and their medical supporters who, if they had their way, would have us drink nothing but water. Even that would have to be filtered. Ugh!

Lastly, there was the usual selection of energy and vitamin pills. I cleared the lot and enjoyed every morsel. Besides being hungry I was concerned as to when – and if – I might eat again.

The thought of having to keep my 'manky' inner-suit on was a bit repugnant so it was a pleasant surprise to find a complete set of clean clothing placed, neatly folded, on the lounger. I was receiving VIP treatment – why? I had the awful feeling that it was the 'last supper' treatment. It was quite frightening.

In the bathroom, after voiding my complaining bladder and showering in beautifully soft warm water, I lotioned my chin and removed a day-old growth of stubbly whiskers with a shave-pad, thinking back to not so long ago, when men shaved with razor-sharp cutting blades. It all seemed so primitive now.

My mouth felt like the bottom of a parrot's cage and I was relieved to find, on the shelf, a bottle of mouthwash that put the finishing touches to making me feel as human as the situation would allow.

I climbed into my new inner-suit. The good quality thermic material felt good against my skin. The new shoes were soft, comfortable and an exact fit – someone had taken a hell of a lot of trouble!

By this time I was beginning to compose myself and asserting some new-found self discipline. After all, I told myself, I had to get used to the idea of living in the contradictory situation of being a 'free' prisoner in solitary confinement. If it wasn't so scary it would be laughable. I didn't feel at all like laughing.

Putting the cup and empty containers back into the waiting cabinet I gathered up the new coverall suit from the lounger and held it at arm's length for inspection. The plain silver-grey colour was relieved only by black pouch-pockets on the chest and thighs. On the left breast, shining silver against the black backcloth, the numbers 242 were crowned by the letter 'B' and I guessed, quite rightly as it turned out, that for the next eight months at least, this was my new 'name'.

I slid a hand down the neck-to-crutch opening, separating the fastening pads and stepped into the suit. Touching the pads together I surveyed the result in the reflector on the wall and had to admit I looked pretty smart. Better than I could have afforded myself. Pity it was prison garb.

At eight o'clock, to the very second, the door whispered open again and my earlier caller stood waiting. Another thing to get used to – people not knocking.

'Follow me,' he grunted, turning on his heel and striding off along the plain white-walled corridor.

Swallowing a sharp retort, and the little pride I had left, I did as I was told, falling in behind him like a devoted spaniel puppy, noticing the small tear in the seat of his coverall.

'Hope you get piles,' I thought benevolently.

By late morning, after a thorough medical examination in which I coughed, breathed heavily in and out, stretched, bent over, had every orifice probed, gave blood, urine and sputum samples, and succumbed to every imaginable humiliation and embarrassment – all of which proved my own diagnosis correct – I was taken by electric car, with my guardian angel, to the City Main Station where we boarded the inter-city 'bullet' train to be whisked off, unseeingly at over 150 kpm, to London.

My efforts to converse with my escort met a blank wall of silence and I wondered if he was under orders to ignore me. I had offered him my wrists for handcuffing but his only response was a shake of the head and a fleeting grin of amusement at my naivety.

From Waterloo Station it was just a car ride through the grey dismal suburbs to the city centre and equally grey dismal building that contained the plush offices of the oil company.

Not surprisingly I was pleased to arrive, and to see the back of my silent, unsmiling, travelling companion.

What with one thing and another, I felt depressed. Very depressed. As low as a snake's belly – an underground one at that. A blind man at a strip-show would have been happier.

My welcome, to my delight, was warm and friendly. The staff treated me as a normal trainee, not as a convicted fraudster, and I felt free, or as free as my restricting wrist-monitor would allow.

The Duty Manager showed me where I could take a quick wash and brush-up before leading me into the staff restaurant to meet with the two other, recently arrived, trainees on my course. Introductions were made over a sumptuous three-course meal – served by an attractive waitress, no less.

Alistair Paget, a granite-faced Scot, was a middle-aged Ship Manager in his early fifties, I guessed, who had been sentenced to eight voyages for malicious damage to his ship's power-plant during a drunken frenzy after learning of his wife's infidelity. He was, understandably, a bitter man.

Malcolm Blane, the third member of our small team, was a quiet, reserved, Assistant Ship Manager in his thirties, from London. He was to serve three voyages for disobedience of a lawful command. He would say no more than that. He was a nice chap; perhaps the command hadn't been too lawful!

Malcolm was a pleasant fellow but I wouldn't care to be shipmates with Alistair for very long. He was arrogant, ignorant and opinionated. No wonder his wife had left him. He probably thought Malcolm and I were a couple of wimpish wallies.

The next morning in the classroom, a bare pre-fabricated detached building furnished with school-type desks and chairs guaranteed not to let you fall asleep, our course lecturer introduced himself as Martin Bovek, a tall, slim, high-cheeked man with a vague hint of an Eastern European accent who would, I'm sure, be a hit with the ladies. At first his slightly patronising manner was an irritant and caused our loveable Scot to indignantly demand what gave him the right to preach to experienced ship managers as though they were first-trippers.

Quietly, and with the self-confidence of the supremely able, Martin gave a quick resumé of his forty years at sea, his various commands, and that he had been a major figure in the design and operation of COBVs.

Happily, this put our Alistair in his place. Peace reigned. Martin knew his subject and put it across in an informative and amusing way.

We sat back, uncomfortable in the unyielding chairs. He had our attention.

Almost without pausing for breath – he had obviously done this many times before – he told us that at the end of this short course we would remain at the centre to await a ship. Our wait could be anything from days to weeks. The Company to whom we were assigned operated three Cobbs from the London offices but other European countries, mainly France and Norway, controlled numerous others. In emergency we could be sent to one of them. Apparently I was second on the waiting list.

The Cobbs were, to all intents and purposes, nothing more than massive, floating oil-storage tanks sharpened at the bows. At half a million tons dead-weight each, they were powered by nuclear engines that gave them a speed of a little over twenty knots.

They carried crude oil from Bandar Abbas in Iran, loading from offshore pipeline terminals, to Bantry Bay where unloading was by similar means.

The uniqueness of these vessels was that they were totally controlled by computers in London. Computers operated everything on board: the starting, stopping and speed variations of the engines; the navigation; courses to be steered; avoidance of other ships; and even the docking and undocking at the terminals. Computers were the ship's captain, officers and engineers.

'You,' he said, scanning our three disconcerted faces, 'will each be the solitary human beings on board. You will have no duties other than to monitor and report. In the unlikely event of failure or malfunction of any system (there are so many back-up systems built-in) you will inform London immediately by Sat-link, even though they will probably be already aware of it. They will either (a) give you instruction for rectification or (b) fly out a technician. The only way you can over-ride the computer to gain manual control is by the input of an unlocking code given you by the control centre.

'Each day, at twelve noon GMT, you will contact London by Sat-link to receive any instruction or message they may have for you. Failure to meet this schedule will result in a spot-check of you and the system, and may result in possible repercussions not beneficial to you. At that time you will have the opportunity to pass any requests or messages to them.

'At each terminal the vessel will be docked by remote control. Personnel will be put on board by VTOL (Vertical Take-off and Landing aircraft) for any necessary maintenance, repair and re-storing. At such times you will not have contact with them; you will confine yourself to your personal quarters on the starboard side of the accommodation block. They will gain access to your storerooms etc, by external doors that will automatically lock your internal access doors.

'In front of you' ... he paused to point at our desks, 'are lay-out drawings of the accommodation block right at the very stern of the ship. You will see the internal and external access doors clearly marked. You will also see that you have every amenity including a small swimming pool. On the port side, opposite your quarters, are the fridge, freezer and dry-storage facilities that will afford you a wide choice of food and a varied, nutritious diet.

'Over your quarters, is what we call the "bridge", where no doubt you will spend a great deal of your time. It has all-round visibility and contains all the instrumentation needed for the safe conduct of the ship. You will see engine monitors, course indicators, Sat-Nav indicators, Radar, Sat-link communications etc, etc. Alarm bells will alert you to any and all malfunctions. Astern of all this is an exercise area above which is your gravity-launched escape capsule. It is fireproof, fully provisioned and has an electric engine to give the craft a range of two hundred kilometres at a speed of five knots. It also has an in-built Position Indicator Beacon (PIB) that will enable rescuers to home onto you.

'You will have a personal computer terminal for your own use, such as Word Processing, E-mailing, or just playing games.

'Your on-board movements will be confined to the area of the accommodation block. Should you wander outside of this area sensors will alert London. They will check on your whereabouts and why you are there. Acceptable reasons are hard to envisage and I should warn you, gentlemen, that any transgression will be punishable by additional service.'

'Remember,' he smiled, 'you are prisoners under sentence.' He gave a look of sympathy. 'This afternoon you'll be given a short talk on the psychological effects of loneliness and living alone. I strongly recommend you listen to it, but that's enough for this morning. Let's go to lunch, shall we?'

The 'short talk' was a long dreary monologue given by an equally long and dreary professorial type who, undoubtedly, had qualifications in anaesthesia and hypnotherapy. It was hard enough trying to keep awake, let alone listen, and we were grateful when he decided *he* had had enough.

The next day in the simulator was, in contrast, interesting and professionally stimulating. Almost like being on board a ship, very realistic.

Unfortunately it was cut short at mid-day when Malcolm – who was first on the waiting list – was ordered to fly out to Cape Town for onward transfer by VTOL to the outward-bound COBV 2 at sea. Her 'master' had died of a heart attack and Malcolm was pleased to learn that the body had already been taken off the ship, as he trotted off with his bags like a schoolboy bound for the tuck-shop.

Martin decided this was good enough reason to 'call it a day' so in relatively good spirits I returned to my room, happy with the knowledge that I was now 'next in line'.

Lounging around in the Company's so called 'rest-room' was not my idea of pleasure – not that I was on a pleasure trip. The room itself was comfortable enough with deep leather armchairs, TV, and newspapers. It was the hanging around all day and trying to avoid the joyful Scot. Meal-times were the only break in the boredom. Worst of all was being aware that these days were not reducing my sentence; only sea-time would do that.

We were not permitted outside the training complex which, in a perverse way, was fortunate. The views from our rain-streaked windows were of the brick-walled surrounding buildings and the flooded concrete courtyards in between. Staff members told us that it hadn't stopped raining for almost a week! No wonder they called West London, Wet London.

The days seemed unending but eventually, after only four days, Lady Luck smiled upon me. I was snoozing, slid almost horizontal in the deep armchair, still holding my crumpled, half-read newspaper collapsed on my chest, when Martin burst into the room making me jump awake. 'Chop-chop Gordon, old chap,' he shouted urgently as I hauled myself upright. 'Get your bags packed.'

'Why, what's happened,' I mumbled, still only semi-conscious and trying to focus heavy eyes.

He took hold of my arm to assist my sleepy leg muscles get me on my feet; I shrugged his hand away, tearing the newspaper in doing so. 'We've got to get you to Bantry Bay, PDQ,' he said impatiently. 'The chap who was on her has been re-arrested and taken away and she is just about ready to sail. So get a move on. I need you ready to go in half an hour.' ... I needed no further urging.

The flight from London Central Airport – where seventy years ago the world's busiest docks hosted bustling ships of all nations – across England, the Irish Sea and Southern Ireland, took a relaxing two and a half hours and by mid-afternoon I was stretching my neck to see out of the aircraft's small window as we decelerated over the narrowing stretch of water wedging into the craggy brown-green hills of County Cork.

Tall aluminium chimneys of the great oil refinery, tops flaming like candles, stood pointing up to the overcast sky, like obscene finger gestures, as though disdainful of the tangled mish-mash of steaming pipes, obese storage tanks and scruffy buildings around their feet.

Small coastal tankers and other miscellaneous craft lay alongside the black oil-stained jetties. Others criss-crossed the harbour, trailing dirty-white wakes through the scummy surface of the dark Atlantic sea as the aircraft lost height and swung onto a new heading for the VTOL landing pad.

Then I saw her in the distance. It could only be her.

Nosed against the off-shore terminal she looked like an ugly, rusting block of flats with a white cottage stuck, apparently as an afterthought, on her after end, like a wart on a witch's nose. She was light-ship (empty) and the vast expanse of her red-rusting hull, normally underwater when loaded with oil or ballast-water, gave her the appearance of a gigantic, dilapidated, floating warehouse.

COBV 3 was not a pretty sight – but then, neither is a prison.

The noise of the jet engine decreased to a purring whine as the aircraft came to a hover above the landing site, then increased again as the altimeter wound down until, during the last few metres, they became a screaming, roaring crescendo to cushion the landing.

As soon as its wheels touched the ground the pilot cut the throttle and the jet's noise dropped dramatically to a soft whistling wail. Within minutes the cabin steward had opened the fuselage door and lowered the folding steps to the tarmac. Stiffly I unbuckled my seat-belt and stood up, shaking one leg at a time to restore circulation, stretching and straightening my back as I took my hold-all bag down from the overhead racking.

I was about to step out of the exit door, slightly crouched to avoid the reduced head-height, when I heard a voice shout, 'Thorpe?' I looked up to see a drenched, windswept figure of a man in a long, soaked, old-fashioned raincoat who was splashing across the tarmac through the deluge of rain like a panicking duck in ankle deep water. He was waving both hands across his face like a windscreen wiper then extending them towards me, palms forward in a pushing gesture. Obviously he was trying to attract my attention and signalling for me to stop where I was. Perhaps he had an umbrella stuck up his jumper and didn't want me to get wet ... Although somehow I doubted that.

Breathlessly he reached the steps and held on to them, head down, like a geriatric with a zimmer-frame, as he panted, 'Stay on board. We've got to go straight out to your ship. She's waiting for you.'

I stepped back to allow him to crawl wearily up the steps and into the aircraft as the cabin steward shut and twist-locked the door behind him. He held one palm face-out to me as though to say 'Wait a minute' as he pushed past and disappeared onto the flight deck. Resignedly I replaced my bag up on the rack and sat back down on the seat to await his return. He was back within a minute.

'Sorry about this, old chap,' he wheezed (Oh, no, I thought, not another 'old chap' type). 'Got to get you straight out to your Cobb.'

Still breathless, he sat down opposite me, his chest heaving, as rainwater ran down his face from his drenched hair, soaking his shirt collar and dripping from his nose, lips and chin like crystal clear blood.

'She's finishing unloading and started pumping her ballast,' he spluttered, spraying me in the process. 'We can get her away as soon as you are on board.'

An answer died on my lips as the pilot gunned his jets into an eardrum shattering roar as we lifted off, vibrating heavily. Someone was in a hurry.

Unable to speak, I looked down onto the floor and concentrated my attention on the ever increasing puddle around the sodden shoes of my new-found soggy friend, watching it sway from side to side like the ebb and flow of a tide-flow, filmed at fast speed, as the aircraft rolled its way to where my 'flag-ship' awaited my arrival.

There was no side-party to greet me as I stepped down onto COBV 3's pipe- and valve-covered deck that stretched forever into the distance, the length and breadth of several football pitches. No Junior Officer to welcome me aboard with an obsequious smile and salute. No Steward to carry my bag and lead me to my quarters. Just the bedraggled oil-man standing in the aircraft's door pointing and shouting, 'Go in that door there.'

I walked hurriedly across the fifty metres from the landing spot and opened the indicated door in the superstructure. Stepping in, I looked back to where the VTOL was already winding up with increasing decibels, raring to take-off. A hand waved from one of the fuselage windows, but I didn't respond. He would soon be back in his warm, comfortable home, probably with an equally warm wife or girlfriend.

I clamped the door closed, shutting out the outside world, for how long? ... I felt very alone and unwanted, like a broom in a cupboard, as I turned to face my future.

I was in a short, brightly lit alleyway. On the left were three doors marked 'Store', 'Exercise-Room', and 'Laundry'. To my right were two stairways, one leading up and one going down. Between them another alleyway went left. I turned into this one and found three more doors. The one in front was marked 'Store', the one to my right labelled 'Galley', and the open one opposite said 'Lounge' so I went in this one and dumped my bag down onto the carpeted floor.

It was pleasantly warm and tastefully furnished with a large curtained-window looking out along the whole unending length of the ship's hull to the distant murky shore and the silver candlestick chimneys of the refinery.

I looked around my new home. A huge library of books lined one bulkhead (or should I say 'wall' in this day and age) and I hoped that many of them would be to my taste. A large, comfortable-looking settee occupied most of the opposite wall and a warm-brown leather armchair stood in a corner facing a wide-screen TV combo with rows of discs beneath.

Suddenly, I was overcome with emotion as I realised this was where I was to live for many months to come; completely on my own with no contact with anyone other than those I would see from my window as they boarded by VTOL at the terminals, and the impersonal, disembodied voices that would speak to me on the Sat-Link each day.

My legs gave way and I slumped down into the armchair, elbows on knees, as I buried my face into my hands and cried, pathetically and full of self-pity.

How long I sat there I don't know. It was like being in a world of emptiness, an uninhabited void. How was I going to cope? Was life worth living? I had no one to live for now that Mother was dead. I truly felt like ending it all. Me, the big macho guy who had always considered suicide as being an act of cowardice, the easy way out.

Fortunately the blue-mood passed away and common-sense returned as I realised, with a shock, that probably big-brother was watching me. I felt ashamed and embarrassed and stiffened my resolve to become positive.

Just then I felt a thump and felt the familiar gentle vibration of the deck through the soles of my shoe. The ship's engine had started.

Levering myself from out of the armchair I crossed to the window and was amazed to see the distant shoreline of the Bay swinging past our bow. We were moving, we had sailed!

Recalling the ship's lay-out from the drawings we were shown at the training centre, I ran out of the lounge and up the stairway to the bridge. It was exactly like the simulator except that now there was sound. Everywhere, electronic equipment and computer gadgetry hummed and whirled. Lights flickered, digital read-outs clicked, and screens flashed ever-changing imaging information. It was all very Hi-tech, certainly more than I had ever encountered before and I thanked God for the time spent on the simulator. At least I knew what it was all about even though I had nothing to do. I had no control whatsoever over events.

The all-round view from the bridge was awesome. The sensation of standing doing nothing as everything went on around me was eerie. I was mesmerised yet professionally fascinated as the ship's bow swung round 180 degrees away from the receding refinery as the electronic pilot and auto-helm took us seaward between the radar-reflector-topped buoys marking the deep-water channel. It was as though I were a spectral being looking down on a modern-day *Marie Celeste* and I could not help but wonder what I could do, or would do, if anything went wrong. But of course it didn't.

I was so engrossed in what was going on that I forgot to look astern to see my last sight of land for weeks as it disappeared below the darkening horizon at the far end of our turbulent wake.

The ship breathed quietly as it headed seaward, gradually sinking lower into the Atlantic as the pumped sea-water ballast continued to fill her empty tanks for stability. Westward we steamed (well, it doesn't sound right to say we 'nucleared' does it?) for a hundred Ks, out into the vast ocean to comply with International Regulations that required all oil-carrying vessels to distance themselves from any land – other than when arriving at, or departing from, their port of destination – after the environmentally catastrophic oil-pollution caused by tankers in the late 1900s.

I stood spellbound by all this electronic wizardry, watching the day die and the blackness of the night close around us.

The glowing light of the ship's speed indicator showed that the powerful nuclear engine, sealed below deck from my prying eye, was thrusting our great hull at almost twenty knots through the heaving seas driving in from the storm-tossed Western Ocean, that would have a lesser vessel rolling and pitching uncomfortably.

Only an occasional shudder could be felt as she shouldered aside an exceptionally large sea. The rise and fall of her bluff bow was imperceptible against the vague horizon seen only as a dividing line between two differing shades of black. These titanic Cobbs drove *through* most seas – not *over* them.

Straddling my hands on the side edges of the RPIP (Relative Position Indicator Plot – a sloping, almost horizontal, electronic chart-like screen on which the ship's position was the central point) I saw the tracing echo of the Irish coast many Ks astern of us. Far away on our port side, another ship appeared on the plot as a moving dot of light trailing a wake behind it, like the tail of a tadpole, to show its course. Had this distant ship come anywhere near us, or indicated the remotest chance of hazarding our progress, the computer would action a collision-avoidance alteration of course to keep us well out of harm's way. Good thing too. The impetus of a Cobb took it a distance of fifteen K's to come to a stop from full speed once the engine was shut down.

I leaned heavily on my hands; head drooping, as a wave of weariness swept over me. I had had a mentally and emotionally exhausting day. I wanted to fiddle with the range-changing knobs on the plot but I felt too tired. Anyhow, I had months ahead with nothing to do but fiddle.

Listlessly I turned away and made my way down the stairway from the darkness of the bridge into the brightness of my accommodation, squinting my eyes defensively against the relative glare of the soft lighting.

As tired as I was, I could not resist looking into the galley. It was spotless.

Stainless-steel sinks and draining boards gleamed. Kitchen and cooking utensils, micro-wave ovens, mixers, blenders, and a variety of other gadgets, stood on wipe-clean work-tops, everything in pristine condition. Even my bleary brain recorded the fact that it would be my job to keep it that way.

Staggering, almost drunk with fatigue, I crossed back into the lounge, avoiding the temptation to flop down in the armchair, and entered the cabin. All my heavy eyes saw was the bed as I kicked off my shoes and, leaving a crumpled heap of clothing on the floor, fell into it pulling the cover up over my shoulders, tucking a fistful under my chin as I mentally and physically shut down.

Chapter Three

A white ball of light shone on my closed eyelids and they fluttered open and shut several times. Gradually my brain awoke and ordered my sightless eyes to focus. The light from the porthole shone straight into my face. Where was I?

Reluctantly memory returned and for a few moments I lay wallowing in a depression of misery. I had two alternatives, I told myself; I could buck up and face the future positively, or jump overboard. I was too much of a coward to even consider the latter so, in reality, there was no alternative.

I swung my feet onto the floor, sitting upright on the bed, dragging several deep breathes into my lungs then exhaling slowly through whistling lips like someone cooling a spoonful of hot soup.

On the bulkhead, alongside the porthole, two polished glass-faced clocks swam into vision through my tear-filled eyes. Why two? ... Was I seeing double? I ground both eyelids closed, squeegeeing the tears away to roll down my cheeks. Clarity returned and my brain clicked into living mode. Of course! ... one would be GMT and the other automatically controlled local time. My identification of the quandary was assisted, just a little, by the two large labels beneath each clock.

The GMT one became the cynosure of my rapidly clearing eyes. It was 11.30 hours and I had to make a Sat-Link call to London at noon!

Twenty-five minutes later, a hot cup of tea on the table in front of me and a thick slice of toast – half eaten – alongside it, I was seated upstairs facing the Sat-Link console, re-familiarising myself with the various knobs, dials and switches. Very simple really.

At noon, as the second-hand of the bridge clock swept across the figure twelve, I switched on the set, punched in my given code number and spoke into the mike. 'London, this is Cobb 3, Cobb 3, – Over.'

Immediately, as though in the next room, came their response. 'Cobb 3, this is London. Thank you ... Out.'

Well, that was short and sweet, I thought. So much for chatty conversation. Guess they were not as lonely as me.

Down below again, in the bathroom, I studied myself in the reflector. God, I looked gaunt! Dark rings under my eyes made me look like a ninety-year-old Hallowe'en mask. I rubbed a fist across my bristled chin. Sod it – why should I shave? No one was going to see me. Deep down in my troubled self-conscience it registered as the first sign of a decline in personal standards so I surrendered to my better self and pulled out a shave-pad.

My routine for that first day was to become – with variation – the pattern of everyday life.

Breakfast was always eaten on the bridge, sitting on the cushioned swivel chair gazing out over the empty sea and the closed circle of a hazily visible horizon. From this position I could not see the bow-wave made by the ship's stem thrusting relentlessly into the white crested waves, nor the creaming sea-water rushing aft along the hull in its hurry to be left behind, in peace. It was as though there was no movement. The ship was silent and still, like a straw upon the surface, drifting – eternally. It was only when looking aft and seeing the long, straight, churning wake disappearing astern that an impression of movement could be gained.

The remainder of the mornings became a ritual of cleaning and tidying that lasted until the noon-time Sat-Link call to London that varied only in the change of operator at the other end. One made the probably unsupervised mistake of wishing me 'Good morning'. That was a one-off rare occasion that I entered in the ship's Log as 'an unusual occurrence'.

Also at midday I would note our position and record it, with any relevant comments, in my personal diary and ship's Log whilst enjoying a light snack-lunch.

Early afternoons were spent in the exercise-room where, in the early days, my efforts were short and desultory. But, as the voyage progressed, they became longer and more vigorous. More anti-boredom than anything. This was followed by a pleasurable swim in the long but narrow pool in the temperature-controlled area, always eagerly anticipated. At least twice a week I would luxuriate in the relaxing sauna.

The remainder of the afternoon would be spent, usually, sitting up in the bridge with a book, or doing a crossword puzzle from out of the several books full of them in the library. I had no one to write to, and in any case, had little to write about.

Apart from the swimming, the highlight of each day was preparing and cooking an evening meal in the galley. At first I could not cook. I never could cook because I never had to. Now, by reading the instructions on the tins or packages, I began to enjoy it – even experimented with my own recipes as the weeks went by. Some of my concoctions, such as bacon and egg sprinkled with curry powder, would disgust a cordon-bleu chef (and probably everyone else), but I only had myself to please.

Evenings were a regular routine. An hour or so sitting on the bridge, dreaming and relaxing. Feeling the gentle tremor of the engine, listening to the ship's silence and the electronic clicking of its brain. Watching the dying sun lower itself smoothly below the horizon. Looking at the plot expecting to see ... nothing.

Each day was the same. Only the flickering figures of the Sat-Nav recorder informed the empty bridge of our changing Latitude and Longitude as we voyaged southward, crossing the equator and down through the South Atlantic.

In my enclosed, controlled environment I was unaware of outside temperatures, or the changes of weather, other than what I could see from my window and portholes. So, without the availability of charts, I had to mentally plot our progress, estimating for my own interest when we should alter course eastward across the foot of South Africa, passing the Cape of Good Hope (roughly our half-way mark) and then northward into the Indian Ocean. Seeing how much my estimations differed from the actual turn.

Nothing ever appeared on the plot. We were too far offshore. The only exceptions were the echoes of tadpole-shaped ships that twice lit up the extreme edge of the screen; dozens of Ks away and too distant to cause any concern.

As we neared the end of our outward journey my visits to the plot became more frequent as I eagerly looked for a trace of the Omani coastline that should appear way out to port. Then, late one morning, there it was. Just a streak on the edge of the screen at first, gradually becoming a firm echo, like a white cloud, as it took shape. I soon recognised, from previous trips to the Gulf, the unmistakable headland of Ras-al-Hadd – known to seafarers all over the world as Razzle Head. Only one more day to Bandar Abbas, I said to myself, excited as a youngster on his first date as I watched the ghostly image drop lower on the plot until it disappeared off the screen altogether.

By nightfall another milky echo appeared, this time on the starboard edge of the plot as we neared the Iranian coast, still many miles below the rapidly darkening horizon. Flashes of memory sprang into mind as I recalled earlier voyages through these same waters, back in the 1990s, sailing to and from the Abadan and Mena-al-Ahmadi refineries at the northern end of the Gulf, sweltering in tankers that were far smaller and slower than a Cobb, and without air-conditioning. Nevertheless, with all my present comforts I would still prefer those days when, as a young navigating officer, I had few worries or responsibilities. Then I had a future, a career, and I was free.

We were approaching the busy, and relatively narrow, Straits of Hormuz through which countless bloated tankers, deeply laden with the desert's liquid black-gold, passed on their endless shuttle-service distributing their precious cargo to the fuel starved ends of the Earth. Land was echoed on both sides of the plot now and tadpoles began to appear on the screen, wriggling and squirming like the images of organisms viewed through a powerful microscope. I watched, professionally fascinated but helpless, as this lumbering vessel altered course and speed to avoid them, like a driverless dodgem car at a fun-fair.

I hastened below to the galley to stock up with a flask of tea and a plateful of sandwiches full of deliciously greasy bacon, grilled in seconds and plastered with tomato ketchup, to sustain me through the long moonless cavern of an Arabian night. I was determined not to miss anything.

Back on the bridge I stood leaning against the plot, seeing the land echoes encroaching on either side, and the ever-increasing number of tadpoles. It looked like Piccadilly Circus but when I used binoculars to sweep the surrounding sea I could see ... nothing. Not one light, other than the glistening diamonds of stars seemingly set in a sky of black velvet. Nor a glimpse of a low shadow of land; it was still, as yet, hidden below the Earth's curvature.

Occasionally the distant, dark-shape of our bow, with its stumpy, stick-like mast faintly outlined by the ethereal glow of its white forward-shining mast-head navigation light, swung a few degrees one way or the other. The clicking of the engine rev-counter and the variation of the underfoot vibrations indicated small changes of course and speed as I kept my lonely vigil. Alone except for the robotic bridge-crew.

By midnight, the Straits ahead had narrowed to less than one hundred Ks and was full of tadpoles. In front and behind they squiggled on the same course, in company with us. On the other side of the separation zone they swam like a shoal of salmon against the tide, steering in the opposite direction. Lights were all around us and our engine revs dropped to less than half speed as we almost drifted along at a comparatively slow ten knots maintaining a safe distance from the friendly white stern-light of the ship ahead while others followed us faithfully and trustingly. I wondered if they were fully manned, or like this one – a ghost ship.

Morning dawned to starboard. Dull yellow and copper coloured streaks lit the sky over the low-lying desert land, becoming brighter each passing minute until, eventually, the sun showed a wary edge, like a peeping-tom expecting discovery, before climbing dramatically into the sky and flooding the sea with sparkling light and warmth to mark the start of another day.

By mid-morning, the off-shore pumping terminals – huge islands of structural steel – were a few Ks ahead. Going dead-slow, with engine barely turning, we were drawn towards one of them guided by radio beacons and sensors between its two steel latticed jetties that engulfed us like the loving arms of a skeletal mother as we crept along at snail's pace until, with an imperceptible clunk, our bow locked on and we were secured.

Almost immediately, huge flexible pipelines swung aboard, connected to our on-deck facilities and began pumping-out the millions of litres of sea-water, now contaminated with oil, that had been our ballast from the UK. Only a couple of decades ago, certainly in my tanker days, this ballast water would be discharged into the sea before docking; a practice quite rightly brought to a stop by environmentalists. Now it was pumped ashore into filtering tanks to be cleaned before being returned to the sea.

As each tank was sucked dry of water so it began to refill with glutinous crude oil. The pumping switch indicator board on the bridge flashed madly like a pin-ball machine as the numerous pumps and valves, on and below our main deck, were switched open or closed by computer. So finely and accurately controlled was this operation that the load-line painted on the ship's side barely rose or fell in relation to the water-line, a feat no old-time tanker pump-man could hope to equal as he dashed around his cluttered deck doing the same job by manually turning big, stiff hand wheels.

As I watched in amazement, a loud whining, whistling noise heralded the arrival on deck of a VTOL. As its jet engine wound-down, three Arab looking men leapt out and started unloading cartons and crates of bottles that they carried the few metres to the superstructure and out of my view. To see other human beings after nearly a month of solitary confinement was fantastic. My hands shook with excitement as I reached for the handle of the external door to meet and greet them. I had forgotten the rules … the door was locked. I rushed back to the lounge window, flattening my nose against the glass, and a few minutes later they came back into view and re-boarded the aircraft. My eyes followed them hungrily, I was so desperate for company, but they did not even look back. I sat on the armchair and cried until I fell miserably asleep.

In the very early hours of the next morning the gentle trembling of engine movement woke me. I jumped to my feet, back to my window-of-the-world, and was surprised to see we were drawing away from the terminal.

We were loaded and moving, re-tracing a course back to Ireland. Half of one trip to be scratched off my sentence calendar.

Chapter Four

I had been fully employed most of the day on the bridge doing absolutely nothing, bored out of my skull, staring sightlessly along the vast expanse of the tanker's pipe-covered deck that was already weeping red tears of rust. I could not even bother to read a book or tackle a crossword puzzle. My morning swim and sauna had left me tired and listless. What a state to be in! Life was like being in the centre of an unmoving circle of ocean, empty and unchanging except for a ridge of swollen clouds, like dark boulders, way ahead. It was like living in a void. The ocean, seen from my lofty viewpoint, appeared restless rather than rough although I had no doubts that the seas would be mountainous seen from sea-level.

Only two thoughts were occupying my semi-comatose mind. The curry that I would be heating up for my evening meal and the read-out on the Sat-Nav position indicator clicking, like a muffled grandfather clock, on the after bulkhead as it flicked through the early thirties south latitude. I knew that, at any time now, our bow would be swinging to starboard onto a westerly course to take us around the Cape, back into the Atlantic, homeward bound to the UK.

But why was I getting so excited? ... there was no one at home waiting for me, not even a relative. No one to wave a welcome as we docked. No one standing on the quayside wanting me, a middle-aged orphan. I was feeling sorry for myself again, even more so when I realised I probably would not be allowed off the ship anyhow. Not even to walk around the refinery. 'No harm in asking, though,' I said to myself, making a mental note to ask London at the next Sat-Link call.

I leaned back in the cushioned swivel chair and swung my feet up onto the instrument console between the blank screen of the RPI plot and the Sat-Link transceiver set, watching the cooling sun drop through the evening sky, like a deflated balloon, expecting a hiss of steam as it kissed the shivering horizon that ate it up, like a tasty cheese, until it was gone.

Existing lights on the console became brighter and night-lights switched on as the fog of darkness filled the bridge and another day wound down as the diamond stars glinted to greet the yellow-faced moon.

It was at that moment that my world seemed to stop.

Suddenly, without warning, every light went out. Every source of noise stopped. No hum, no buzzing, no whine, no clicking. Nothing. It was as quiet and as black as a forsaken grave. Total silence except for the continuing vibration of the deck underfoot. Jesus, it was scary and my heart thumped, like a Boy Scout's bass drum. What the hell was happening? There was no emergency lighting to my knowledge. Perhaps the designers had not envisaged this could ever happen. I groped around ... feeling for what? I could not see a thing. At least the engine was still running, but even that didn't prevent me from being frightened – very frightened. And there was not a damn thing I could do. Eventually, common-sense returned and my heart-rate dropped to only twice normal.

'Don't panic,' I told my inner confidence-manager. 'There's been a total systems failure somewhere. London will sort it out.' I prayed I was being honest with myself.

Meanwhile COBV 3 plodded on; half a million tons of unlit, unstoppable and uncontrolled ship, plus one dead-scared passenger.

In London, the following day, newspaper sellers stood silently – not like the old days when their cries of 'PAPER, PAPER, READ ALL ABOUT IT' rang around every street corner of the capital – contemplating their rapidly dying trade as they shivered in the cold, early morning mist. Even the latest news item – reduced to two words on the poster trestle beside them – failed to attract a rush of customers already well-used to violence in a world where brother fought brother, religion fought religion, colour fought colour and race fought race. That it was on their own doorstep didn't seem to matter a hoot. It was not the first time the City had been targeted and it wouldn't be the last.

The majority were not even interested in the story behind the two boldly dramatic words 'CITY EXPLOSION'. At that early hour they would be more interested had it been another rail strike to give them the excuse of a few days off.

Tom Suthers read those headlines on the front page of his paper as he stood waiting, miserable and half-awake, for the Commuter Transport Shuttle to take him into the City. His immediate and uninterested thought was 'Another bloody terrorist bombing'.

He was about to fold it under his arm when his eye caught the words 'Occidental Oil Company' in the text beneath the headline. 'Blimey,' he thought. 'That's my place,' and he re-opened it ... interest aroused.

Yesterday evening he read, *a huge explosion ripped apart the European offices of the Occidental Oil Company in the heart of the city. Three security guards and eight other employees were killed in the blast that completely demolished the buildings. Many more are injured, some seriously, and the death roll is expected to rise. State police fear it to be the work of persons as yet unknown and officers of the Anti-terrorist Unit are at the scene. A spokesman for the Company said, 'This is a crippling blow but we will rise again from the ashes. Our thoughts at this moment are for our dead and injured colleagues, and their families.*

One of the injured, a supervisor in the ship control department said there was concern for the safety of the Company's three unmanned bulk-oil vessels now uncontrolled somewhere at sea.

The Company declined to comment on this.

The article went on to describe the success of Occidental Oil and its excellent safety record and promised further details as soon as they become available.

Tom re-folded his paper and tucked it back under his arm. 'Suppose I should still go in and see what's happening,' he muttered to himself as the old lady at his side tilted her head and gave a questioning look.

Chapter Five

I awoke with a start. My legs ached where they had been tucked up tightly under my chin in an attempt to keep warm. Last night, as the dark, dead bridge became cold, I had fumbled my way downstairs into the dry-store and found a couple of old woollen blankets and a thermal sheet. With these under my arm I groped my way to the cabin, climbed into my bed without undressing, covered myself with the blankets and a thick duvet, rolled up into a foetus-style ball and went miserably to sleep.

The cabin was like an Eskimo's ice-box as I swung my feet onto the deck, wrapping the duvet tightly around my shoulders. Christ, it was bitterly cold! As cold as a grave in winter – and just as dead, except for the unheard rumble of the engine, still turning. Obviously London hadn't got their fingers out yet. I'd have to get some sort of plan organised, when I could crash my frozen brain into gear.

First priority, warm clothes. Then food.

To my knowledge there were no cold-weather clothes on board. Who would have thought they would be needed? However, I did find more blankets in the store from which I fashioned a ragged cape-like coat. Over thermal inner and outer suits it was just about sufficient to keep me from freezing to death.

Food was no problem, there was plenty. Unfortunately most was useless without means of heating it. Dehydrated meals by the hundred were nothing but packets of powder without hot water. Tins of meat, vegetables, curries and sweets were stacked high in the store. All perfectly edible providing one could eat them cold and congealed.

Water, thank goodness, was plentiful. Bottles and bottles of it.

The fridge and freezer were well stocked with fresh milk, bread and vegetables. Providing I kept the doors closed it would be days before they defrosted. At least I wouldn't starve for a while.

I took a corned-beef sandwich and a glass of cold milk up to the bridge and looked around the lifeless, unlit instrumentation and the empty surrounding sea. Where the hell were we?

By guestimated dead-reckoning we must be a few hundred K's south of the Cape's latitude. Occasional glimpses of a weak and watery sun through the overcast sky indicated we were heading something west of south – say, roughly 200 degrees True. I strained my memory to visualise the Southern Ocean. I had never sailed these waters before. It must be best part of three thousand Ks from the Cape to the Antarctic ice edge. At twenty knots that was about four days' steaming. Four days for London to get their act together and sort things out. The alternative didn't bear thinking about. Then I had a brain-wave. If there was no power my wrist sensor wouldn't work. I was free! Free to go wherever I pleased. Under the circumstances it wasn't even funny. At least I could explore outside my 'confined area' now. Perhaps find a way into the engine-room and – if necessary as a last resort – sabotage the engine so that we would drift until found by the inevitable searchers. Anything was better than going further south into sub-zero temperatures, and ice.

Fearfully, I unclipped the external door and stepped out onto the deck expecting a bolt of lightning, or something, to strike me for disobeying orders, but nothing did. The weather was atrocious and I wasn't acclimatised after six weeks of being cosseted. It was bitterly cold and wet. A freezing, biting wind swept over the deck, driving flurries of sleet before it. I felt like Scott of Antarctic fame. Clouds, like black boulders, scudded low across the sombre, cheerless sky and within seconds I was like a block of marble, though not so valuable. Carefully I worked around the superstructure from hand-hold to hand-hold, with the wind trying its best to whip the blanket coat away, and me with it. There were only three or four doors, heavy watertight ones like the gold-vault doors at the Bank of England, all locked and bolted.

The nuclear engine-room was a tightly sealed unit to unauthorised personnel. That was me.

Dispirited, but eager to get out of the weather, I returned inside ... so much for freedom.

Making the most of the shortening daylight I searched through all the store-rooms and lockers with a fine-tooth comb looking for anything to make life more comfortable and bearable. All I found, of any use, were more blankets and six bottles of three-star French brandy. I've never been much of a drinker but what the hell. Why leave it for the penguins?

Lunch consisted of the usual corned-beef, cold baked beans, and a tin of sliced apricots with cream. It tasted reasonably good – I was hungry.

All afternoon I sat huddled in the deep leather armchair, mummified in blankets, dividing my time between reading a book to take my mind off my predicament and lowering the level in the brandy bottle. I don't remember falling asleep or going to bed. I told you I wasn't much of a drinker.

There was no change come the next morning except that I had a troop of stampeding elephants doing the Cornish clog-dance in my head. I was cold, cramped and aching in every joint and muscle, and still London hadn't mended the fuse.

I could not move my head – I dared not – so I lay, immobile, submerged under half a dozen blankets, and drifted off into merciful sleep again.

It was past noon when I awoke for the second time. The elephants had moved on but my head was like a lead ingot on a fragile neck. Any sudden movement would have been fatal. I shuffled into the bathroom, from necessity, swathed in blankets like an Indian beggar and blissfully cleaned my teeth, rinsing away the cloying taste like the inside of a Chinese wrestler's jock-strap; not that my nautical experiences had included that delight.

A decent shave was out of the question without hot water and I didn't fancy the idea of a cold-water scrape. My two-day-old stubble would stay where it was, psychologically helping to keep me warm.

After an unsuccessful hair-of-the-dog, and the inevitable corned-dog sandwich, I eased my growing concern by loading the lifeboat (sorry, the escape capsule) with as much eatable food, water, blankets etc, as I could find. 'Now,' I said to myself, 'I am as ready as I can be for whatever comes,' and returned to the armchair, book and bottle.

Next day – the fourth since my personal Armageddon – I moved my blanket igloo to the bridge, spending most of the time scanning the horizon with binoculars looking for the ice that didn't materialise. So much for my make-do navigation. One thing was a certainty, we would hit it. On this course it could not be avoided. It was only a matter of when.

Naturally I was frightened, very frightened. So frightened that I left the bottle well and truly corked that night as I curled up in my bed like a cringing dog. If anything was going to happen I would need my wits about me.

It was in the early hours of the morning when the collision threw me violently out of bed, onto the floor, a tangled bundle of bedclothes.

Stunned and petrified I clambered to my feet knowing full well that it was the ice. There was nothing else down here to hit. Strangely, I experienced a sensation of relief as I staggered up to the bridge cocooned in a duvet and skinning my shin on a hidden, unidentified protrusion in the process. At last the worrying and apprehensive waiting was over.

The windows were solid black shapes until I pressed my nose against the cold moistness of the glass; even then all I could seen was a vague dull-whiteness beyond the dark expanse of the ship's deck. My most frightening concern was the continuing beat of the engine, now changed to a heavier, labouring pounding as the propeller cavitated in its own water, pushing our great bulk harder and further into the ice-floe.

The next few hours of agonising wait seemed an eternity until a glimmer of lighter sky appeared on the horizon. Gradually, as though reluctant to awaken the world, the low canopy of cloud changed from its Stygian black night cloak to the leaden-grey sunless Antarctic day.

The view from the bridge window gave the impression of witnessing a scene being lit by a dimmer-switch being very slowly turned to reveal an appalling sight. The distant landscape was a sparkling, virginal white but surrounding my doomed ship – still being forced into the ice by an unstoppable engine – a carpet of glutinous, slimy, evil smelling crude oil was spreading over the ice as the ship's precious cargo poured out from huge gashes torn in the hull. Astern, the surface of the sea was a heaving layer of black treacle on and in which oil-coated figures swam frantically without progress. Ashore, on the ice, other creatures staggered and fell into the deadly sludge, dying by the hundred even at this early stage. Were they birds, penguins, seals? ... I couldn't tell.

The stringent, sickly stench of oil was thick in the air, stinging my eyes and causing a burning sensation in my throat. A wet cloth over my face, covering mouth and nose, helped a bit, but for how long? ... it was getting worse.

Then I noticed that the forward end of the cargo-deck had sunk to the level of the ice and it was obvious that our blunt bow was not only being driven into the ice, it was also pushing under it as the bow sank. Furthermore, the sinking bow was causing the ship's stern to rise higher. I had to get out while there was still chance.

Pausing just long enough to collect my wallet, and the brandy bottle, from the cabin, I ran aft to where the escape capsule was poised – ready and waiting – on its sloping launch-ramp, like a lifeboat on a slipway. I climbed the short iron-runged ladder, slipping twice in my panicking haste, and slid feet first into its space-like interior, closing and clamping the watertight hatch behind me.

The almost horizontal, coffin-like launching seat into which I had to squeeze myself was claustrophobic to say the least. My hands shook as

I secured the safety straps around my body and forehead, ready for lift-off, or in my case, drop-off.

Clamping my jaws tightly together and scrunching my eyes closed, I lifted both hands to the overhead release mechanism and pulled it down, like an aircraft ejector seat. For several heart-stopping seconds nothing happened then, with a slight rumble and grind, it started to move. I had the sensation of gathering speed and then a floating freedom, like a glider, as it dropped the twenty-odd, stomach-churning metres to splash into the sea ... or where the sea should have been. Instead, it came to a violent and abrupt halt as it crashed down on a concrete-hard ice-floe that had been swept around the ship's stern. The bow of the capsule caved in followed by a solid mass of ice-rock. My whole, panic-stricken body-weight felt as if it was being forced down into my boots as the capsule toppled off the floe and into the sea.

Freezing sea-water rushed in through the shattered bow, up my tethered body and poured into my gaping mouth, wide open with shock in a silent scream, as we slipped quietly down into the cold, dark depth of the Antarctic Ocean.

Epilogue

Two days after the bombing of the Occidental Oil Company's offices in London the following information was released to the Press.

> The Company is pleased to announce that the death toll from the bombing of our London office has not increased. All injured employees are now out of hospital. State Police have found indications that the bombing is attributable to a terrorist organisation – as yet not named.

> The latest news on the Company's three bulk-oil vessels is:

> COBV 1 has today been driven ashore on the coast of Pakistan, eighty kilometres west of Karachi. Salvage tugs are on their way to her and the only person on board is reported as safe and well. The ship was nearing the end of her outward voyage and was not loaded. She is undamaged and there is no danger of oil pollution.

> COBV 2 was in a French shipyard at the time of the explosion and not affected in any way.

> COBV 3, unfortunately has disappeared. Its last reported position was Latitude 28 degrees 40 minutes South. Longitude 51 degrees 25 minutes East. That is approximately three hundred kilometres south west of Madagascar.

Search and Rescue aircraft of the South African, Argentine and Chilean Air Forces are systematically covering the vast area of the South Atlantic. There have been no radar or radio contacts so far. The search will continue.

This ship was fully ,loaded with crude-oil from the Iranian oil-fields. Oil pollution experts from all over the world are gathering at Cape Town.

Three days later another press release was made.

The Company regrets to advise that the South African Government has sent the following communiqué to London.

An aircraft of the South African Air Force has sighted the half-sunken wreck of COBV 3 on the ice-edge off the coast of Enderby Land in the Australian Dependency of Antarctica. There was no sign of its one-man crew. The area around the wreck, for many kilometres, is heavily contaminated with oil from the ship and heavy loss of wild-life is expected. Pollution experts are expected to leave Cape Town within hours for the wreck site.

The South African Government is in emergency session and close contact with other Heads of State is being maintained.

No further information is available at this time.

An article in *Britain Today* quotes Professor Ian Douglas of the University of Cape Town, one of the world's top experts in Environmental Pollution as saying ... 'It is my opinion that the recent spillage of millions of litres of crude-oil from the Occidental Oil Company's ship in Antarctica will prove to be the worst oil pollution in history, by far. Many thousands of sea-birds and animals have already died. Countless more will die in the future. It will take several decades, at least, before the contamination is clear. The damage to the environment and wild-life is inestimable.'